Tommy Glover's
Sketch of
Heaven

JANE BAILEY

CONSTABLE • LONDON

CONSTABLE

First published in Great Britain in 2005 by Constable & Robinson Ltd

This edition published in 2018 by Constable

Copyright © Jane Bailey, 2005

1 3 5 7 9 10 8 6 4 2

The moral right of the author has been asserted.

A CIP catalogue record for this book is available from the British Library.

ISBN: 978-1-47212-840-9

Printed and bound in Great Britain by Clays Ltd, St Ives plc

Papers used by Constable are from well-managed forests
and other responsible sources.

Constable
An imprint of
Little, Brown Book Group
Carmelite House
50 Victoria Embankment
London EC4Y 0DZ

An Hachette UK Company
www.hachette.co.uk

www.littlebrown.co.uk

For the greatest creations I have ever had a hand in:
Anna and Lucy

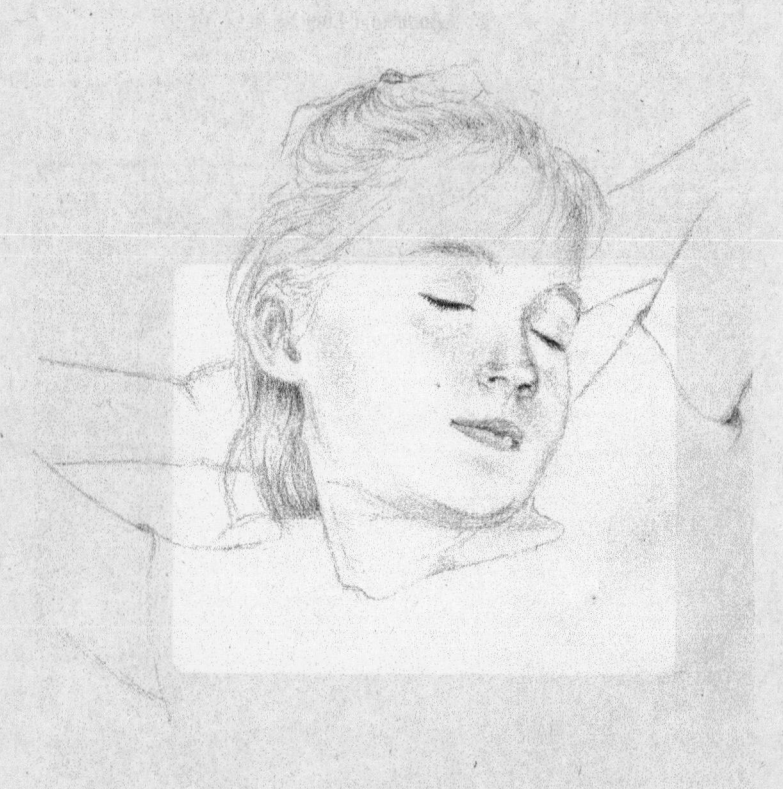

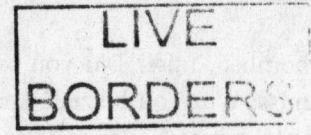

April showers

People watched me like foxes. There was an intrigue about me which had nothing to do with my thin face and my scruffy accent, but it was a long time before I understood the furtive glances, the sly exchange of looks.

I need to tell you my story. Not just because you have told me yours (and it beggars belief, it really does. All these years, and I didn't have a clue . . . not a clue). The thing is, mine is a different story to me now, now that I'm grown up. I told it – most of it – the other day for the first time in eleven years, and as I was telling it things kept dawning on me – hitting me, real swipes from the past, making connections. It was when I started teaching practice here last month. There I was, all ready to stand and learn, take in those half-familiar surroundings – join in a bit maybe – when Miss Pegler said she was off to the station and would I stand in for a while. Meeting some person about plans for the new school building, and it was important. She wouldn't be long (and of course she was all morning). She said perhaps the children would like to hear about when I was a girl in Sheepcote.

Well, that was the last thing I wanted to remember, as you can imagine, but the door closed behind her and up shot all these hands: Miss, miss, tell us about the war, miss. Wuz you bombed, miss? Did you see a Lancaster? You from London, miss? Wuz you blitzed? And their cut-in-half exercise books, their burry Gloucestershire accents, the pong of inkwells and desk polish and the stove hurled me back in time. I can smell it now . . .

From the moment she picks me in the village hall, I am confused about Aunty Joyce. There aren't many of us – maybe only half a dozen bussed as far as Sheepcote. We're six weeks ahead of the big evacuation in June, but our homes have been bombed so we're urgent cases. We're all given an apple, and it's so long since I've had one that I can't remember how to eat it, so I'm still munching, cross-legged, when the posse of women come in and crowd around the coat hooks at the back of the hall. They are all wearing hats or headscarves and some have gloved hands, which they put to each other's ears while they're talking. We are looked up and down and plucked out like teams in a playground, and ticked off on the clipboard by an eagle-beaked billeting officer and sent out to disappear with a stranger into the afternoon sunshine.

There are only two of us remaining, myself and a boy, when we're told to stand up. There's a beautiful film star and a woman with a face like a potato. Face-like-a-spud chooses the boy, and he picks up his gas mask. But then the film star says she can't have a girl. With instant sympathy, Spud-face offers to swap, but the other one looks me up and down then opens her beautiful clamped lips and says she can't take anyone, after all. Her sympathetic companion leaves with the boy, and the billeting officer gathers her papers and goes out of the door defiantly, leaving us alone.

"Come on then," say the full red lips, and she walks so fast I can hardly keep up with her.

* * *

Our old neighbour has a book of fairy stories with beautiful colour pictures. The fairies flit through green fields and hedgerows, make clothes out of flower petals, and perch on red toadstools. I've always imagined these things to be part of myth, along with the fairies. But as I follow this beautiful lady up the pale stoned lane I'm overwhelmed with a sense of walking through these book illustrations. Everywhere there is green. Pink, yellow and white flowers lean out from either side of the lane as if waving and cheering us on our way, and overhead the trees hold hands in an archway of green. I've had a glimpse of this in the bus from the station, but now I'm up close and right inside this reek of pollen and dung, a smell which will always whisk me back to that hybrid moment of awe and apprehension. I feel the person I have been slipping away already, and the animal I am begins to stir. I sniff the air, I crane my neck to see the invisible songsters that fill the leaves, I draw deep breaths of pungent countryside.

A bicycle bell sounds behind us. "Joyce!"

We turn and see a woman in WVS uniform pushing hard on the pedals of a tricycle with a full basket on the back. As she catches up with us she plants a flat brown lace-up on the yellow ground and smiles keenly. She has the clean determined jawline of a fighter pilot.

"Joyce, can I say 'knickers' to you?"

My lady manages a smile.

"Would you like to see my collection? Why don't I cycle on up to your house and you can take your pick?"

At the end of our walk is another picture from that story book. A row of three terraced cottages of yellow-grey stone, and a cream-painted door barely visible through a tangle of strange leafy stems and purple flowers.

The knickers lady has dismounted and is joyously waiting for us. There is an exaggerated swing to her arms as she follows us up the path with such energy that she nearly swipes me in the face.

Inside, the dark hallway leads us to a back parlour smelling of soot and paraffin and onions.

"And this must be . . .?" she says, smiling at each of us in turn. My lady finds the tag hanging from my coat button-hole, flips it over and reads: "Kitty Green." Then she selects some suitable items from the basket that has been brought in, holding them between thumb and forefinger.

"Kitty! What a pretty name!" says the knickers lady. She studies me intently. That look again — a mixture of pity and anxiety. Is it only with hindsight that I can recognize a nerv-ousness in that smile? There is so much to take in all at once: new colours, new landscape, new faces, new accents, new smells. Perhaps I do smell trouble, but it gets lost in this scrum of new aromas.

And so I am kitted out in second-hand woollens, one skirt that is too short and one that is too long and, on my lady's insistence, four pairs of knickers (all on the baggy side). I have only ever had one pair and made do without on washday. Even though the visitor insists that all her clothes are spot-lessly clean, my lady plops the underwear in a pot for a boil, just in case. Then she makes me take off my clothes and stands me in a tub in front of the range while she opens the range door, picks up my clothes with a pair of wooden tongs, and puts them on the fire.

"'Ere, that's all I got!" I protest, but she is unmoved.

The visitor looks down at her basket and bites her lip. "My name's Miss Lavish!" she says suddenly, holding out her hand, and then in a whisper, "My first name's Lavinia — isn't it ridiculous?"

I shake her hand. It is the first time I've been touched since I left Paddington station.

"What's your name, then?" I ask my lady.

"Mrs Shepherd." She pours warm water on me from a jug, and I can smell carbolic soap.

"Joyce . . ." Miss Lavish looks at her and then at me. There is a silence. My hair is being pulled through a tiny-toothed comb and gusts of exasperation are being breathed down my neck. "Mrs Shepherd is a very kind lady." Miss Lavish gathers her things and walks towards the parlour door. "And I'm sure she'll let you call her Aunty Joyce if you behave yourself."

My head is yanked hard by the comb, with a sigh. "Aunty Joyce then," says Aunty Joyce flatly. "Honestly, you should see the nits in this. Absolutely lousy! The size of *woodlice*!"

Miss Lavish opens the door smiling. "Lavender and geranium oil. That'll do the trick. I'll leave you to it then, Joyce. If there's anything you want . . . remember I'm just next door!"

Then she gives me that look, searching already for something in my face. She smiles and is gone.

People watch me like foxes. There is an intrigue about me, which has nothing to do with my thin face or my scruffy accent, and it is a long time before I understand the furtive glances, the sly exchange of looks. For I am a stranger like any number of strangers in wartime, but I am something more. I am set amongst two strangers to each other: Mrs Shepherd and her husband. I am in the intimate space of each, where no one else has ventured or been able to venture, and I am observed like litmus paper.

Knitting for victory

Aunty Joyce dries my hair vigorously with a crisp towel. She says nothing, and all I can hear is the scrunch scrunch inside my scalp as she yanks my head around. Then she packs me off to play in the garden in unfitting clothes, so the sun can dry the rest of it.

Out the back is a long garden planted with vegetables on the right and full of chickens on the left. The path through the middle leads to the back wall, the ash heap, a shed and a curious small hut covered with creeper, which must be the lav. The back wall is low and made of the same lemon-grey stone as the house, with upright stones piled on top. Every now and then there is a gash in it, showing the bright yellow stone underneath the shell. Over the wall is a field rising slowly up to the sky. I have never seen an unbroken horizon like this, and I stand and gaze at it in disbelief. Straight ahead, in the distance, is a beautiful story-book tree, and over to the left are farm buildings and barns. I can see people moving about the landscape, bent over the golden grass, bending and straightening up, and hear the tat-tat-tat of a machine some-where out of sight.

I sit down on a wooden crate and imagine my mum's arms, trying manfully not to cry, but I do. A tortoiseshell cat comes trotting out of nowhere and rubs her entire body against my legs. Back and forth she goes, pushing the whole length of herself into my legs, and I take comfort in her velvety fur. I imagine her to be delighted, startled at the strength of my affection, unused to warmth of any sort in this cold and silent home.

After half an hour or so Aunty Joyce emerges in the sunshine and pegs up my newly boiled knickers without looking at me.

"What's the cat called?" I venture.

"Oh . . . her. Kemble. My husband found her at Kemble station. When he got back, there she was in the guard's van. Reckons she got on without a ticket, and never wanted to go back."

I nod slightly, as if to say 'I see', but I have no idea what she's talking about.

"Daft name really. Good job she didn't get on at Bristol Temple Meads!" Aunty Joyce laughs. I chuckle too. Then she looks at me for a moment or two with curiosity rather than kindness.

"Come on! Let's find you an egg for your tea, shall we?"

She beckons me over to the chicken coop, and I approach gingerly. One hen squawks and runs across me flapping. Their eyes stare at me, blinking upwards with their bottom lids, and their heads do strange jerky movements back and forth. They don't like me, I can tell.

"Come on." Aunty Joyce opens a hatch door in the coop and reaches out for my hand. Her hand is cool and still damp from washing, and she places mine under the warm breast of a ginger hen. It flutters off indignantly, and I see two eggs, then three, four, in the straw bedding.

"She didn't lay them all, did you, Gloria?" She picks two up and nods at me to take the other two.

"Won't she mind?"

Aunty Joyce shakes her head, and I cradle the eggs, stuck with dirt and feather down, one in each hand.

For tea we have boiled eggs with deep orange yolks and cut-up toast, which Aunty Joyce dips into her egg. I copy her: it is delicious. I can't believe I'm having egg, and I can't believe where it came from. I'm not so sure about the two green leaves which are next to it on the plate. Aunty Joyce attacks hers with a knife and a fork. I try to copy her but end up using my fingers. I take one nibble and feel like spitting it out. She rebukes me for moving on to the bread and jam, but it is scrumptious. The bread smells sweet, and the jam is runny and full of dark fruit.

These small miracles hold back the tears.

After tea I am marched back down the lane to the village hall. I am convinced Aunty Joyce is going to return me as unsatisfactory goods. Despite the sense of rejection, I am relieved. Now I may get to be sent home and see my mum.

But inside the hall a group of women are sitting in a circle on steel-tubed canvas chairs, and as we get closer I see that they are all knitting.

"Joyce!" they all say, but it is me they are looking at.

There is Miss Lavish smiling at me and there, once again, is Face-like-a-spud, pulling a chair up for me. "You knit before? Come and sit here, my love, and I'll show you how tiz done."

"I'll show her," says a baggy-faced lady. "I just finished my gloves, look. I'll show her what to do."

"Suit yourself."

"What's your name then?"

"Kitty," answers Miss Lavish on my behalf. "We've already made friends, haven't we, Kitty? Remember my name?"

"Lavinia Lavish," I say, and because I haven't come across the name before, I say it without an accent.

There is a chuckle.

"And while we're here," whispers Miss Lavish, eager with delight at her own swipe at convention, "you can call me Aunty Lavinia!"

"So long as she don't call you Aunty Lav!" says Baggy. More chortles. "I'm Mrs Tugwell. But you'd better call me Aggie, then." Perfect. Baggie Aggie.

It gets better. Face-like-a-spud is Mrs Tabby Chudd, there's Mrs South with a very tight mouth, and Mrs Marsh with a small moustache, and of course Mrs Glass with the very big arse.

One woman looks like a tramp, and doesn't introduce herself. She certainly gives off a breathtaking stink of stale sweat, and the others seem to have shifted their chairs a little away from hers. Baggie Aggie is plump and smiley and she wants to teach me to knit. I can already knit a little, but choose not to reveal this, because I'd like to amaze them with my fast learning. Suddenly, I see a small chink of affection, and I am desperate to impress.

But after their avowals of intimacy, the women launch into conversation as if I'm not there. After ten minutes of guidance by Baggie Aggie's fat hands, I am left to get on with my knitting. They talk about their families, the war, the vicar, the evacuees, they even talk about me. It's as if by concentrating hard on my stocking stitch and displaying more intense interest in my 'egg cosy' than it deserves, I have successfully convinced them of my non-existence.

Aggie Tugwell, the grocer's wife, knits and speaks very fast indeed. Because she has a boy and a girl of school age, she aligns herself with my beautiful Aunty Joyce and takes great delight in offering her a stream of advice on diet and routine, although it is clear that Aunty Joyce never seeks advice from anyone. But Aggie's needles dart like her tongue, and if it weren't for the need to take a breath no one else would say a thing.

Tabby Chudd-like-a-spud runs the post office with her husband and is the proud mother of Betty, a girl in the top standard at the school, it seems. There is barely a sentence uttered that doesn't relate to Our Betty. Even the Allies' advance into France can't escape: "Talking of advances, you should see Our Betty's handwriting . . . !" And there is little doubt that when the war is eventually won, Betty will have had something to do with it, in one way or another.

Aunty Joyce is not so much quiet as unrevealing. She surprises me by babbling along with the rest of them about who is the best living actor and what is showing at the Plaza and who was seen holding whose hand and a new wool shade, 'ox-blood', and where you can get a decent piece of haddock if you're prepared to take the bus. From time to time they look about shiftily and get their teeth into some local no-gooder. This is the best bit of all, because I get to hear the shadiest gossip and to see their true colours. Only Aunty Joyce holds back a bit, and dear Miss Lavish tries to find the good in everyone.

Then suddenly, to my delight, the old tramp in the corner will break her silence by puckering her warty lip and snarling, "Tosser!" And conversation carries on as if she has merely noted that it is chilly for the time of year. Although she seems like a tramp to me, I soon find out Mrs Galloway has a respectable background as a carrier's wife and lives in the almshouses, too world-weary to wash at her one cold pump and too adrift from her life to care.

When Aunty Joyce puts down her knitting and counts how many there are for tea and cocoa there is a rustle of anticipation. As soon as she is in the kitchen they turn their eyes on me.

"How are you settling in, my love?" "She's all right, you know, our Joyce." "Don't be put off – she've 'ad a 'ard time."

I tell them that I am fine and that I have had a lovely tea with a real egg, except I had to eat leaves and we don't eat leaves back home. They all chuckle and call me a card. I think maybe they don't believe me.

"You wait till you meet Mr Shepherd. He's a *train driver*, he is! He's a –"

I am already picturing myself perched cheerily by his side travelling the length of Britain in the driver's cab, when there comes a snarl from the corner: "Tosser!"

The first night at Weaver's Cottage is a complicated one for me. To start with Aunty Joyce shows me a chamber pot veined with tiny cracks and says, "Now you know where it is, there's no excuse. I won't have any dirty bed-wetting in this house," and she shoves the thing under the bed with a look of disgust. I never need a chamber pot at night, and my indignation is softened by the thought of how surprised she'll be by my clean sheets and empty chamber pot in the morning.

The next thing I know I'm being shoved beside the bed myself.

"Kneel," she says. "We say our prayers kneeling, not in bed like some folks."

I look up at her for guidance, and fumble with my hands until my palms are touching. She sighs as though this is yet more confirmation of the horror of taking me into their home. No doubt she'll tell her husband I don't even say my prayers and that all Londoners are clearly heathens.

"Close your eyes. I suppose I'll have to start you off: 'Dear Lord, thank you for delivering me safely to Sheepcote, and for the good food on my plate, and the cleanliness of this house.' There. Now you carry on."

I swallow. She seems to have about covered everything. If thank yous are all you're allowed to say then I'm stumped.

"Um . . . Dear God . . . look after Mum and Dad for me . . ." I open one eye and see Aunty Joyce nod her approval. "Don't let Dad be killed and don't let Mum be killed by a bomb on the munitions factory . . . or the twins . . . and may Granny James and Dad and Mum and the twins all live till they're at least a hundred . . . that's it."

"Amen."

"Our men."

She ushers me into bed, pats my arm and blows out the candle before closing the door behind her.

I've been itching for this moment all day, so that I can cry in peace without being seen. But it is not so easy.

I look into the dark. It is the darkest dark I have ever known. I cannot remember life without blackouts, but there is something different about this, which terrifies me.

There is no sound of people walking about outside. No steady burr of vehicles going past. There are no merry voices spilling out from the pub next door, no sirens, no one shouting to put lights out. There is just a curious sound of a kettle on full steam coming from outside. It turns out to be the trees rustling. And there is the odd howl of a dog – or is it a wolf?

After a few hours of terror I hear muffled voices downstairs. There is a man's voice, and then the creaking of stairs. A few more creaks and clunks, then silence. I fumble for the matches and light the candle and fill the chamber pot. The shadows make me catch my breath. A moth flutters past my face and I let out a little squeak of horror. Everywhere I look there are spiders and moths clinging to the walls. They are within inches of the pillows, moths with wings folded ready to flap flap flap; spiders with enough legs to sprint across your face, down under the bedcovers – anywhere – in the folds of your nightie – anywhere!

I head for the landing and see the other door. It opens into their room: two mounds in a double bed, a dark wardrobe, a dressing table, and the strange musty wood smell like the inside of pianos. I creep under the covers next to Aunty Joyce.

In the morning, I wake up in my own bed.

And by the way, if you never go to school . . .

I am placed in Standard Three, in a shared classroom with Standard Four. Both years are taught together as eight- to ten-year-olds by a young teacher called Miss Hubble. I like Miss Hubble. She is bright-cheeked and alert with a smile for everyone, very thick ankles and a passion for wild flowers. Everyone knows she will make a joke sooner than use the ruler if you blot your work or forget how many pounds in a hundredweight. On my first day she gives me an exercise book, cut in half, for 'HANDWRITING'. When she discovers my blank page halfway through the lesson, she keeps the sneerers at bay by giving me a foxglove and some campion from a jar on her desk and thanks me for offering to stick them in the book for her. At playtime she whispers that she will help me catch up at the weekends.

Standards Five and Six, on the other hand, are taught by the sour-faced Miss Miller. People say she is a spinster of the Great War and is angry with the whole world because her stock of possible husbands has been blown to bits and used as compost for foreign flowers.

The children in the next two Standards, aged between twelve and fourteen, are taught by the headmaster, Mr Edwards, and they call him 'Boss Harry'. Boss Harry is no taller than the women but seems a giant. He lost three brothers in the Great War, in which he fought himself, and he keeps a slim pale cane in a cupboard above his desk. These facts together increase his height by a good few inches.

Boss Harry takes us for 'poetry'. He stands by the window, facing out, and spouts lines about lovers and soldiers, birdsong and heartbreak, in a strong melodic voice that I will later discover is from South Wales. We watch his chalky hands clasped behind his black jacket, and we enjoy not having to do anything but sit. We like it especially when he becomes angry, because it is exciting. No one ever knows for certain what he will do next. And one thing that is guaranteed to make him angry but unable to use his cane is Miss Miller, twice a week. She vents her anger with the world through music. Every Wednesday and Friday she hands out an assortment of percussion instruments and bangs away at her untuned piano to the arbitrary thrashing of triangles and tambourines. Through this ear-splitting racket she entreats her avid class to howl out a song. She shrieks it out, line by wretched line, crashing away at the keys until Boss Harry (whose sensitive ears were made in the Land of Song) is unable to ignore the onslaught coming through the partition wall. He turns the colour of foxglove and has to face the window to avoid showing us his slitted eyes and gritted teeth. She will punish him this way for ever for being the only eligible widower this side of Stroud, and he not willing to give her the time of day.

It's been years since I went to school properly, and I find sitting still in squashed rows very difficult. What with all the evacuees there are three or four of us to every two-seater desk, and our elbows can barely move. I am on the end with my bum half on and half off the bench. And I learn early on that 'vacuees' are deemed no better than gypsies in the order of things, since it is always a gypsy or an evacuee who is sent to flush the toilets at the edge of the playground. This has to be done three times a day, and I am chosen in the playground by Miss Miller on the very first day. I'm sent with a gypsy boy called Stef who is to show me the ropes.

There, bordering the fields, is a row of holes in the ground with square wooden seats. The cubicles reek of shit and sour urine. I need to use them myself but after Aunty Joyce's boiling, the elastic in my knickers was so limp that she had to tie a knot in it, and now I can't get them down.

"You pull this and the shit gets chucked into the field," he says, pointing to a handle. "Do it!" And then for no reason he picks up a sharp stone from the filthy floor and holds it close to my cheek: "I could cut you!"

I soon see that the gypsies enjoy the new evacuees because for once they are no longer the lowest of the low. And there are two more groups of children who are grateful for our arrival.

The first are the evacuees who arrived at the beginning of the war. Tired of being the scapegoats for every problem in the village, they relish the opportunity to pick on new arrivals. They make fun of my accent, which was once theirs, my inability to read and write any better than the reception class, and they laugh at my unfitting clothes.

The second group of children who welcome our arrival are those from the boys' home. They can sympathize with us for being brought up by strangers, but only until we get letters from home.

And from this melting pot of seething rivalries we bubble over at the end of the day and make our way through the lanes. But walking home turns out to be worse than play-times. At least at playtime you can play hopscotch by yourself and pretend to be busy. You can make yourself invisible in the playground, provided nobody gets bored and begins to notice those they've excluded. They reckon British Bulldog was banned last year because it always turned into a vicious battle between evacuees and villagers. Children were trampled on, fingers were broken, lips were split. But still large groups of them are always having a go, until Boss Harry spots them from his schoolhouse window and comes down to ring his handbell furiously.

On the way home it's different. There is no restraining bell. Children scatter in all directions. Some go down the road to a neighbouring hamlet, some across the valley to the farms or up the hill to the church. Others, like me, troop on past the church, through Sheepcote, and carry on up to the Fleece, where things start to get nasty.

By now there are about ten children, and a score or so more from the boys' home. I am walking ahead on this first day as fast as I can, but keeping my knees as clamped as possible, because I am now desperate for a wee.

One of the girls runs up behind me and lifts the hem of my skirt. There are hoots and giggles.

"Hey! Droopy drawers!"

I don't look back. Then a boy's voice:

"'Er can't 'ear you! 'Er can't read and 'er can't write! I don't s'pose 'er can *say* nothink neither!"

This time a stone strikes me on the shoulder. It hurts. I try not to feel it, and keep walking. I'm going to wet myself if I don't get home soon.

"What you *doin'*?" booms a new voice. "You can't 'it girls! Get lost – go on! Get on home, you!"

There are a series of whistles and teasing whoops, and the owner of the voice runs up to me. "You all right?"

It takes a few moments for me to pluck up the courage to look at him, in case it's another trick. "I'm okay . . . fanks!"

He's a much older boy, thirteen or fourteen maybe, and he has kind eyes. He smiles at me, and I look down at the road, at my squirming knees and my heavy feet, which threaten a leak with the impact of each boot.

The rowdiest of the troop seem to have tailed off.

"Where you from, then? London?"

"Yeah."

"Hey! You seen bombers, then? Seen doodlebugs?"

"I got shrapnel."

"Hey!"

"Got loads at home. Brought a few bits wiv me though."

He comes to a standstill. The rest of the group are turning right down a path towards an iron gate marked "Heaven House", only I don't have time to work out the sign because I am on a mission. I hurry on.

"My name's Tommy, by the way," he calls after me.

I cannot, I *cannot* stop now. Running, I turn my head, so chewed up with gratitude and guilt, and mutter, "I'm Kitty. I'll show you the shrapnel – you can 'ave it!"

I can already feel the sore heat of it running down my thighs and, as I head up the path to Aunty Joyce's, I leave a dark trail in the stone. Then I stand on the doorstep and let it all come out. When Aunty Joyce opens the door it is over. I greet her in a pool of shame, desperately hoping that the big boy did not watch me running home.

My Uncle Jack

Uncle Jack turns out not to be such a tosser as I expected. At least, not at first, and then later . . . I'm not sure what I would call him.

The first thing I see is his boots by the door: huge black hobnails with leather like orange peel. They stand on yesterday's *Gloucestershire Echo* in a ten-to-two formation, making them look strangely balletic. Inside the parlour his dark blue jacket hangs on the back of a dining chair like a living thing, its pockets bulging with tins and its arms curved forwards. There is an intense musky smell to it, half sweat, half smoke, and the usual paraffin and sulphurous cooking smells of the parlour are stifled by a waft of vanilla tobacco. There is a man about.

It is a long time since I have lived with a man, and I am nervous and excited by his presence. He comes in from the back door carrying wood, his pipe still in his mouth. He grips it between his teeth and tries to smile at me, but has to deposit the logs and take out the pipe for me to make sense of his greeting.

"Hello! You must be . . . Kitty, is it?"

"Yes. Kitty Green."

"Kitty Green!" He holds out his hand and it is huge and warm. His face is smudged with dust and smoke, which makes the white of his eyes gleam a brilliant blue. "Jack Shepherd. You can call me Uncle Jack if you like."

I smile weakly, not sure what is expected of me, and afraid to break any unspoken rules.

"You'll be well looked after here, at any rate," he says, sinking into one of the two armchairs by the range. "Joyce is a good cook – I dare say you've never eaten anything like it, have you? Pass me that box in my pocket there, will you?"

I go to his jacket and reach in the right-hand pocket, but he shakes his head and indicates the left one. I reach in my hand and feel string and paper, two-inch stubby pencils and something cold like a screw. I close my hand around the tin and take it over to him. I flinch as he knocks his pipe sharply on the stone hearth around the range. Then I watch as he opens the tin and out springs a ginger tress of tobacco, which he expertly tugs at and stuffs little wisps into the bowl of his pipe. The smell takes me back to the waiting room at Paddington station, where my dad – home on leave – said, "Remember, you show them toffs. Behave yourself, be kind, and no fackin' swearing! You show 'em!" Then it wafts me back to my Uncle Frank and Aunty Vi's, where we stayed for two years before my mum had the twins and before Aunty Vi went doolally and got sent to a home. It wasn't Uncle Frank who smoked the pipe, but his mate George who used to come round sometimes. It smelt a lot like this. Suddenly I am there, in that soot-smelling living room and the bedroom with the damp encrusted wallpaper and my mother's arms around me all night. Before the twins she used to do that. Dad had been in the army so long I couldn't remember any different.

Uncle Jack looks young enough to be in the army. There

is no grey in his brown curly hair and under his blue over-alls he looks quite sturdy.

"Now you're to help your Aunty Joyce, mind. Up at the farm in the mornings and weekends, and help with the house-work after school. Isn't that right, Joyce?"

He calls, but Aunty Joyce is in the pantry. She holds open the beaded fronds that separate the pantry from the parlour and says to me, "You better come and help me, then."

I help her prepare tea. Before the week is out I will know how to scrub potatoes, boil eggs, top and tail beans and make pastry. But on this particular evening she makes a point of everything I can't do, as if emphasizing to Uncle Jack how useless I am, and he looks up from his paper with sympathy, as if to agree with her unspoken assertion that I am lucky to be with them, considering the hovel I must have come from where everyone says 'cor blimey' and they don't even have a change of knickers or know what a vegetable is.

I suppose I don't actually think this, but in that instinctive way children have, I know it.

Uncle Jack works ten-day shifts: any time from two o'clock in the morning to ten o'clock at night. Whenever he comes home after 2 p.m., or as near as train times will allow, Aunty Joyce always insists on having dinner at teatime, to allow her husband a full hot meal. So on this first evening with Uncle Jack we have liver and onion, potato and cabbage.

When we sit down to eat, I still have not let go of my mother's arms around me in Aunty Vi's spare room, and I am not hungry. Nonetheless, I pick up my knife and fork like Aunty Joyce did yesterday, to show willing. Uncle Jack instantly clamps a large hand on mine and forces my fork to the table in a frightening rebuke. He looks at me intently and his frown turns to a sort of sympathetic smile, as if to say he understands my impetuous animal need to scoff anything on my plate, but here we do things differently.

He bows his head and Aunty Joyce does the same, clasping her pretty hands together against the tablecloth.

"For these and all Thy bounteous gifts, oh Lord, we give Thee our thanks. Amen."

"Amen," says Aunty Joyce.

"Our men," I agree.

We tuck in, only I have even less will than ever to tackle the liver now that I have so much to live up to. I watch from the corner of my eye to see how they hold the meat down with the fork, then saw at it with the knife. I try to do the same, but it is tough, and a piece of liver flies off the plate and speckles the tablecloth with gravy. Aunty Joyce rolls her eyes, and gives Uncle Jack a distant "You see what I have to put up with?" look, to which he replies with a magnanimous look which says, "We cannot expect too much of her."

By now, the dissected liver – whose name was enough to put me off in the first place – is sprouting little tubes, which fill me with such revulsion I move on to the potatoes.

"Well, have you made any friends at school?" he asks me with his mouth full of liver.

"No, not yet. Well – there's a bigger boy called Tommy. He's my friend."

They exchange glances. Aunty Joyce puts down her cutlery and I swear she flares her nostrils at Uncle Jack. He, in turn, points his fork at me: "Don't go messing with Tommy. Do you hear me? Keep well away from that boy."

"But why? He was kind to me. I –"

"There are no buts. You do as I say or you'll find yourself in Queer Street!"

I never do find out where Queer Street is, but in my dreams it is always a bit like Weaver's Terrace in Sheepcote.

They move on quickly to another topic and, although they

occasionally lob me a question or fill me in on local information, most of the time I am able to assume my knitting
club pose, and make myself completely disappear.

It seems there is a Lady Elmsleigh they do not approve of
because her father would have done things differently, she
doesn't go to church and she smokes. She is a 'naytheiss' and
worst of all she is a 'soashliss'. Then there is a man called Mr
Fairly who looks after the boys' home, and he is a good, God-
fearing man and a 'lay' preacher. Apparently Uncle Jack is
going to become a 'lay' preacher at the church too (I imagine
him brooding on a pile of hymn books), although before he
married Aunty Joyce he used to be a 'methodiss'. I am not
sure if it was a downwards move marrying her or not, but
he is now Church of England, because his family wouldn't
let him be a methodiss any more. Whenever things go a bit
wrong or whenever someone gets upset, Uncle Jack towers
up and quotes things Jesus would say in this situation.

One thing I soon learn about Uncle Jack anyhow is that
he seems to know God really well. Sometimes he says things
like "God wouldn't turn his nose up at your liver and onion,
even if it has gone cold now! No! God would have no qualms
about cabbage!" or sometimes, if he is offered a flagon of
cider by a neighbour, "God isn't a prude! Oh no! God is a
kind, friendly God, who'd enjoy a good pint along with the
next man, as long as it wasn't on a Sunday!"

Indeed, God and Jesus are ever present in the Shepherd
household and seem to pop up in every room on a regular
basis. And although I labour hard at Sunday school to work
out the difference between the Father, the Son and the Holy
Ghost, God and Jesus seem remarkably interchangeable at
Weaver's Cottage. Usually, if he can't find a good quote from
Jesus on any particular subject, Uncle Jack will attribute it to
God. Thus God likes rice pudding, God enjoys sums, God does
not think it a good idea for thirteen-year olds and eight-year

olds to play together. God likes clean nails and God did not waste his time going to the pictures to see Betty Grable.

But the things that God finds most abhorrent are 'the sins of the flesh'. They are talked about an awful lot by Uncle Jack, and for me they recall only the limp pink meat wrapped in bloodied paper for a ridiculous number of ration points.

Uncle Jack is really quite a jolly man, I conclude, after a week or so. He has a reassuring certainty about him. He is whatever he is with absolute conviction. He blunders his way through biblical references with such cheerful evangelism that he could convince even the most cynical eight-year-old. Most of all, he is a tonic after the dour, uncertain world that Aunty Joyce seems to inhabit.

Nonetheless, neither of them is quite ready for me. When the liver is cleared away (I help take the plates to the sink) they have 'afters'. I can hardly believe my eyes when a giant wedge of cake is put on my plate.

"Facky Nell!" I say.

"*What?*"

"Facky Nell," I repeat, a little more cautiously.

Uncle Jack is momentarily lost for words. Aunty Joyce stops cutting the cake mid-movement. I look from one to the other. Uncle Jack swallows hard.

"We do *not*," (his voice starts as a whisper and gets louder – very loud) "I repeat *not*, use language like that in this house."

"Like –?" I begin.

"Go to your room!"

I look wistfully at the wedge of cake, my eyes filling with tears and my firmly closed lips beginning to move this way and that on their own.

In my room I see the cupboard door in the corner and think I might hide in it, but it is locked. It was locked the last time I tried it too. I am so shut out of everything and utterly lost. I sink on to the cold bed and cry and cry until my face is sore with tears. Then I fall asleep under the moth-spattered walls.

You like tomaytoes

On Sunday morning I awake to the sound of church bells. I am in the single bed alone, despite having crept in with Aunty Joyce again last night.

The church seems very small to me, and very old. I sit between Aunty Joyce and Uncle Jack in the pews and copy their every move, although I can hardly take my eyes off the timber-beamed roof and the pretty-coloured glass in the windows. I kneel when they do, mouth prayers when they do, and open my mouth to sing, just like them. Red and violet are the colours that intrigue me most as they fall in chunks of light across the pews. They come from Jesus in the window: he is wearing a crown of thorns and rolling his eyes up to the sky. I must admit I feel a bit sorry for him, but frankly, it's not what you want to see on a Sunday morning, is it? It could be a bit more cheerful. In the front pews are the boys from Heaven House and Mr Fairly with his wife. We sit directly behind Mr Fairly, because Uncle Jack insists we are as far forward as possible. Tommy turns round and smiles at me and I smile back. He turns round quickly. I'm sure Aunty Joyce sees, and I am very, very smug. At least she can see that *someone* likes me.

But Aunty Joyce seems to be smiling a lot more than usual,

and even takes my hand as we walk down the aisle on the way out. The vicar, a thin unhealthy-looking man with brown teeth, greets everyone as they come out of church with utter indifference.

"Well done, Jack; well done, Joyce. I'm glad to see you managed to take one. Well done. We must all do our bit." And he smiles at me, but half-heartedly, as though he really would rather be down the pub.

After matins and dinner comes Sunday school. This is a group of seventy or eighty children led by Miss Didbury at one end of the village hall. I notice Miss Didbury is the same buzzard-eyed lady as the billeting officer. It is strange to return to the hall where I waited to be chosen and where I have knitted for England.

We kick off with more hymns I don't know, because I don't know any hymns. Then we sing " . . . Praise from the great and jelly ghost . . ." I will get the hang of that one. It's a laugh.

We're divided into groups, each taught by an assistant: an older girl or boy recently graduated from Sunday school. I am with Violet. We listen to stories about Jesus and Violet shows pictures of him. He had pale brown hair, a brown beard and blue eyes. He wore satin robes and sometimes rode a donkey. Jesus came from another country. Does anyone know where Jews came from, wonders Violet? I do. I know people in London who are Jews. They come from Whitechapel and they go to a synagogue. None of the ones I know have blue eyes, so I tell them. Everyone laughs because of my accent. I laugh too because I think maybe I'm being funny.

Violet smiles nervously. "You don't go to a synagogue, do you, Kitty?"

"No."

"You go to church, then?"

"Nope."

More laughs.

"She's a vacuee, Violet. She don't know what church is, do ya?"

"They all got nits in London, so don't sit too close!"

"They don't speak proper up there."

"They don't read nor nothink."

My eyes begin to sting and I fold my lips to stop them from wobbling. Violet hushes the children firmly and finds an excuse to give me a picture of a donkey to stick into my *Life of Our Lord* book. Then we all draw pictures of what God gives us each day, sing another round of 'Jelly Ghost' with Miss Didbury, and go home or to 'cadets'.

On the way back I see Tommy waiting by the church gate. I put my hand to my mouth, because I forgot to get him my shrapnel. As I approach he takes his hands out of his pockets and moves towards me.

"Yes?"

"I was wondering . . . I'm going up Lady Elmsleigh's after tea to see the Americans. They got tents everywhere and lorries up there an' all. Wanna come?"

"Okay," I say.

"Meet me at the end of the path – to Heaven House."

"Righto!"

I march on homewards, pleased as punch and just a little bit smug again.

Running down the lane I can hardly believe Tommy is there, waiting for me like he said. He is so grown-up and handsome I can't help thinking he's waiting for someone else.

"Hi there!" he smiles as I come panting up to him.

"Hi!"

I am overwhelmed by his sad brown eyes and his earnest face. I hand him a small canvas sack, and when he has looked inside he places a loud exaggerated kiss on the top of my hair ribbon.

"I never seen so much shrapnel!"

"It's everywhere in London." I try to be cool, but I'm reeling from the kiss. "Our home got blown to bits."

"Never!"

"It did. We had to go an' live with our Aunty Vi, but then Mum had twins and Aunty Vi had a . . . nerviss breakdown, so Mum went to work in a munitions factory in Somerset only they don't take children only children under two in the crèche . . . so . . . I had to come here."

I pretend to look at the hedgerows as we walk along, but really I am taking in his manly brow and jaw, and his trumpet ears and downy soft cheeks which are still those of a child. His hair is thick and dark and too long on top, and he has a few freckles on his nose that I haven't noticed before.

"You didn't tell no one you were meeting me, did you?" he asks.

"No – why?"

"Best not to, that's all."

I don't want to upset him, but I want to know what's going on.

"Don't they like you, then, Aunty Joyce and Uncle Jack?"

"Not much."

I frown, and say the first stupid thing that comes into my head.

"Not because you're from the boys' home, is it?"

He gives a breath of a laugh.

"No. No, far from it. They'd love to show their merciful charity to a poor orphan. Looks good in church."

I hate these mysteries.

"So —"

"Soon as I get out of school I'm joining the RAF and then you won't have no more bombing in London, you mark my words."

"You can't, you won't be old enough." He has changed the subject and taken me with him.

"I can lie about my age. I'm fourteen in March, an' I'm leaving school then. Any road, I've got a way in."

"How do you mean?"

"Jonathan Crocker, right, he went to school here an' he's a fighter pilot. He come back last year for a visit an' he told me he'd take me up in his plane next time he comes. Jonathan Crocker. He's going to get me in."

"Oh!" I'm fairly certain Tommy can look after himself, but I've seen planes collide. "I hope you don't get shot down."

"I won't," he says very seriously. "Though I don't s'pose anyone'd care if I did."

"I would."

He beams. He has lovely teeth. "You're the only person who's ever said that," and he puts his hand on my shoulder like a big brother. Or a sweetheart, perhaps. Well, I can dream.

Lady Elmsleigh's big house has become the focus of attention this week. Not long before my arrival some thirty tanks and twenty lorries parked up around her estate and tents were put up in the grounds. Young American soldiers hang about in twos and threes, roaming the fields aimlessly, starting up their lorry engines, turning them off. They offer us rides, give us Lucky Strikes and gum and chocolate, and all for the pleasure of our company. They seem bored and homesick, and perhaps because of this they seem more approachable than our own soldiers, who we hardly ever see except on leave.

They seem less formal even than the Home Guard, who

take everything a bit seriously. These Americans play cards with us, wrestle with the boys, and take the clips from their pistols so we can play with them. It's the closest any of us has been to an army of soldiers, and we love it.

Some of the kids become errand runners for them, and we're all happy as Larry to bring them fresh bread or eggs in exchange for the glamour of their company. We start to loiter after school, listening to stories of faraway places called Maine and Utah told in film-star voices. The stories are rarely about themselves, and are based on whatever we want to hear: cowboys, Indians, Hollywood. When we do ask them about themselves they turn out to be mostly from farms and miss their mothers. A few of them have girlfriends, and I love to ply them with questions about their romances. The girls have names like Loretta and Dolores that conjure up such beauties I hardly dare look at the solid, dumpy girls they show me in their pocket photos.

Aunty Joyce and Uncle Jack often guess I'm up there with the other kids, but I don't let on I'm with Tommy. They're so busy getting huffy about Lady Elmsleigh that it doesn't dawn on them.

Aunty Joyce is big in the WVS, you see. She spearheaded working lunches for land girls and prisoners of war, organizing mobile soup kitchens from local milk carts. She was the driving force (believe it or not) behind the weekly 'knit for victory' sessions at the village hall.

The leader of the WVS, however, is Lady Elmsleigh, herself a local champion of ways to support the war effort. There is a curious relationship between Lady Elmsleigh and Aunty Joyce, because of course Lady Elmsleigh does not believe in God. Uncle Jack is intensely suspicious of her, certain that she is a bad influence on the village. She is a 'soashliss' and a 'naytheeiss' and she smokes cigarettes.

When her father Lord Elmsleigh was alive, the whole

village voted along with the government because he was a Tory MP. Now the whole village seems soashliss. That's how it is and that's how you always choose your party here. Fair enough. But there is talk that one of her brothers died fighting for the 'communiss' in Spain. Uncle Jack finds this all highly dodgy.

There is widespread sympathy for her, though, because her husband died in the Great War, her eldest son was shot down over Germany, and her second son is missing, presumed dead. What's more she holds regular fêtes for the whole village and parties for evacuees, orphans and war-workers, where she lets children trample freely on her flower beds and grown-ups gawp at her posh rugs and blue-patterned porcelain lavatory bowls. It is also rumoured – although no one can know for sure except the grocer, and he is sworn to secrecy – that it is she who has anonymously paid off all the outstanding debts 'on tab' of the poorest families in Sheepcote. It is the anonymity of her kindness that clinched it for her with most of the villagers. For everyone knows that if they had performed such a generous act they would have wanted to bask in its glory, although Uncle Jack proclaims it "only what you'd expect from the gentry".

As for smoking, he tries to muster up some moral indignation on the subject, but the truth is he loves his pipe and it is a tricky one for him. Nonetheless, cigarettes are a sign of decadence and gluttony in these times. It simply isn't right and proper that any woman should be seen smoking when our boys on the front line are going short of vital supplies. Everyone knows you should leave cigarettes for the men.

What he doesn't know is that the vicar and his wife are addicted to tobacco, and that their entire black market supply comes from Lady Elmsleigh. I heard it at knitting group. Uncle Jack thinks the frantic expressions exchanged between the Reverend Mr Harrison and Lady Elmsleigh are caused by heated debates about the existence of God, and not the surreptitious delivery of Players cork-tipped to the holy pocket.

As for Americans, they are just bad news all round as far as Uncle Jack's concerned. I don't know what he bases this on, but I've heard a few interesting things whilst turning out socks and mittens. Baggie Aggie reckons some poor girls are so hard up they're *selling themselves* to the Americans at the air base down the road, although they talk in such funny nods and whispers sometimes at the Sheepcote Women's Voluntary Service that I never do work out who exactly bought them and where they put them. One thing is certain, the Americans up at Lady Elmsleigh's have not bought any. They're too busy mooching over their dumpy girlfriends, their mums' meat pies or their ol' farm dogs.

At any rate, when Uncle Jack and Aunty Joyce ask where I've been they are so bent on grunting over Lady Elmsleigh and Americans they forget to ask who I went with.

Then one day, in early June, they all disappear: the Americans, the tanks, the lorries, the tents. We go to see them after school and they have gone, leaving only a debris of tin cans, bald grass and tyre marks. We never see any of them again, although one or two of them leave behind more enduring mementoes which we discover only later. They quite literally put life into the village, then they go and lose theirs in two feet of sea water on a foreign beach.

Shagging

People say there's another huge wave of evacuees leaving London, and I'm lucky to have a place already. But at home with the Shepherds I still don't feel very at home. Aunty Joyce seems to scrub everything in my path with carbolic soap and makes me wash my hands so many times a day that calluses are beginning to appear on my knuckles. In fairness, Aunty Joyce also seems to wash herself a lot. An awful lot, as a matter of fact.

Another thing that's odd is that there seems to be an intruder in the house, and it's not me. I've got used to saying my prayers and saying grace, but I can't stand God following me about everywhere. Uncle Jack goes on and on about him like he's an old mate, but an old mate that I will never get to meet, so there. Everything that happens is an opportunity for a little extract from the Bible. I've never read the Bible, but I can't see what all the fuss is about. They all live in places with funny names where they drink wine instead of beer and wear sandals and go about on donkeys and camels saying 'thee' and 'thou art' to each other for no earthly reason. And there are no pictures in it. Not even black and white. I can't see the point. It makes Uncle Jack feel important, though. (I'm sure he can't have read it all because he sometimes has trouble with words in the *Gloucestershire Echo*.) He seems to be in some kind of competition with Mr Fairly Himself, who is also big on biblical references.

The day of the Sunday school picnic starts off well enough, with salmon sandwiches and a tomato for everyone up at Lady Elmsleigh's big house. There is tug-of-war and pass-the-ball-under-your-chin, and what's left of the Sheepcote Brass Band with four old men, three cornets and a bugle. There's even a boogie band laid on by members of the American air base a few miles down the road, but that is for later in the afternoon.

First it's time for the Sunday school to do their bit. We give a small play in which Joe Bunting stars as Jesus and in which I mercifully do not perform, and the whole joyous sun-baked event is rounded off by some hymn singing and the fateful 'Jelly Ghost'.

We sit cross-legged on the grass, and the Reverend Mr Harrison leads the singing in a dapper linen suit and straw boater. Because I am looking at him, I don't notice Miss Didbury's face change from blissful content into rage, and I'm surprised when she rises from her canvas seat to interrupt the vicar.

"Stop! Stop! Stop!"

We all fall silent and crane our necks this way and that to see what's happening.

"I'm sorry, vicar." Miss Didbury has gone mauve. "*Who* was that?"

Everyone looks at each other dumbly.

"*Who* is singing . . . *who* is singing . . . 'jelly ghost'?"

Some children titter. What a daft question. We all are, aren't we?

"*You!*" cries Miss Didbury, panting at me. "You are making fun of the Lord's anthem! Stand up!"

I scramble to my feet, heart pounding and knees like the jelly ghost.

"What are you singing?"

I begin to tremble. "Jelly ghost, miss."

Everyone laughs treacherously.

"Be quiet! Repeat after me, young lady: 'Praise from the great angelic host.'"

Every girl wants to be a young lady, but somehow when you're called it by a grown-up it sounds really quite nasty. I swallow. "Praise from the great and jelly ghost."

More titters are silenced by Miss Didbury's blood-filled face.

"HOW DARE YOU!" Then in words clipped as sharp as blades, "Repeat . . . after . . . me . . . 'angelic host'."

I haven't a clue why I have to keep repeating it. I listen intently.

"Repeat it! Angelic host!"

Maybe 'ghost' is wrong. I take a deep breath and try to steady my voice: "And jelly coast."

More pitiless laughs. Miss Didbury calls me out to the front of the seated multitude, pushes up my cardigan sleeve (there is a lot of pushing to do) and slaps me over and over again with her Sunny Songs for Sunday School. Slap! Slap! Slap! Slap! Slap! I feel my lips trembling, but not because of the pain, nor even because of the humiliation of being punished in front of the whole of Sheepcote. I am devastated by the clenched teeth and pursed lips of this woman who seems, for no reason I can fathom, to hate me with all the spite in the world.

The vicar hangs his head awkwardly, shuffles from one foot to the other, and scratches his nose. Then he rubs his hands together and says with a little too much joviality, "How about some campfire songs? 'If you're happy and you know it . . .' Ready, everyone? One, two, three . . .'"

I go back to my place and clap my hands and stamp my feet with happiness along with everyone else, then as soon as the songs are over I slip off to find Tommy before Aunty Joyce or Uncle Jack get their hands on me. The brass band starts up and I scamper past the food tables where the poorer children are stuffing paste sandwiches down their shirts and jumpers, and weave my way through the boogie orchestra which is just setting up. I see Miss Hubble arriving on the back of a motorbike with a black American airman. She waves vigorously at me, totally unaware of what I have been through. They both look so glamorous, and I am pleased for her being with him, and pleased that she wasn't there earlier, because if she had been I would have wondered why she let it happen and did nothing.

Tommy reaches out an arm from behind the summer house and pulls me in towards him. He stands facing me sadly, and rubs my arm. I look back at him frowning, and can think of nothing to say.

Every time I open my mouth, it seems, I may well make someone angry. I'm determined to get to the bottom of it, and there's only one person I can ask.

"What's facky Nell?" I ask Tommy as we escape down the lane.

He gives a little laugh, and looks at me to check I'm being serious. "It's like swearing."

"Why?"

"What d'you mean, 'Why?' It just is."

"What's it mean?"

He looks a little coy. "It's like shaggin'."

"Ah . . ."

"You know shaggin' 'don't you?"

"Yes." I do know shagging. As a word. I haven't a clue what it's about.

"So . . . what's it mean?"

"Shaggin'? You don't know what it means?"

I shake my head. We walk on in silence. Then Tommy stops and looks at me.

"Come on!" he says, taking me by the hand. "I'll show you."

He helps me over a gate and leads me through some knee-high barley. I am full of anticipation, part excitement because this is an adventure — and part fear, because I have been warned about Tommy, and maybe I am about to discover why.

When we reach the other side of the field he helps me over another gate and on to a path which runs between some old corrugated iron huts and chicken coops. There is an old, disused caravan on the left-hand side, with bits of old upholstery hanging out of it.

"Where are we?" I ask.

"The Lovatts."

He grips my hand tighter and I feel a little thrill shoot up my arm.

"What's the Lovatts?"

"Just a smallholding. Used to be a big farm, now it's just bits and pieces."

He leads me into some bushes at the side, and I see there is another small path. I follow him, still holding his hand, until we stop in front of some wooden boxes. He opens a clasp on one and I can hear scuffling. I see now it is a hutch, and he's holding a large brown rabbit.

"Hold this," he says, and the rabbit scrambles furiously up on to my shoulder. I frantically try to pull it back, feeling its claws in my neck. But Tommy takes it back from me and places it in another hutch he has just opened.

"There," he says. "Watch."

We watch together, as two rabbits twitch their noses up

and down at us, then at each other. Soon the one rabbit has shuffled over to the other rabbit from behind, and seems to be nudging it. I look at Tommy curiously.

"What are we looking at this for?"

"That's shaggin'," says Tommy.

"What? That?"

"Yes. That's how they make babies. That's how babies are made. The male shags the female."

I stare at the cage in disbelief. He unfastens the cage door again, takes out the reluctant male by the ears and replaces him in his own cage.

We saunter back along the paths.

"Well, I won't say facky Nell again if it's swearing. But frankly, I can't see what all the fuss is about."

Tommy laughs.

"So is jelly ghost shaggin' as well?" I ask.

He laughs again.

"There's nothing wrong with your jelly ghost. You can say it as often as you like. It's just that they wanted you to sing 'angelic host'," he pronounces it in a very posh accent, "and they thought you were making fun of them."

We weave our way back through the barley.

"What's the angelic host?"

"A bunch of angels."

We reach the gate.

"Do you believe in angels?"

"No . . . do you?"

We lean on the gate together, looking out across the green and golden valley.

"Nah."

They are not angry with me when I get home late. In fact, Uncle Jack's face is a picture of sympathy and concern.

"That Miss Didbury needs taking down a peg or two," he confides.

"Jumped-up old hag," adds Aunty Joyce, handing me a cup of Ovaltine.

Although it soon becomes clear that it is not concern for me but venom for Miss Didbury that drives their unusual sympathy, I lap it up with a mixture of joy and relief.

"I've told Leslie time and time again she's not the woman for the job. And Mr Fairly agrees with me. But does he listen?"

Aunty Joyce shakes her head. "She doesn't have a clue how to deal with children."

"Not a clue."

"Daft bat."

"So full of her own importance!"

Maybe it is the Ovaltine, maybe it is the glow of the fire in the range, I don't know, but I feel so reassured that I take a notion to join in.

"Po-faced old twat!" I suggest.

They both stare at me in that same blank-but-indignant way sheep stare at you when you go in their field. Then they start to look not unlike Miss Didbury.

Uncle Jack makes me wash my mouth out with soap. It stings a lot. I start to cry and Aunty Joyce says I'm a very rude girl and makes me wash my hands three times.

I say my prayers trembling by the bedside, and round them off with: "I'm sorry God about the rude words but I don't know what's swearing and what's not and nobody will tell me, anyway, I don't see why Aunty Joyce and Uncle Jack are so horrible to me and why they are so horrible to Tommy. Please let me understand why they don't like a poor orphan boy. Otherwise, to be honest, I just don't think I can believe in you any more –"

"Shut up! Get into bed!"

I scramble into bed, and she approaches me with a candle.

"What's all this nonsense about Tommy?"

I have hidden my face under the covers.

"Kitty? What's he been telling you?"

I peep just above the covers. "Nothing. Just you don't like him."

"That wicked boy! What a . . . !"

There is a sharp intake of breath, "Now you listen to me, Kitty. Tommy Glover is a *bad sort*. A bad *bad* boy. You are not to go near him again, do you understand?"

She blows the candle out before I can answer, and I am left in the dark once more.

Command rescue

Even through the summer holidays, Sunday remains a busy day for me. Church is still followed after dinner by Sunday school, which is followed by a unique Sheepcote club called the 'Sheepcote Commando Cadets', an inspired creation by Mr Fairly from the boys' home to help with the war effort. I am now a fully fledged member of the SCC, which is really just an offshoot of the Sunday school and consists of the same children donning their commando gear immediately after prayers. The uniform, devised by the vicar and Miss Didbury, is a black beret and khaki jacket with black trousers for boys, black skirt for girls. Because only one boy has a black beret, most of the Sheepcote Commando Cadets wear red, blue, green or brown berets, or else woollen bonnets or balaclavas in a selection of interesting colours and patterns.

For most children, this is the highlight of their week. Our activities include map reading, tracking, signalling and first aid. We do collection rounds with an old pull-cart. We leave empty sacks outside people's houses and call back later to pick them up, full of paper, magazines for the air forces, or sometimes scrap metal for munitions and planes. But most interesting of all are the Civil Defence exercises. These are performed in conjunction with the APP and the Home Guard, and usually consist of a mock-up air raid in which numerous German V1 bombs take a notion to give Sheepcote a direct hit. Sheepcote Commando Cadets are needed to play the wounded, and some thirty-odd children are happily dispatched to the four corners of the village and surrounding fields with labels on their coats, and told to wait to be rescued.

My first time I'm sent to lie outside the post office with a 'badly mutilated torso – severe bleeding' and Tommy has to slump by the baker's with mustard gas poisoning. Miss Didbury has 'severe burns' and has to be lowered from Mr Tugwell's 'blazing' upstairs window, which involved Mr Tugwell (the grocer) and Mr Marsh (the milkman) tying her up zealously with ropes. Baggie Aggie Tugwell (who only has 'mild concussion') looks on enviously. The vicar, who has 'lacerated legs – delirious', plays his part so well that the Home Guard think he has completely lost it. Miss Didbury is black and blue all over and vows she will never take part in another exercise. The vicar finds screaming at members of his congregation a tremendous release, and looks forward to the next operation. I don't know what a torso is so I hold my leg and roll around on the pavement for a long time, moaning in agony, until Mrs Chudd from the post office tells me she can't hear the telephone, and I'm carried off on a stretcher to the village hall. Poor Tommy comes off the worst. Since the treatment for mustard gas poisoning is to wash the skin, the APP set up screens around the baker's, strip him naked and give him the coldest shower you can imagine. He reckons mustard gas isn't a threat any more and this is just plain barbarism.

On another occasion he is sent to the field next to Lady Elmsleigh's with 'head injury and severed leg', where he lies for three hours waiting for rescue. Then it begins to get dark, and Lady Elmsleigh spots him and invites him in out of the cold. She gives him tea and drives him back to Heaven House, tartly reassuring Mr Fairly that he would have bled to death by now anyway.

Uncle Jack is dogged by the same fantasy as every man in Sheepcote, and there is something about the long stretch of the war that sharpens its allure. It is, quite simply, to be a hero.

It is all very well for the men in the armed forces. They just have to be absent from daily life to become heroes. For all anyone knows they may be sharpening pencils in some hidden barracks, but they wear a uniform, and that entitles them to the same awe as those who regularly blast Germans to bits and lose body parts. But, for those doing Essential Work, like Uncle Jack on his railway, it's not so easy.

You can see he wants so much to make a difference. He longs for people to look at him the same way they look at the young servicemen who walk indifferently into shops but have women almost genuflecting in respect, awe and lust. If he were to share his thoughts with any number of Sheepcote men he would find he's not alone in his fantasy heroics, for they too probably rescue maidens from pillaging Germans and heave friends from the flames of battle on a daily basis.

The trouble is, Uncle Jack has spent his life preaching against vanity, even though his ambitions to stand at the golden eagle in front of a packed church are fuelled by the very same thirst for glory. Even with his manly composure and the attention of a full nave, he cannot command the same mystique as the American soldiers with their wretched chewing gum. And despite years of striving, it seems he cannot even challenge the indifference of his wife, let alone the utter unamazement of an entire congregation.

Then one day he sees his opportunity, and decides to grab it. It is on one of these very training days, in fact, where men, women and children are proving their potential heroism to a considerable audience.

Things are coming to a ragged sort of end, and people are tidying up, when there is a shriek from the upstairs window of one of the council houses. Looking up, Uncle Jack sees his chance. Young Mrs Nicholas is shouting for help, although the day's exercise is definitely over.

Quick as a flash he grabs the ladder that is being loaded on to the back of the APP van and runs to the small front garden. Up he climbs, fearless as a young officer, turning round briefly to check his audience.

"Watch carefully and observe!" he commands Mr Tugwell, Mr Chudd, the vicar and an assortment of astonished onlookers.

The ladder is a little short, and he is still a few feet lower than the victim when he reaches the top. He approaches the window and grabs the young woman brusquely under the arms.

"It's okay. I've got you!"

Young Mrs Nicholas shrieks again.

"Don't worry, I've got you. You're safe now. Just hold on tight!" and he begins to yank her forward.

She screams and beats her fists on his shoulder blades. "I don't want to be fucking safe!" she hollers. "I'm dusting the fucking windows, aren't I?"

Uncle Jack looks up to see what he hadn't noticed before: a man in a state of complete undress standing behind her. Mr Nicholas is home on leave and, seeing his wife leaning out and dusting the windows, has had the sudden notion to disrupt her daily routine. It is while Uncle Jack is trying to absorb this shocking animal fact that he loses his balance on the ladder which, amply helped by the thumps of Mrs Nicholas, moves like the hand of a clock turning a quarter past.

45

Women run from all over to crowd around the injured hero, lying in some redcurrant bushes with badly bruised hip and pride. One of the girls from my Sunday school group, Babs Sedgemoor, whispers in my ear, "She was getting it from behind." I nod sagely, and remember the bunnies.

Miss Lavish stops her tricycle in front of me in a panic. "Whatever's happened?"

"Uncle Jack tried to rescue her," I explain. "But she was just having a shag."

A little on the lonely side

In the night I dream I'm being held in my mother's arms. It's so real I can feel my bottom pressed into her warm lap and my cheek resting against the soft inside of her arm. I swear I actually wake up in the dark and know she's there. But when the morning light wakes me through the curtains, she is gone.

There is no sound from downstairs yet, and I lie for a while listening to the birds and the distant bleating of a sheep. The walls of my room are white with leaves of duck-egg blue winding up to the ceiling in stripes on the wallpaper. The curtains are cream with ladies on horseback riding across the folds. They have red jackets and black hats and smile as they race off to the kill with their little patchy dogs. The room is empty apart from the bed, a chest of drawers and a picture of Jesus, which hangs above my pillow. And then there is the door, that other door covered in so many layers of cream paint the panel ridges are just faint hollows. It is the cupboard I cannot open, but by now I am sure it holds some important clue to Uncle Jack and Aunty Joyce. I am certain that if I can just find the key to it, all will be revealed. I imagine opening it and finding a body or something. I sort of want to open it, and I sort of don't.

On this particular morning I seem to have woken early, and I am aware of something stirring under the bed. When I find the courage to look, I can see nothing, but I can hear some distinct rustling. There's a cardboard box shoved right against the wall with old magazines in it. I reach out and tug at an open flap, afraid I'll be bitten by a rat. Instantly a paw comes out and swipes me on the wrist.

"Kemble!" I croon, a little annoyed at the scratch. "Kemble, come out and let me cuddle you." I pull harder at the box and get another blow from her paw. But I know she'll be in for it if she's found upstairs, so I pull the box right out. The sight of four tiny kittens fills me with such awe that I just sit perfectly still and watch them until I hear Aunty Joyce's creaking tread on the stairs down to the parlour.

Even Aunty Joyce's insistence that we cannot keep the kittens does nothing to prevent this new feeling of light-heartedness. I have four kittens and Kemble has chosen my bed to have them under.

"Don't go getting too attached," she says. "They'll have to go."

"Oh, let her keep them a while," says Uncle Jack.

"Whatever for?"

"It's not fair to take them from the mother this early. Let her suckle them at least. Wait till they're weaned."

"Have you gone mad? Why?"

"She'll only pine for them if she loses them this soon. Think of the cat."

Aunty Joyce slams a loaf of bread on the table, then goes off to the pantry and slams a few tins around on the shelf. Then she comes back and throws a pot of jam on the table.

Uncle Jack looks shifty and says nothing. Aunty Joyce is breathing fire.

"Oh. Think of the cat! Think of the ruddy cat, why don't you? She'll lose her blessed kittens! Imagine how she'll feel! Don't ever ruddy well think of me!" She kicks the range door shut with her foot. I feel I ought to point out to someone that if twat is a swear word then I'm fairly certain ruddy is too, but she has slammed out into the back garden and Uncle Jack does not look at me. He puts on his boots and goes out of the front door without speaking. Her tantrum is not mentioned again, but I'm pretty sure she never has to wash her mouth out with soap.

Summer arrives in full flood. The road outside the cottage has halved in width as the hedgerows expand fatly along its sides. That summer of 1944, working in the fields and the barns, loitering in the lanes, is the summer I remember most of the whole war. I spend it with the other children earthing up potatoes, picking up stones, cutting thistles and rat-catching, or swapping stories against the knobbly trunk of an old oak tree with Tommy.

In the early mornings we're sent off to Farmer Hawking's, up behind the back garden, whose foreman 'Thumper' gives us jobs to do. It takes me nearly a week to learn to milk.

"First you wash them," Thumper says, giving me a wet rag, "then give us a shout an' I'll show you how to hold the udders."

A few minutes later one of the prisoners of war, Franz, starts laughing, and a couple of the land girls join in. Thumper comes back down the line of cows to see how I'm getting on and stands looking at me, his head on one side, smiling.

"What?" I ask.

"Still washing?"

"It takes ages," I look up at them all, and can feel the red of my cheeks and little drops of sweat around my hairline.

"I'm not surprised! You're supposed to wash the udders, not the whole bloody cow!"

There are hoots of laughter all round, but the German prisoner on the other side of me leans on his cow's back and says kindly, "It is a good thing you do. She likes it I sink." He smiles at me. "She gives you more milk, you will see."

My whole body aches with milking, and my fingers grow so stiff I can hardly move them. All I manage is a tiny squirt that barely wets the bottom of the pail. As the days pass my squirts become rhythmic and strong, and Heinrich, the kind German, can find less and less in each udder as he finishes the cows off for me.

When milking is over we all gather in the barn and Aunty Joyce brings out a tray of tea with bread and dripping. The prisoners talk to each other in one corner, although I notice Heinrich is often quiet. He seems to look over at me and Aunty Joyce a lot. I look at her as she puts down her tray and blows the air up her face so that the blonde wisps dance aside. She is flushed, and with her sleeves rolled up and her heavily patched wellingtons pulled over her droopy corduroys, she looks radiant. I have been so tied up in trying to understand her that I forgot for a while how beautiful she can be.

On the way to the fields from the cow barn is the short lane leading back to Weaver's Terrace, and the trees bordering it are in full bloom, forming an arched tunnel of green. On our first day of fieldwork Tommy flies on ahead of me with the other children, calling to me to hurry up. But I stand in the middle of the lane, feet planted firmly on the yellow track, and stare upwards. I am so awed at the plumpness of a full-blown summer, the rampant sticky stems and the sweet woody smell of the air, that I forget to move. My insides pummel at me like a rabbit in a sack, and I don't know if it is homesickness or the overwhelming shock of tender green that makes my face wet with tears.

At dinner time, in these first few weeks, I find an excuse to slip home so that I can check up on my kittens. Aunty Joyce moved them out of the house straight away and stuck them in a tool shed near the lav. I cuddle each one in turn and they let me, until they spill out of my grasp, light as air, and on to the grass. Some days, if Aunty Joyce is not there, I take them into the house. There is a little black and white I call Boomer who always runs up and down on the piano in the front room. Since I've never been invited into this room, I guess it is somewhere I shouldn't go, a bit like Aunty Vi's front room, reserved for visitors only. When Boomer runs up and down the piano it's a devil of a job to get him back out because the door doesn't shut properly. He knocks over the wedding photograph or leaps into the knitting basket and plays with the wool. I can see he's going to be a handful when he's older, but he's definitely my favourite.

Sometimes Heinrich comes with me to see the kittens. He leans over the back wall from the field and looks wistful.

"Ket!" he says sometimes.

"And kittens," I say.

"Is like you. Kitty! You are a kitty, I sink."

I laugh. It is always the same joke, but it is his attempt to make contact. And when I give him a kitten to stroke, he caresses it so hungrily I can feel the great hollow he is desperate to fill, and it is just like mine. We kiss and cuddle the kittens, snuggling their soft fur to our cheeks and necks with matching greed.

Germ warfare

Since Uncle Jack's shifts keep changing, our routine in the Shepherd household revolves around the Railway. When he does an early turn a boy comes knocking at the door in the small hours and shouts, "Jack! Jack! You up?" like he's barking mad or something. And since Uncle Jack is never late for anything, he shouts, "Keep your hair on, you noisy blighter!" and stomps grumpily out of the hallway with his boots already laced up.

I don't always wake up with the call-boy, but on the few occasions his knocking has pulled me out of sleep I have had that sense again that my mum has been with me, holding me in her arms. I can almost feel her warmth taken suddenly away from me, and then I become so chilly I can't get back to sleep.

When Uncle Jack comes home after an early turn, Aunty Joyce always complains about the night's banging, and he curiously changes allegiance, explaining that if he *had* over-slept he wouldn't have been able to get the engine up to steam on time, and the whole system would be running late. The call-boy, he maintains, is an essential part of the well-oiled machine that is the very Great Western Railway. Other times Aunty Joyce complains that his eight-hour shift has lasted nine hours, and he places his black oilskin driver's cap upon the table, tilts his head back importantly, and explains. "What you've got to understand," he says, "is there is no such thing as an eight-hour shift with the Great Western. You can't relieve a train halfway between Stroud and Gloucester, or between Cheltenham and Swindon. The driver stays with his train until the journey is complete. Then – and only then – can he finish his shift." He sits back and taps the flat of his hand on the table. "How would it be if I took a running jump halfway between Stonehouse and Stroud? Hmm?"

Aunty Joyce looks sometimes as though she thinks this might be a very good idea. And although her main irritation is that she can never get dinner on the table at the same time for him, I wonder if she's a little fed up with his evangelical devotion to the Railway and to God, and maybe wishes he would be a little more devoted to her.

Uncle Jack's shifts mean that some weeks Aunty Joyce needs me in the mornings, and sometimes in the afternoons or evenings, so my farm help is never too regular. There are no annual summer holidays for the teachers, and if children can't be at home or in the fields then they're found chores to do at school. Of course, the Heaven House boys flock to the fields, and only the very small ones have to help at school. And since I know I'll end up there too if I can't be of enough use to Aunty Joyce or the farm, I am eager to get some sort of routine going.

When milking is over, Tommy and the others go off to the fields, and I sometimes go with them. But if Aunty Joyce needs me for chores, I stay while the prisoners muck out the sheds and load the heavy churns on to the waiting milk cart, and until Aunty Joyce has finished collecting all the empties on her tray.

After breakfast I sweep the kitchen floor, feed the chickens and pick vegetables from the garden, while Aunty Joyce sits at the kitchen table to consult her second bible, *Gleanings from Gloucestershire Housewives*, before pronouncing on the intended dinner.

The grocer is Mr Tugwell, Baggie Aggie's husband, and he always gives me a wink. Aunty Joyce buys a tin of Spam, some flour and butter or a portion of cheese. She doesn't buy powdered eggs because we have our own, but she never fails to remark on the poor souls in cities who have to rely on the stuff.

"This poor girl never had a fresh egg in her life till she came to us," she says with a self-congratulatory shake of the head. I soon realize how important it is for the world to see what a fine job she is doing with one of the nation's unfortunate paupers. Sometimes, if there's a crowd, I join in: "I thought cows grew on trees till I came here," or "At last I'm free of nits," or, better still, taking off my bonnet and giving my head a good shake, "Look! The nits have almost gone!"

Aunty Joyce usually pats me on the head and smiles at the other shoppers.

She does find it hard to smile, I think. With her curly blonde pageboy hair, her generous lips and wistful blue eyes, there is more than a passing resemblance to Ingrid Bergman. And the butcher, Mr Glass (of wife with very fat arse), often gives her his wrapped pink flesh with a wink and tells her that for a moment he thought he was in Hollywood, even though we are standing ankle deep in sawdust and surrounded by smiling china pigs wearing aprons. She never gives anything more than a wooden smile, but he keeps on trying.

Of course it is hard to imagine why anyone would want to flirt with a man who sports a meat cleaver and wears blood. He often puts his raw bloodied knuckles into my cheek and says, "Hello, my darlin'," and I want to duck. But still, I wish she would loosen up a bit.

I think hard about ways to make her laugh, and start to tell jokes in the shop queues.

"What am I saying, then? Look!" I touch my ear, my eyes and my nose. "What is it then, eh?"

But Aunty Joyce just looks uncomfortable.

"Ear eye nose you!" I blurt out, grinning hopefully. "Get it? Ear, eye nose you! Get it? D'you get it?"

She tells me not to be rude.

"No. See, it's not rude, it's —"

"You're making too much noise!"

"All right," I whisper, "how about this one? One bloke goes to another bloke, 'My wife's on 'oliday,' and the other bloke goes, 'Jamaica?' and he goes, 'No, she went of her own accord!'"

She frowns sternly. My voice has risen steadily and I find I'm belting it out.

"D'you get it?"

Maybe she would tell me off good and proper if she didn't notice the other women in the shop tittering.

"My, she's a card, en' she?"

"You got a right cracker there, Joyce," "Lovely to hear them happy, ennit?" and, from Miss Lavish, "How are your knickers, Kitty?"

"I got plenty more of them up my sleeve," I say, basking in the attention. "Not knickers — jokes!" Everyone laughs. I am a success. "D'ya hear the one about the bear with piles . . . ?"

The shop is in uproar. I am as high as a kite, and Aunty Joyce, praised for her highly entertaining protégée, still only manages to roll her eyes at their mirth.

Back home the day's spoils are lined up on the kitchen table and put into the larder. Now we prepare the vegetables.

I am not allowed to do any chopping, but I scrape the carrots and new potatoes and wash the cabbage or lettuce in the sink in ice-cold water.

Before she lets me do anything Aunty Joyce makes sure my hands are clean. She ties back my hair with a fat kirby grip and sets to work scrubbing my nails for me. Then, to my bewilderment, she washes the tap. In these days of shortages, of thin slivers of soap to serve whole families, Aunty Joyce *washes the tap*. She does this "to stop the germs". I have it in my head that germs are something to do with Germans, so I'm happy to enter into the spirit of things, at first.

"It's no good cleaning your hands if you then go and turn off the tap which you turned on with dirty hands." She looks at me with wide eyes: "*Recontamination, Kitty!*"

After the cleaning rituals she takes down her book from its shelf and reads aloud the recipe for the day's dinner. I always feel important when she reads out to me, and sometimes she even asks me for advice.

"Small tin of corned beef – have we got that, Kitty? Two or three onions?"

I nod gravely.

"A small quantity of lard?"

"It will have to be small," I say.

"Okay. Cut beef into slices and place in bottom of dish . . ."

After reading, she announces one day that Mr South has killed a pig and promised her the head. She starts flicking pages.

"Brawn . . . mmm . . . I fancy a bit of brawn. *Half a pig's head that has been salted or pickled . . . one or more pig's tongues . . . clean out the eye part. Put the head and tongues into a saucepan, cover with water, and bring slowly to the boil.*"

Facky Nell!

I take some newspaper from the shopping basket, sit at the table and begin cutting it into squares.

"What are you doing?"

"Cutting it for the lav."

"We don't use paper that's been *used*, Kitty. We use clean newspaper, that's been *read*."

I stop cutting and look up. "It's all going on your bum, isn't it?"

"Don't be disgusting!" She looks at me with utter repugnance. "Ah! Here we are: *Headcheese: the pig's head is singed, then soaked in salt water for twenty-four hours. It is then taken out, scrubbed and cleaned. A red-hot poker is thrust into its ears and nostrils* . . . blah . . . blah . . ."

I put my hand to my mouth and close my eyes tightly. Aunty Joyce goes on for some time about simmering and liquid. ". . . *take note that the eyes which in boiling will be removed from their sockets are taken out and thrown to the hens. The ears are chopped with the other meat.*"

"I ain't feeding no eyeballs to hens. I ain't eating no chopped-up ears!" I run to the sink and retch.

She looks faint. "Lord above! Now I'll have to disinfect the sink!"

"Please, I wasn't actually sick. You needn't worry!"

"There was a dribble! I saw it! As if I haven't enough to do without all these extra germs!"

She looks so wretched that I begin to feel sorry for her, as well as feeling deeply guilty for having brought so many extra germs into the house.

As the weeks pass, however, I do wonder if Aunty Joyce isn't perhaps a bit barking mad. This household germ invasion seems to keep her more occupied than the German one which is bothering everyone else.

It's one particular event which first arouses my suspicions. I've been up in the fields earthing potatoes and return home to find the house empty. I'm aware of making great clods of earth on the front path, so I leave my shoes outside the front door. There may even be some cow dung on them, for I've been in the cowshed earlier with Tommy. At any rate, I stand by the range in my stocking feet and wonder what I should do. The parlour is spotless, so there's no point in tidying. I go into the front room and open the window to see if Aunty Joyce is coming. There's no sign of her, so I take a newspaper, place it on the front room sofa, and sit down on it tentatively so as not to leave a trace of dirt. I pick up a magazine from the rack on the floor. Mrs Sew-and-Sew is looking smug next to some refooted stockings, and so is a boy whose mother has cut off his overcoat to make him a hideous jacket. I wouldn't be so chuffed if I were him. I'm having real trouble with some of the words, when there is a grunt from the window. I look up and see Aunty Joyce trying to open the window wider with her elbows, her fists clenched tight in front of her. I rush over to help her.

"What is it? You okay?"

She seems surprised to see me.

"Could you hold the curtains right back?" she asks, a terrible expression of pain and confusion in her face. Then she begins to ease herself on to the window ledge and, huffing and puffing, she manages to get one leg over. "Don't let me touch the curtains!"

I hold them back as far as I can, and something shiny and heavy slips out on to the carpet from the curtain hem. She is so busy trying to squeeze through the window without touching anything that she doesn't notice it, and I slip it into my dress pocket.

After launching herself through the window and hurling herself like a paratrooper on to the carpet in front of me, Aunty Joyce completes a small roll and sits up, fists still clenched, relieved. She lets me help her up by the elbow, and

58

when I follow her into the kitchen and she asks me to turn on the tap, I begin to work something out. By now I am fluent in the language of germs, and I see that I'm not the one who's contaminated. I can't pick germs up from the dirt around me: it is Aunty Joyce. She is afraid of touching things – not just because they will contaminate her – but because *she* will contaminate *them*. Dirt affects *her* – not other people – and she alone bears the responsibility for keeping it to herself.

Skeletons in the cupboard

In my pocket is a key.

It fits, of course. I prepare myself for a dangling skeleton as I unlock the cupboard, my blood pumping so hard I'm sure my head must be nodding back and forth like one of the hens.

It is difficult to say whether I'm disappointed or relieved. For there, hanging up, is a row of neatly pressed girls' clothes. A yellow gingham dress, a pink floral one, a blue plaid one and a selection of cardigans. There are pastel summer ones in four-ply and winter ones with collars and pockets in double knit. There is a small pair of corduroy trousers too, and a row of little shoes. I pick one up. It is a red leather strapped shoe, as pretty as can be, but second-hand. I try it on. Although it is slightly too wide, it almost fits in length and is more comfortable than my boots. I try on its partner, and walk up and down the room. Indignation starts to bubble inside me, and I take in deep breaths as I look at this little treasure trove locked away from me for so long. It is quite clear that these were meant for me. Some kind soul like Miss Lavish or Baggie Aggie or Lady Elmsleigh – or maybe even Aunty Joyce herself – got these in preparation for my arrival. But somehow I have not lived up to expectations, and Aunty Joyce has thought the better of it. She was expecting a little girl with glossy ringlets and clean nails, a girl with good manners who never said twat or facky Nell. That I have been a huge disappointment to them is obvious, but I am so hurt I forget that I am precisely what they *were* expecting: a girl from the East End, warts and all. Or if it does dawn on me for an instant, I shove it aside in the fury of realizing that I am not good enough, not worthy enough in some way for these beautiful clothes. Only one thing is clear: for some reason, she does not like me. I have always suspected it, but now I know.

I plod up the lane to the farm sick with self-pity, aching for someone to talk to, to undo the knot of emotions which is tightening around my throat. But my mum is making weapons and my dad is using them somewhere in Burma. There is a loneliness in being away from those you love, and there is another quite different loneliness, of not fitting in, of standing on the outside of everything around you, with alien smells and alien accents and alien emotions. The smells of muck and dung and sap and silage taunt me as much as the frenzied attack on every wrong word I say. And the sun can shine and the flowers bloom and the birds trill all they like, but the withdrawal of touch is like a prison cell. I am eight years old. To live with a woman who recoils from me is the loneliest thing on earth.

I find Tommy on the way to the fields, and we bunk off together, heading to the woods to the west of Sheepcote. As we enter the woods he takes my hand – just sort of holds it out slightly for me, so that I could miss it almost, if I weren't so longing to hold on to someone. We walk through a tangle of low vegetation. I still can't quite believe the way that plants grow. Nothing seems to stop them, and they are everywhere, letting off a stink of juice and sap and pollen. There are tall, indestructible leaves like rubber (he calls these lords-and-ladies) and colonies of leathery leaves, tough as oilskins (he calls these wild garlic); there are stinging nettles with leaves the size of my hand; there are a few ugly spotted orchids that make me catch my breath in horror for fear they might sting (he calls these 'bee-orchids'), and things that spring out at you from nowhere. There are pretty white star-shaped flowers called wood anemones. Tommy says they're sometimes called 'smell fox'.

"Smell fox?"

"Yep. Know why?"

"Foxes like 'em?"

"No. 'Cos they've got poison in their stems. Can give you blisters. Sly like foxes, see."

Tommy reckons that plants were here millions of years before man and will be here millions of years after we're gone.

"They're the most powerful living things on the planet," he says, and I believe him. "Hold the answer to all illness, they do."

He stops now and then to show me a butterfly, and sketches them quickly in his notebook, which he carries in his pocket. When he's finished he tucks the short pencil behind his ear like the grocer or the bread deliveryman. Today there is a tortoiseshell, a wall brown, a meadow brown and a large skipper. There are moths too, wings folded horizontally on the tree bark. I treasure their names like jewels: pale tussock, burnished brass, rosy rustic. There is a buff-topped one that looks like a stick and he makes me hold one, so that I won't be afraid any more at night.

Out of the woods, it is the unbroken horizons that impress me most. There are no jagged edges like in cities, since the villages are nestled into the slopes, and their ageing stone merges so well into the landscape that a thin mist can hide them altogether. Some mornings a whole hill can disappear under the mists.

Even with the arrival of jeeps and combine harvesters, chewing gum and jitterbugging, this little pocket of Gloucestershire seems secluded in spirit. Tommy says the hills were nothing but sheepwalks once, and the land nothing more than herbs and wild grasses to feed the famous – the glorious – Cotswold sheep. Now the drystone walls remain, but the fields are being stuffed with wheat and barley, potatoes and mangolds, and every bit of fallow pasture is ploughed up for the war effort. It's all wrong, according to Tommy. He says we'll never get the fallow land back, and it's storing up problems for the future. The land needs to breathe, to rest, to renew itself. He shakes his head. He's afraid his good earth is ruined for ever.

When the church bell strikes ten o'clock and I'm certain Aunty Joyce will be out, I take Tommy down to the back field behind our house to play with the kittens.

Kemble is lying slumped in a patch of sunlight behind the shed, and two of her kittens are suckling. The other two are bouncing and leaping around the garden, falling over each other and attacking imaginary foes.

Tommy's face lights up. He can't stop smiling.

"Look at that one – he's bonkers!"

The black kitten is doing a somersault over a leaf he has found, then pushing the leaf with his paw so that it moves and he can attack it all over again.

I laugh too. "He can be yours, if you like."

Tommy looks at me, open-mouthed. "You're allowed to keep 'em?"

"We're keeping them till they're weaned. Uncle Jack says so. You can have Bonkers and I'll have Boomer and Heinrich is mad about the little tortoiseshell. He calls her Kitty!"

I pick up Bonkers and give him to Tommy to hold, then

hold Boomer up and smile into his dear kitten face. I try to detect a smile on Boomer's face, but he looks off into the middle distance and wriggles free.

"Best not get too attached," says Tommy. "They won't let you keep him."

I consider this for a moment. Whatever happens I will continue to see Boomer. I'll visit whoever owns him every day, or else I'll hide him.

"It's Aunty Joyce," I say, biting my lip. "She doesn't like me."

"What makes you say that?"

I pick at a few tufts of grass and hold them up to the kittens. "She doesn't like you and she doesn't like me. I know she doesn't like me. She had a whole load of girls' clothes hidden away – nice stuff – and she makes me wear this, and I know what's going on because it's all the right size, and the reason she hasn't even let me try it on is obvious!"

"What?" He looks strangely worried. Almost panic-stricken.

"There's just something about me she can't like, no matter how hard she tries. What is it, Tommy? What's wrong with me?"

He breathes out a long sigh and smiles. "It's not you." He shuffles up closer to me by the wall and puts his arm around me. "These clothes weren't meant for you, look. She collects things."

"No she doesn't."

"Old family stuff, she does. And look, I can promise you, you're very lovable, you are." He gives my shoulder a squeeze, and I flop into it, taking grateful wafts of his woollen sheep-smelling jacket.

When it is teatime I have an idea. I go upstairs and take out the little key from my curtain hem, where I've hidden it. I open the door and select the yellow gingham dress and try it on with the pair of red shoes and a lemon-coloured cardigan. I creep into their bedroom and look at myself in the dressing-table mirror, turning this way and that and smiling at my reflection. It is dinner at teatime today, and I can't wait to see the surprise on Uncle Jack's face when he sees how smart I can look. And Aunty Joyce will wish she'd thought of lending them to me sooner.

It seems foolish now, I know, but that little eight-year-old simply doesn't guess. I blunder in there in the full party frock of their dead daughter and wonder why Aunty Joyce drops the runner beans all over the floor and opens her mouth in slow motion and narrows her eyes and lets out the most terrifying howl anyone has ever aimed at me before or since. I wonder why she leaps on me like a mad woman, tears off the cardigan and orders me to "Get it off! Get it off. You wicked girl!" I wonder why she screams, "How dare you?" so many times, and why Uncle Jack just keeps repeating, "Joyce! Joyce! Joyce!"

Counting ourselves lucky

There are many stealthy sorrows in Sheepcote. There are those you just chance upon, like George, who drives an imaginary Spitfire down the road and makes the sound of an engine. He is a six-footer with the build of a warrior, but his little head hangs apologetically from his monstrous shoulders, and when the village girls tease him – "D'you wanna go out with us then, George?" – his eyes light up and he nods so credulously it would break your heart.

Then there are those you'd never guess at, hidden behind the little lace curtains and the stoic Sheepcote faces, sorrows and secrets that only an invisible person at the knitting group can uncover.

There is Mrs Marsh with the small moustache, whose husband delivers the milk and who's taken in the evacuee, Babs Sedgemoor. She's lost two of her three sons in the war, one by a U-boat and one shot down over France, and she's had no bodies to bury. Her gloves and mittens are perfect, with not a stitch out of place, not a fault in the neat four-ply. Then there's Mrs Glass with the very fat arse, the butcher's wife. She can hardly look Mrs Marsh in the eye with two strapping lads, still too young to join up, and lucky as Larry to be safe on Gloucestershire soil and not lifeless on some strange field far from the smell of home. She is so guilty for it you wouldn't know she forgot to put cold water in the tub some years back and immersed her first-born in a bath of freshly boiled water. The fatal baptism killed her only daughter, and left a furrow on her brow which everyone understands and no one speaks of, at least not while she's there. "I'm a lucky woman," she says eagerly, and with a note of apology for her two healthy boys, safer than they should be in the midst of war; but no one really knows what 'lucky' is any more.

But what of Aunty Joyce? I listen eagerly for snippets about her. Often, on a Thursday, she'll pack me off to the village hall and stay in with Uncle Jack if his shift means he's home. At least, that's what she tells Aggie and the others, but I can't see them having much fun together.

These are good times for me though, because I've learnt that whenever someone is absent, they become the unofficial topic of conversation.

"See our Joyce is busy again," starts Mrs Chudd. "Got work up at the farm, 'ave she?"

"Just spending some time with Uncle Jack, I think."

"Oooh?" A mewling of surprise from Mrs Chudd.

A moment of silence, but Mrs Chudd will not let this one go. "She's such a pretty thing. I wonder she doesn't wear make-up any more. Have you noticed? She could look like a film star with a bit of rouge."

"It's Jack as stops her," says Aggie Tugwell.

"No!"

"He does. I heard that ever since . . . you know . . . he won't let her touch the stuff."

"Get away!"

"Tiz true."

"Well, that don't make no sense, do it? Tiz like he's punishing her."

"Twuz hardly her fault."

"Makes no sense at all."

Clicking of needles. Things are hotting up. I put my nose down and knit furiously.

"These things make people behave in strange ways," says Miss Lavish, generously. "I should think it can tear a couple apart."

"It takes its toll for certain," says Aggie.

"It do that," says Mrs Marsh, her moustache unmoved.

"But tiz no one's fault . . ."

"Well . . ."

"They do say that lad Tommy —"

"No!"

"Well, there was something fishy going on," says Mrs Chudd, pulling decisively at her ball of wool to unravel another yard.

"Tommy would never do a thing like that. I'm sure of it," says Miss Lavish.

"Well . . . that's not how she sees it. I don't know how she puts up with it. Seeing him around."

"She's a saint is Joyce."

"She is that."

Then all faces suddenly freeze as Aunty Joyce turns up with my cardigan and decides to stay till the end. We talk about Gregory Peck and Betty Chudd's amazing arithmetic, and I am left yet again with this notion that Tommy has done something too dreadful to speak of, and also with the more curious notion that Aunty Joyce is, of all things, a 'saint'.

When we get back it's still light, but time for my bed. I go out the back to the lav, and try hard not to think of the many-legged creatures scuttling around the wooden seat and in the murky corners. After I've flushed I go round the back of the shed to the kittens, but they're not in the box. I look under the wooden crates and in the bushes and over the wall. At last I see Kemble and she comes to rub up against my legs.

"Where are those naughty kittens?" She continues to rub up against me, but makes strange mewling noises. "Have you lost them? Let's help you find them."

I search behind the hen coop, in the cinder pile and between the rows of beans. Then I lift the lid of a pail, which is sitting by the shed, and see a pile of wet fur with pink flesh visible underneath.

I drop the lid and it clatters off down between the runner beans. Kemble comes up and sniffs the pail, miaowing pathetically. I take them out one by one and lay them on the grass, but Boomer I pick up in my arms. I hold his little soggy body close to mine. His head rolls right back and I support it in my hand, catching my breath as giant angry sobs build up like a tidal wave.

"NO!" I scream. "No! No! No!" I run indoors, Boomer's little head flopping backwards as I trundle into the parlour.

Uncle Jack covers his face with his hand, but not in shock, more as though he saw it coming. I plant myself in front of Aunty Joyce, face burning with tears and nose running over my lips, ready to rebuff all her excuses.

She looks at me unmoved. It is not the look of a saint.

Sketching heaven

Once again the solace of touch is taken away as I awake. There was a human warmth surrounding me and now it has gone with the sunlight on the curtains.

Yesterday's horror steals over me. I remember my wakefulness for hours and lean out of bed to reach for the bundle I have left hidden beneath it. I unwrap Boomer from my cardigan and stroke his dried fur gently.

I am a bag of nerves and sorrow and anger. I will run away. I will kill myself. I will kill Aunty Joyce, smash this house to pieces, scream in church, stab Miss Didbury, swear in Sunday school, facky, facky, facky Nell! And facky Jesus and facky jelly ghost!

Instead I pound the eiderdown with my fists, grit my teeth, and go straight out of the house without any breakfast, leaving Aunty Joyce standing by the range with a pot full of porridge.

I go to the only grown-up I can think of who might understand my grief. He is still busy milking, but he stops when he sees me with my bundle and my rumpled face. "Look, Heinrich! Look what she's done!"

He stands up, and then immediately crouches down to comfort me.

"He is dead?" He takes Boomer and strokes him affectionately. "And the others also?"

I nod, blotchy-faced, folding my lips as tightly shut as I can, but then erupt into ferocious sobs: "She did it! Aunty Joyce! She drowned them all in a bucket! She's a cruel witch! She's a witch!"

Heinrich puts his arm around me and pulls me in close. I can smell the reassuring cow odours of his jacket and the musty woody smell of his neck and hair, and suddenly everything feels a little bit all right. This is the consolation I need, the rescuing warmth of an embrace, the fragrant comfort of human skin.

"Don't cry, Liebling. Don't cry."

I gulp in the balsamic wafts from his closeness, unwilling to let go. He strokes my hair. "I sink Joyce she is a gentle woman. I sink she will not hurt any creature without a good reason."

And I realize, looking up from my burrow, that she is standing there – behind me – and he is looking at her as he speaks. She is blushing.

There is a silence as they look at each other, and I start to feel sick. I pull away, but Heinrich says, "Come with me."

I am grateful to get out of her presence. We go off together to a neighbouring barn and pick up some wood, leaving her standing in the cow barn.

He makes me a cross with 'Boomer' carved on it. Even working at speed, he is deft with his knife on the wood.

"I will make a more important one later," he smiles. "You bury him now."

Aunty Joyce is going round with her tray, and I catch her looking at us as I dash off with my tombstone and corpse. Maybe she is sorry now. Maybe I'll get into trouble later. Either way, I don't care.

* * *

Tommy is horrified, of course, and we shoot off across the fields towards the lanes and then down to the stile and our special meadow. The cowslips have all but gone, and tall thistles take their place. We run and run as if the very force of our movements will burn up our anger. Over the next gate, and the next, until we're looking right across the valley.

"All this . . ." he pants, sweeping his arm across the panorama, ". . . all this will be ours one day."

"How d'you mean?"

"After the war . . . everything'll be shared up, as it should be."

I look out at the green and golden fields as they rise up the slopes beyond the stream, the pretty hamlet perched near the top and the sheep grazing sleepily on the hillside.

"This'll be our bit," he says, decisively. "And this is where Boomer would've roamed. So this is where we should bury him." We will have to bury the other kittens later.

He breaks off a piece of branch and starts to dig under a beech tree, while I try to take in the heady news that I have a future with Tommy.

It is a long, mucky job, but when we've finished we sing 'The day thou gavest Lord has ended', which is what is always sung in church when one of our lads is shot down. Then, since drowning was the cause of death, we throw in 'For those in peril on the sea' for good measure.

We slump down for a rest after the service, and he pulls out his sketchpad.

"You're good at drawing," I say. "I wish I could draw."

"You can."

"No, I can't. I'm crap."

"You draw a picture just being there. You *are* a work of art."

If he is taking the mickey there is also a look of tenderness, which unnerves me, and makes me rub my nose in my sleeve and ask, "What's that then? A worker fart?"

He smiles and lies back in the grass. "You're funny."

I am pleased. Being funny is the best thing that has happened to me lately. "Are you going to be an artist?"

"One day. First I'm going to be a fighter pilot. I'm going to join the RAF as soon as I leave school, remember?"

"I'm sure you'll have to wait a bit, even if you lie about your age."

"I told you. I got a *way in*."

I pluck sulkily at the grass. I don't want Tommy to die. If I feel like this about Boomer, how will I feel about Tommy?

"D'you believe in heaven?" I ask.

"Dunno . . . s'pose . . ." Then, seeing my downcast face, he says kindly, "Actually, yes. I'm sure Boomer's in heaven, look."

I lie back in the grass. It is only here in Gloucestershire that I have ever been able to lie in a field and feast on the complete dome of a changing sky: the giant clouds fleeting across the blue above, but the distant ones stretched around the horizon like elastic bands. The hills have become covered in a thick-piled blanket of green, as trees emerge from nowhere and puff out their soft plumage. I can feel the warm earth beneath me and I can see the shape of it: the horizon goes all the way round in a giant circle.

"I wonder what it looks like – heaven."

Tommy blows out his cheeks and turns over a new page in his pad.

"You live in Heaven House," I add. "You should know."

He cackles and begins to draw. His bitter laugh startles me a bit.

"What's so funny?"

He says nothing, but carries on drawing.

"What you drawing?"

"Heaven," he says, and I close my eyes against the sun as it comes out from a cloud. I suppose I ought to feel unsafe with him, after all the things I've heard, but I don't. I feel perfectly at ease. I run my fingers through vetch and clover and trefoils. I hear the gentle friction of his pencil on the paper, the chirruping of two blackbirds who seem to be singing "You say potaytoes and I say potartoes," and I feel this is where I want to be right at this moment.

"Why did she do it, then?" I ask.

"Bitter, I reckon."

"What about?"

"Search me."

I open one eye as if I might just do that.

"Summut wrong, anyway," he says, continuing to draw.

"Why don't they like you, then?"

"Did they say that?"

"No, you did."

"Well . . . it's complicated. I don't really know. You'd better ask her."

"All right, I will." Fat lot of good that does me, though.

"On second thoughts," he says, "perhaps you'd better not . . . I dunno . . ."

"Stop saying that! I want you to tell me now! Please, Tommy."

He draws furiously. "Look, I can't say, really. She thinks I done a bad thing . . . there was rumours . . . an' she believed them. She used to like me, see. She liked me a lot. I mean, she was going to adopt me an' all."

"*Adopt* you?"

"Well . . . yes."

"Oh God, that's awful! I mean, for her to like you so much and then . . . it's awful!"

He nods and scratches his forehead, frowning at me.

"What changed her mind?"

"Like I said . . . dunno really . . ." He shrugs. Then he looks up and into the middle distance. "It was brilliant. It was like . . . I had a family of my own. Uncle Jack – he liked me too . . ." Then he looks at me again, but at my neck, not my face.

I know how much it hurts to be away from my family. I know the real nausea of homesickness. I flinch to think of his loneliness, to think that he has never had a family, that he has come close to feeling what it was like only to have it whisked away from him. Tears come easily today, and my eyes begin to well up.

"What happened to your own mum and dad?" I ask.

"Mr Fairly said they left me there soon as I was born. Didn't like the look of me, he says. Says I'm not a very lovable person."

I sit up indignantly. "Well, that's rubbish! He's talking through his bum!"

Tommy breathes a laugh.

"I'll be your sister," I say. He studies my face anxiously, tenderly.

"I will," I say, and then, "What's that sound?"

"Stay absolutely still. Don't move a muscle."

I freeze. The sound is getting louder, and it is coming from behind me. It is almost like footsteps on gravel, but hollower, more muffled. Louder it comes, and louder.

"Now turn around," he says, smiling.

There, at my shoulder, are the hot wet nostrils of a cow, who is chomping at the very grass I'm sitting on. The head sways up and down, and I can feel the breath warm on my neck. What a sound!

I beam at him, and he knows it has given me pleasure. "There you go!" he smiles, tearing off the sheet from his pad.

"Hey, I thought you were drawing a picture of heaven."

"Oh . . . well." He gets to his feet and turns away from me awkwardly.

I pick it up and open my mouth. Then I shut it again. "Crumbs."

There is something incomplete about it, with more white paper than tentative pencil marks, but there is no doubting what it is. It is a portrait of me.

There, I've said it again

Term ends. Spurred on by the impact of Tommy's picture of me, I decide to present Aunty Joyce and Uncle Jack with a picture I have been painting at school for two weeks. The title Miss Hubble gave us was 'Friends Talking', and I have painted a masterpiece.

"Thank you," says Aunty Joyce, chopping cabbage at the table.

"Where shall I put it?" I ask, but I have already put it in pride of place on the dresser, propping the thin paper in front of a plate.

"That's nice," says Uncle Jack, trying to show an interest. "What is it?"

I point out the lollopy figures with heads like balloons and weedy legs mixed up with thick chair legs. "It's the knitting group," I say in disbelief. "See . . ." I point out the gangly arms and the brown wool – as thick as my paintbrush – streaming from each shovel-like hand. "That's Miss Lavish – never-been-ravished . . . that's Mrs Chudd – face-like-a –"

"*What* did you say?"

Uncle Jack suddenly takes out his pipe. I think perhaps I'm going to make them laugh, so I repeat it.

"Miss Lavish – never-been-ravished!" I'm smiling, waiting for them to smile too.

Uncle Jack leans forward from his armchair and says very, very slowly, "Go . . . and . . . wash . . . your . . . mouth . . . out – now!"

"But –"

"Now!"

I try to think how I could've made such a terrible mistake this time. It must be 'ravished' that is causing the problem, but when I think how I know this word, it's just my dad home on leave, seeing my mum washing up and rushing towards her crying, "Oooh! I could ravish you!" and plonking a kiss on the back of her neck. Is kissing a dirty word in Sheepcote too?

They both think my half-smile is a sign of insolence. But I am so deeply hurt, and so embarrassed by my hurt, that I find myself playing with the edge of the table and humming. I walk over to the sink with lips trembling, still trying to trot out a little hum, but sobbing inside.

Ravishing soon begins to change its meaning. Mrs Chudd is obsessed with the idea of Germans entering Sheepcote by force and ravishing all the women, young and old, in their own back rooms. She has stories from her sisters or sisters' friends' neighbours about how one woman in the Channel Islands was tied up with good strong rope and bent over her kitchen table. "You wouldn't believe it, but she still 'ave the rope burns. Oooh . . . ! They're brutes, you mark my words!" And then there is the German who tortured her sister-in-law's friend's piano teacher, and made her do 'monstrous things' to him until she confessed to the whereabouts of the ARP headquarters. She always takes a deep breath, closes her eyes and exhales slowly, "Filth!"

I can't imagine why the German would want monstrous things done to him. Was he mad? Had war wounds made him a bit confused, or was he punishing himself for being such a baddie? And what was he doing with dirt? There's a connection here, I think, with Aunty Joyce's disinfecting, but I can't quite make it out for now. These knitting sessions are brilliant, though, and sure to reveal all at some point.

Another thing Mrs Chudd is fond of doing is being a woman.

"Don't forget, Aggie – it's hard in this war, I know: you're a war worker, you're a cook, you're a mother . . ." and here her voice would deepen huskily, " . . . but you're also a *woman!*"

Everyone nods in vague agreement, for they have heard it all before. I find it an intriguing statement coming from someone who resembles nothing so much as a potato. I suppose it is important, if you look like Mrs Chudd, to remind yourself occasionally that you are not in fact a root vegetable. Poor Mr Chudd! However does he cope? The postmaster is a quiet slip of a man who means no one any harm.

On one occasion I arrive first at knitting group, with Aunty Joyce trailing up the road behind me. Tommy is there playing a beautiful tune on the village hall piano. I've never heard him play before, and the little point of hair on the back of his dusky neck, and his magical fingers dancing over the keys to produce such sweet unexpected music, make me love him even more.

"What's it called?" I ask.

He turns round, surprised, and stops playing abruptly. "It's bollocks."

Aunty Joyce appears at the doorway, and the sudden silence seems to become even more intense.

She stares at him: a chilling, haunted look that makes me

bite my nail. And Tommy stands his ground, gazing back at her with such a curious mix of hurt and defiance that I don't know what to make of it. There is something between these two that is so powerful it fills the hall, and I am utterly relieved when Aggie Tugwell breezes in. "Oooh! Someone get the stove on! Tiz chilly in here today!"

Aunty Joyce makes her excuses and says she can't stay, and I feel confused. But as soon as she's gone, Tommy apologizes for being in the way, and starts to go. Then Lady Elmsleigh, arriving laden with old jumpers to unravel for wool, insists he must stay and play for us all, at least for a few minutes.

So as the chairs are set out and everyone straggles in, Tommy plays. People smile in approval and start on their socks and balaclavas. Then he finishes his piece, closes the piano lid, and says he must be off.

"That was beautiful, Tommy," says Lady Elmsleigh, looking up from her circular needles. "What's it called?"

"Bollocks," I inform them.

Everyone stops knitting and looks at me.

"That's what you said, wasn't it, Tommy? You said it was Bollocks." I look at him, hopefully.

Lady Elmsleigh starts to laugh, and this gives everyone else leave to laugh too. I'm not quite sure how I've managed to entertain them this time, but it seems to be a success and I feel sure they're not laughing at me. Even smelly old Mrs Galloway seems to be laughing wheezily: "Tiz all bollocks if you ask me!"

Tommy leaves, but only after Lady Elmsleigh has extracted a promise from him that he'll come and play her piano whenever he wants to. This causes a little ripple amongst the two-ply, but no one is going to discuss him with Lady Elmsleigh there.

Instead they move on to their favourite topics of local gossip: love and lust. Lady Elmsleigh doesn't seem to mind, and I don't count. The thing is, these women have a strange way of forgetting there's a child present even after I've just spoken, or else they are so determined to exchange news that they ignore the fact. It's true I have perfected the distracted look, and they happily believe that I really am in a constant daydream. I can frown over a mistake, or gaze wistfully out of the window, mouthing the words of a song, and no one cares a jot what they are revealing to me about the inhabitants of Sheepcote.

It's at knitting group that I learn to spell. I only ever went to school for a year, if that, and I have a dim memory of the alphabet and buying things from a pretend shopkeeper. Aunty Vi taught me to read a bit, but I never really got started on writing. Since Miss Hubble's been helping me out, I'm beginning to get the hang of it, but it's the knitting group that really gets me going on the spelling. This is because occasionally, when they're on a very fruity topic, they do pay lip-service to my presence. They might speak of some girl getting in 'ti-ar-oh-you-bee-elle-ee' and some couples in Sheepcote (notably Jack and Joyce) are thought to have not made 'Hello VE' for years. Essiex is mentioned quite frequently, and I want to correct them and say I know it's pronounced 'Essex', because my Uncle Frank comes from there, but then I'll give myself away.

As the weeks go on, though, I learn to spell with a zeal that surprises Miss Hubble, and I begin to throw myself into knitting for England with glee. Sitting cross-legged on the floor, clicking my needles quietly and producing intricate cable patterns while breaking the grown-ups' code, I am declared an asset to the Sheepcote Knitting Circle.

Careless . . . or do you just care less for me?

I go to Miss Hubble's house – or the classroom – for an hour or so every Wednesday, before tea. I copy out rows of the same letter, we practise sounds, I copy out poems, and she even helps me write letters to my mum.

And then it all begins to bear fruit, because one morning I get a letter.

My mum is not much of a letter-writer, but she does use joined-up writing, and I have to ask Aunty Joyce to read it for me. She plonks the tea-cosy on the pot and begins:

'Dear Kitty,   Thank you for your letter. My you can write now too. I'm so proud of you. What a pity you don't like it . . . ' Aunty Joyce hesitates briefly. '. . . there. I'm sure you will get to like it, even if the lady does seem a bit . . .' She looks up, but I am running my nails along the chenille table-cover, '. . . of a sourpuss. She probably just isn't used . . .' More hesitation (I comb the tablecloth ferociously, without looking up). '. . . to children.'

"Hmm," she says to herself.

'Well don't you worry the war will be over soon. And I hope to be coming up to see you Saturday week. Well must go to catch the post, Lots and lots of love, Mum.'

"She's coming!" I yelp. "When's Saturday week?"

Sourpuss informs me it is in eight days' time, and I can

hardly contain my excitement. In fact, I am so busy picturing showing Mum the hens and how I can milk a cow that I forget to feel sorry for Aunty Joyce. Perhaps if she would just show a little hurt it would help. But she simply clears away the breakfast things poker-faced, and it doesn't seem to be worth apologizing.

Tommy is not happy about my mum coming. I can tell by the way he says, "That's nice for you," and looks all put out. I have to scoop him out of his sulky misery by promising to introduce him to her and asking if he can come and live with us. Then we are both excited, and the eight days pass slowly but busily. We set rabbit snares together, and run home through barley fields high as my waist and awaiting the harvest. We go into town on the back of a cart and sell our rabbits, then use the money for fourpenny tickets at the Gaumont to see *Going My Way*, and a bag of chips on the way home.

When the appointed day arrives I am up early and Aunty Joyce puts a blue ribbon in my rigorously brushed hair. She makes me scrub my nails and pull up my socks, and Uncle Jack has polished my shoes.

We wait at the bus stop for the eleven o'clock and I am bubbling over with all the smiles I will smile when I see her, my mum, after so so long.

It is five minutes late and I fiddle with my collar as the passengers get off. One old lady and a GI.

"Ta-ta, then," the bus conductress says to the old lady's back.

"Ta-ta – I'll tell Iris you wuz asking after her."

And with a laugh and a clink of her money bag, the bus is gone.

We wait for the ten-to-twelve but she isn't on that one

either. I feel so bereft I can hardly breathe, but I refuse to give up. We go to the post office to see if there are any messages, but Mrs Chudd just shakes her head decisively: "No messages, my love."

We go to the shops until the next bus, when Aunty Joyce goes home but I hang around. And so the whole day is played out in this way, with me hanging around the bus stop for ten minutes before each bus is due, and then wandering off to kill time before the next one.

At seven o'clock Uncle Jack comes and takes me home.

Guess I'll hang my tears out to dry

My mother's non-arrival is a huge betrayal. In a world where there are murdered kittens and dead girls' clothes and rampant germs and words too dangerous to speak, I was certain my mum would provide some reassurance, certain she would be my champion in every way, and I would be safe. But now that she's let me down I am more alone than before, and I have to put up with knowing that they're whispering about her. Now they'll never know how normal I really am, and how much someone can love me.

Still, Aunty Joyce seems to mellow a bit during the days that follow. She lets me make cakes with her on Sunday, and on Monday she tells me I'm a real help to have around on washdays.

With all these germs to contend with, you'd imagine washday was the highlight of Aunty Joyce's week. Actually, I don't think she enjoys it that much, although the other women say, "She dun 'alf do a good line of washing, do Joyce," and a good line of washing is the greatest compliment a Sheepcote woman can have.

On washday – always Monday – the parlour and the back kitchen turn into a steam bath, with all pans on to boil and a ruthless stench of strong soap. In the corner of the back kitchen a metal tub encased in stone is filled with water, and underneath it a little trapdoor in the stone is opened, coal is shovelled in and set alight. It takes an age for the deep tub of water to reach boiling point, and as it does the windows start to stream. Our faces turn a deep pink, our skin becomes clammy and our clothes stick to us.

Some weeks, a mystery lidded pail is brought in from the back yard, and I watch at a distance as Aunty Joyce pours a bloody liquid down the sink, then vigorously washes some rags under the cold tap as if it is a race against the clock. She drops them in one boiling pot, and handkerchiefs and knickers in each of the others.

When the tub is ready, in go the sheets and shirts, and Aunty Joyce pumps them up and down with a wash dolly. Meanwhile, as I'm home on holiday, she lets me do some scrubbing of dirtier items on the washboard in the sink. When I've finished I put them in the tin bath ready for rinsing, but she always comes and washes each item again, finding stains I just can't see, however hard I try. After the first few weeks I stop questioning her, and accept that my washing will never be quite up to scratch.

The tin bath is set up on two chairs near the boiler tub, and when things are ready she fishes them out with wooden tongs and slops them, steaming, heavy and lethally hot, into the cold bath for a rinse. She tells me to stand well back and screws her face up at the hot snakes of material that she eases at arm's length into the icy water.

We always have the wireless on all morning for washday. We listen to Music While You Work, the news, and all sorts of songs that get us humming and singing along. Aunty Joyce is a bit shy about singing at first, but I hold the broom handle and pretend to be Carmen Miranda or The Squadronaires and she rolls her eyes as I belt out 'I, yi, yi, yi, yi I like you very much' or 'A Little on the Lonely Side'. I can never catch all the words so I get lots of things wrong, and that always makes her smile.

On one particular occasion I make her smile a lot, and it is so lovely to see her in this mood I lark around even more.

"When April showers they come your way,
They bring the flowers that bloom in May,
So when it's raining, have no regrets,
Because it isn't raining rain, you know —"

I point the broom handle to her mouth to make her join in, and both together, very loudly, we sing:

"IT'S RAINING VIOLETS!"

She giggles. Aunty Joyce actually giggles. At one point I even notice her hips swaying to 'In the Mood'.

"Aunty Joyce . . ." I capitalize on our new-found intimacy to ask the question that's been nagging me for some time. "Why don't you have another baby?"

I see the back of her housecoat freeze for a moment, then her elbows start to move again, and her head bows. All I hear is the slop and scrunch as garments are rinsed at the sink.

"Aunty Joyce . . . ?"

She doesn't turn round, but flops a wet wrung pillowcase on the draining board. "We could do a lot of things if things were different . . . But there! They're not. We must just make the best of it."

I feed one of Uncle Jack's shirts in between the rollers of the mangle and turn the handle very slowly. "My mum always says, it's not what you *could've* done if, it's what you *can* do *despite*."

"Your mother's a very smart woman." She turns a little to see me and lowers her voice. "But then, your mother hasn't had to put up with what I've been through."

I am indignant. I think back to the bombed-out houses,

the babies' rattles, photograph frames, bits of leg, half-eaten pies, peeping through the rubble.

"A lot of people have," I say.

She clenches her lips and wrings some poor garment to death. "Well, I can't bring her back, can I? I can't ever bring my little Rosemary . . . back . . ."

It is the first time I've heard the name, and we catch each other's eye as if she has let slip a huge secret.

"You could have another one."

Her eyes are on me with such fury I'm afraid she's going to lose it altogether like when I wore Rosemary's clothes.

"I could *what*?"

Maybe she misheard. I take up the challenge, hopefully: "You could have another baby. I know it wouldn't be the same an' that, but it would be just as lovely, and then you wouldn't have time to be so sad."

She is gasping for air like a drowning woman, and I suspect she may not like the idea.

"You don't understand!" she hisses through the steam. "How could you? You're far too young."

Actually I'm quite grown up. Miss Lavish and people like that always stop me and Aunty Joyce in the street and say things like "Poor mite, away from home – they grow up so fast in a war" or "It's the children I worry about – they've been robbed of a childhood." I'm convinced that because I've suffered, I understand all suffering. And maybe I do understand much of it, but I have no idea of the sad demons inside Aunty Joyce. But there it is. I think I have her sorted. I think I have the whole world sorted, and that in my new war-enhanced, child-wrenched-from-the-bombing status, I have wisdom beyond compare, so I frown at a wet sock and say glibly, "What don't I understand? I'd've thought a new baby would be better than no baby."

Aunty Joyce takes in a long slow breath and seems to forget

to breathe out. It is a long time before she speaks. After much thwacking and wringing of garments she sighs again and says, "Even if you're right, Jack would never . . . would never agree."

"Oh, why worry about that? Anyway, he'd crack up when he saw it. Just think, it might be a little boy next time and Uncle Jack could take him on the trains. You could call him Glen or Frank – or Gregory – and you could knit him blue woollies, and when he grows up he'll sing on the wireless or act in the pictures and you could have a load of grand-children. Just think –"

"Stop it! And don't you dare say anything to Uncle Jack, for pity's sake."

I fall silent, hurt that she doesn't see I'm trying to help.

"I'm sorry, Kitty, but you don't understand. Having a baby . . . the man needs to . . . to agree. A woman can't have a baby by herself . . ."

I can't get the hang of this agreement lark. Of course you can have a baby on your own. My Aunty Babs had a baby and she wasn't even married. I'm sure you don't have to get anyone's agreement.

"I don't think that's right, Aunty Joyce. If you really want a baby, then I don't think Uncle Jack has much say in the matter."

She brings over a bucket full of wrung clothes for me. I try to read her face: it's not cross, it's more troubled.

"A baby can't just happen, look. It has to be made . . . and that's . . . where the disagreement starts. There!"

She plonks the bucket down decisively as if that's an end to it. I picture Uncle Jack and Aunty Joyce making a baby from modelling kits, carefully gluing bits of balsa wood together – like the boys do in school – and suddenly having a row over where to put the nose. Suddenly I remember the rabbits. I wonder if Aunty Joyce knows the Facts of Life, and how she managed to have Rosemary without noticing she'd been shagged first. Perhaps Uncle Jack just nudged her a bit while she was asleep. She looks very hot and bothered, and I think it might be too cruel to tell her the true facts at this moment. Anyway, a good Bing Crosby song starts up on the wireless and I jump up to grab the broom handle again.

"Imagine I'm Uncle Jack:

> I dream of you
> More than you dream I do.
> How can I prove to you
> This love is real?"

I'm so busy exaggerating my passion to the broom handle, it is a few moments before I notice she has turned away and taken a deep breath again, and she is not smiling.

I sit at the mangle and feed the rinsed garments into its rollers, while Aunty Joyce tries by the sink to wring out the larger unwieldy items. I am not allowed to help as I see her wrestling with a sheet like an enormous steaming serpent about her neck.

Glorious things of Thee are spoken

It is August, and for the past few days Uncle Jack has been practising the lesson he will read in church. He stands in front of the range with his Bible lifted high in front of him, and spouts forth the gospel. It is something about the Sun of Man and separating sheep from goats. Aunty Joyce looks up from her darning from time to time and tells him to mind he doesn't drop the 'h' on this word or that, or to keep his shoulders back.

When Sunday comes I find myself all caught up in Uncle Jack's excitement as the first hymn ends and he makes his way to the golden eagle for the lesson.

It is the first time I've listened to it properly all the way through. There seem to be some sheep sitting on a king's right hand, and some goats sitting on his left one. So it is either a very giant king or these are some pretty small animals. One way or another it doesn't sound too comfortable, but it does sound interesting, and I'm quite keen to hear what the king's going to do about it. Uncle Jack, who looks very small behind the golden eagle, and has been mumbling a little with his head down, suddenly catches Aunty Joyce's eye and must remember her advice, for he thrusts his shoulders back and booms out: "*THEN THE KING*

WILL SAY . . ." (he is loud for a few seconds) *"to those on his right . . ."*

Mr Fairly is listening with his head tilted back, giving the impression of a connoisseur awaiting the moment when he might be called upon to give his marks out of ten. His eyes are fixed on the uppermost panel of a stained glass window (Jesus with some sort of shepherd type) which tilts his nose in a distinctly up position.

"Then the righteous will reply, 'Lord, when was it that we saw you HUNGRY and fed you, or thirsty and gave you drink, a stranger and took you HOME, or naked and clothed you? When did we see you ill or in prison, and come to visit you?' And the king will answer, 'I tell you this: . . ." he catches sight of us again and booms out, *" . . . ANYTHING YOU DID FOR ONE OF MY BROTHERS, 'OWEVER HUMBLE – HOWEVER 'UMBLE – YOU DID IT FOR ME.'"*

I have been lulled by his soft rolling accent, but now I lift my head and listen intently.

"Then HE will say to those on HIS left HAND, 'The curse is upon you; go from my sight to the eternal fire that is ready for the devil and HIS angels. For when I was HUNGRY you gave me nothing to eat, when thirsty nothing to drink; when I was a stranger you gave me no HOME; when naked you did not clothe me; when I was ill and in prison you did not come to my HELP.' And they too will reply, 'Lord, when was it that we saw you HUNGRY or thirsty or a stranger or naked or ill or in prison, and did nothing for you.' And HE will answer, 'I tell you this: anything you did not do for one of these, 'owever HUMBLE – HOWEVER 'UMBLE – you did not do for me . . .'"

Everyone rustles and rumbles to their knees. I peek out from between the fingers which cover my face as he walks proudly back to his seat. I think Aunty Joyce and I both feel relieved that it is over, and I feel oddly protective of him as he kneels beside me in a sweat. I stick two thumbs in the air to show my approval, and I can't help cupping my fingers and commenting, in a loud whisper, "Fackin' ace!"

He shoots me a furious glance, and she rolls her eyes in despair. I put my palms together and pray loudly:

"Our Father, which art in Heaven, Harold be Thy name . . ."

The next day we are just starting tea when there is a visitor. It is really frustrating because there is half an apple pie to finish up and I have been looking forward to it. But it turns out to be someone Uncle Jack and Aunty Joyce are honoured to see. At last I am to meet Mr Fairly Himself.

He comes alone and strides into the front room before Aunty Joyce has time to suggest it. Uncle Jack is soon up from the table and wiping the jam from his mouth. He barges past me with an outstretched arm for Mr Fairly.

"Mr Fairly – Charles, delighted to see you!" He seems to have got a new voice altogether. "To what do we owe this pleasure? Do take a seat."

I loll around the doorway pretending to examine the paint-work. He is shorter than Uncle Jack but somehow quite imposing.

"This must be Betty!" he booms, smiling, as he catches sight of me fingering the wallpaper. I step forward and look him in the eyes. They are pale blue with pupils like full stops.

"I'm Kitty," I say. "Not Betty."

Aunty Joyce laughs like a bell chime and whisks me away to make a cup of tea. "She's from London!" she chirps over her shoulder, as if to apologize for me, and hisses, "Don't be so rude!" as soon as we reach the parlour.

We watch the kettle boil on the range and say nothing. Every time I'm about to open my mouth she sends me to fetch cups or wash spoons. From the front room we can catch words like 'unhealthy' and 'stop' from time to time.

"I should've made a cake today – I was going to, wasn't

I? Oh hang! I haven't even any biscuits. What am I going to offer him? Look in the biscuit tin, Kitty."

I lift the lid of a rectangular tin and a stale smell comes out. There is half a malted biscuit that must have been there for weeks.

"The apple pie!" Joyce is triumphant. She snatches it from the table and cuts a huge wedge from it, placing it in one of the china bowls we never use from the dresser.

I hold open the door as Aunty Joyce takes in the tray.

"Tea, Mr Fairly – Charles."

It is as if they have been given leave to call him by his Christian name but can't quite believe they deserve it.

"I'm ever so sorry there's no biscuits, but would you like some apple pie?"

"Well, really, this was only a fleeting visit . . ." Then he eyes the pie and moistens his lips. "Well . . . it does look delicious, Joyce. Perhaps I will be tempted. But then I must fly."

Aunty Joyce sits with them and I am shooed away as Mr Fairly munches his way through half of our evening meal. I alternately sit by the shoes in the hall or drape myself around the parlour door, listening carefully.

"I've told Jack it's got to stop . . . I'm worried for the girl. She's only – how old is she? Nine? Eight? Well . . . I ask you . . . I'm afraid boys of thirteen . . ." and then his voice becomes lower and it is harder to make things out. " . . . Boys' home lads . . . Tommy . . . there's no . . . what he'll get up to . . . but you . . . the blame if anything happens to her."

Then his voice is suddenly louder: "Please – now I've upset you, Joyce – I'm so sorry." And I can hear Aunty Joyce sounding muffled and upset, and then offering him more apple pie, and he accepts!

Out pops Joyce's head smiling meekly; she says, "Fetch

some more pie, there's a poppet, and use a clean plate! And put the kettle on!"

He's just finishing the pie, when Aunty Joyce springs towards my tray in the hall and grabs the pot. "More tea?"

"No, thank you, I'd best be off." He stands up, brushing the crumbs from his trousers on to Aunty Joyce's spotless floor rug. "I hope you don't mind my calling round, but you can see how serious this could be."

"Of course. Indeed," says Uncle Jack, in his voice borrowed from the Gaumont cinema screen. "Well, many thanks for letting us know, Mr Fairly – Charles."

"Bye-bye, Betty!" he says, stroking me under the chin, and beaming.

"Bye-bye, Mr Hairy," I say in my own best toff's voice. He chuckles amiably.

"And you look after Mr and Mrs Shepherd, now. They're very special people."

Aunty Joyce and Uncle Jack glow as they see him off.

So, that is Mr Fairly. He has come with a very mysterious message. He is smiling and friendly and important. And he has eaten all our pie.

You may not be an angel . . .

Now there is a new mystery. A few days after Mr Fairly's visit Uncle Jack stops my extra lessons with Miss Hubble, and forbids me to visit her again. This makes no sense at all. It can't be because they're afraid of stuff I'll write to my mum, because I can write my own letters now, without anyone's help. Something is going on, and I want to know what it is.

In an effort to keep me away from Tommy, Aunty Joyce packs me off as often as possible to play with another evacuee girl of my own age, Babs Sedgemoor. Babs lives near the pub with Mrs Marsh (of the small moustache and lost sons) and Mr Marsh who delivers the milk with his white carthorse called Boxer. Babs was evacuated four years ago when her mum was killed in the Blitz. Her dad is a prisoner of war somewhere. I like Babs. She has straight jet hair and eyes as blue as Elizabeth Taylor's. In fact, when she shows me Boxer to stroke I could swear I'm in the film *National Velvet*. She's got a local accent though, because she's been here so long, and she seems to know a lot of things I don't. She tells me Mrs Marsh can't bear to see the young men working in the fields or in reserved occupations when hers have died for their country because it isn't bloody fair. Babs thinks it isn't bloody fair either, and I agree. She says she feels like Mrs Marsh too, sometimes, when she sees Sheepcote children with their mums and dads. Although I point out that not many of them have got both parents at the moment.

"Still," she says, "it's not bloody fair." And I agree.

Some days we play skipping with Iris Holland in the street. Iris has tight little pigtails and embroidered pockets. We sing "Kitty's in the kitchen, doin' a bit of stitchin'" and "Vote vote vote for little Iris . . ."

Iris says her mum doesn't like her playing with me, and when I ask her why she just snorts and says it's because I'm friends with Tommy Glover and he's 'a bad sort'.

"He's not," I say.

"She says he's trouble."

"Why's that then?"

"Dunno. Says he killed someone or summut. Don't bother me. I'll play with who I like, I will."

But one day Mrs Holland comes calling down the street, "Iris? Iris!"

"Oh, bugger," says Iris, and she has to go home and stick stamps in her savings book.

It is on this day, when Babs and I are left alone with two ends of a skipping rope, that I spot a strangely familiar figure coming up the road. It starts as little more than a blob of colour, and turns into a woman with a baby on each hip and the unmistakable penguin walk of my mother.

At first I feel put out, not just because it is unexpected, but because I'm with Babs and I can't be as overjoyed as I'd like when I know she'll think it bloody unfair. But as my mother comes close and bursts into a look of joy, and I see the beads of sweat and her exhausted fat calves, I make a run for it, almost knocking her over in my hugs and kisses.

"Steady on! Phew! God Almighty, I feel like I've just climbed bleedin' Everest! It's like carrying two sacks of potatoes with these two. Here y'are – you wanna hold one?"

She hands me one of the twins — Peter, judging by his knitted blue jerkin. I smile at him, and he looks at me indifferently.

"Look, Babs!" I shout, trying to include her. "It's my baby brother, Peter. And this is Shirley. And this is . . ."

"Hello, Babs, I'm Kitty's mother."

Babs smiles with one side of her mouth, and takes Shirley to hold only because my mum plonks the baby in her arms.

I want to throw my arms around my mother and squeeze her tight, but I'm hampered by the baby and the presence of Babs. It is something I look forward to later on.

"This where you live then, is it?"

"No, I'm further up the road — I'll show you."

"Gawd Almighty! More mountains to climb! It's dead pretty though, I'll grant you. You landed on your feet here, didn't you?"

I start up the road, and Babs hands the baby back to my mother. We climb the gradient in the noonday sun and, although I'm over the moon and showing it on my face, my back is burning with guilt as Babs looks after us till we disappear around the hedgerows.

Aunty Joyce greets us in a flap. She hasn't done her hair and she hasn't made a cake and the parlour is a tip and whatever must Mrs Green think of her?

"You keep a very tidy house, Mrs Shepherd," reassures my mum. "I should've let you know but I only found out yesterday I could have the day off. An' it's so difficult with twins — I can't tell you," and all the time she's looking around her as if she's in some kind of palace. That's because we're in the Front Room. I'm proud to think Aunty Joyce deems my mother fit for this privilege, but it's a daft place to take us.

"Oooh, I'm sorry, Mrs Shepherd, you 'aven't got anywhere

I can change Shirley, 'ave you? Only it's been a long journey an' they're both sopping wet, but Shirley's worse than that. Phwoar! Bet you can smell it too! What a welcome, Shirl! That's no way to say hello!"

When she stops for breath Aunty Joyce takes her into the parlour and the back kitchen. I need hardly describe Aunty Joyce's face as she fetches a bucket, fills it with water and bleach and holds it out at arm's length for Mum to put the soiled nappy in. Then she tells me to take it outside.

When all the fuss is over, my mother gets talking to Aunty Joyce about the journey and the munitions factory and the crèche for the twins, over a nice cup of tea. I forgot how much my mother talks. On and on she goes about this and that, and I am still waiting for the moment when I can hold her like she holds me in my dreams.

"I hope our Kitty's been behaving herself, Mrs Shepherd." She gives me a wink and holds her free arm out to stroke my head. "Must be hard, takin' in other people's children, 'specially not havin' any yourself. I don't blame you, mind, believe me. I'm tellin' you, you're well out of it! No offence, Kitty — you're a darlin' an' always have been — hope she is with you as well, Mrs Shepherd — no, but what I mean is you can't *imagine* how hard it is with *babies*."

Aunty Joyce folds her lips together and looks at the rim of her teacup.

"I'm still breastfeeding, you see, so on the train — blimey, can you imagine? — it's not so bad at work, we have breaks and there's the crèche — oooh! I don't know what I'd do without the crèche. Working there's been the saving of me, really . . ."

I have an idea.

"Mum, let me show you the chickens! Come on!" I pull at her hand and after some flustering I get her into the sunshine of the back garden. She stands for a moment in awe at the view. "Lord above. Look at that! Fancy you living in a paradise like this!"

I feel an enormous pride showing my mother around, especially when she sees the eggs underneath the hens. "Blimey! Whatever next!"

When we go back in, Shirley and Peter are just about sitting upright on the rug in front of the range, and Aunty Joyce is shaking a jar of dried beans in front of them and making them smile. My mother has brought the twins with her because she thinks I want to see them, but she is wrong. It's not that I don't like them – they're very cuddly and much more interesting than when I left. It's just that they seem to take up all her attention, and she hasn't seen me for months. I suppose I resent them in their little knitted jerkins, so when I see them teetering gleefully on the floor with Aunty Joyce, I seize my opportunity.

"Come upstairs and see my room! Is it okay, Aunty Joyce? I'll only take her in my room and I've made the bed!"

"Made the bed?" says my mum, already following me upstairs. "And pigs might fly!"

I give one fleeting nervous glance at Aunty Joyce, half expecting to go back downstairs and find the twins drowned in a pail of water with a lid on top, but I selfishly carry on with my plan.

It works. We are alone. I fling myself at my mother and don't let go. I nuzzle into her and breathe in the milky breasts, still heaving with feeding. I am supposed to cry now: that is how I have always imagined this meeting. But somehow nothing is quite how I expect it to be, and there are no tears inside me, only mild irritation. I wish she would stop being so talkative and so pally with Aunty Joyce. I wish she would be like the mothers at the pictures whose eyes fill with tears in a soft-focus haze and say, "Oh Kitty! Oh Kitty, my little love! What have they *done* to you?" But she doesn't.

"I want to come home!" I say, in a pathetic half-whimper. "Please, please take me home."

"We haven't got a home no more, love." She says it in that half-jokey way I'm beginning to resent.

"But I miss you! I don't care where you are, I want to be with you!"

I cling on tight, and she starts to soften a bit. She crouches down to my level and says, "I can't have you at the factory because you're over two. I can't stay in London with you, love, because we'll all be killed. There's doodle-bugs all over the shop. And in any case the war'll be over very soon . . ." She strokes my hair and kisses my cheek. "An' all I want is for us all to be *safe* and together again when it's over . . ." The tears come now, and I sob into her best blue dress, adding spots of wet to match the damp patches under her arms. "There, there . . ." She holds me very tight, and when I look up I can see that she is crying too, only very quietly, and trying not to let it show. "Be brave, my little sweetheart, and I'll be back to fetch you home before you know it."

Then, as quickly as it started, it is over. She has got out a piece of paper and a pencil from my school bag and is drawing around my foot.

"I'll get you some nice new shoes next time I come."

My mother looks out of the window and I join her, feeling cheated by this arrest of emotions. As we look out we can see Aunty Joyce with the twins, one in each arm, crouching down by the hen coop and showing them the chickens. She is talking to them in a sweet voice, which I've never heard before, and she is *smiling* at them.

"She's not such a bad old stick," says Mum.

"You don't know the '*alf* of it . . . !"

I start recounting everything I can think of to get some sympathy, and my mother does listen, but I never again get that moment of warmth when her eyes welled for a second and she abandoned herself to me. I'm so confused I don't know what to do next. I feel strangely betrayed by events, frustrated beyond belief.

When we go downstairs, there are the twins again, billing and cooing and weeing and pooing and giving my mother every reason to be distracted from the main purpose of her visit: me.

When we see her off at the bus stop I feel swizzled. (Even so, I don't forget to tell her *exactly* what sort of shoes I would like: red with a bar.)

The bus disappears around the bend of the road, and I am devastated. It's not bloody fair.

Blueberry Hill

It is the thick of summer, a time of heavily leafed trees rustling overhead and lazy love songs predicting lovers returning. I've no idea when I'll see my mum again, and with Tommy banned, I feel heavily rationed in love. I don't know how many times Tommy and I manage to see each other, but those secret meetings seem to fill the summer.

One Sunday, during cadets, eight of us are selected for the paper collection. The vicar opens the shed at the back of the village hall, and Tommy and Will Capper pull out the cart. It's simple enough through the village, but for the farms we tend to split up into groups of two. Neville Adlard, a scruffy Heaven House boy, my age, with long eyelashes, keeps pestering Will Capper about having a go at the cart, and as soon as Will gives way Babs is on at Tommy to let her have a go. Of course Tommy is off like a shot and, grabbing two flattened cardboard boxes from the cart, he signals me to follow him.

"We'll collect up Russells," he shouts back to the group, meaning the farm on the opposite valley. "See ya!"

And we're off.

Up the lane, over the five bar gate, through the cow field, over the stile, across the smaller stream, up the next field, over the next one, until we're in our field: our valley.

It is so steep here that even the war has left it to pasture: sheep on the top slopes, cows at the bottom near the lush grass of the stream.

As soon as we arrive I can feel something almost like music, a galloping through the whole of my body, and instead of flopping down with exhaustion, I whirl about, running circles, arms outstretched. Gallop, gallop, gallop. There is space – so much space. We both spin, we soar, we are airborne.

Gasping, breathlessly we cling on to our oak tree. Tommy knows the feelings I have in this place, and I know from his eyes, darting and smarting and invigorated in the nippy wind, that he shares them.

"Come on!" he says, handing me a flattened box and setting his own on the grassy slope. "I'll race you!"

He sits on the cardboard and pushes with his feet, and before I can do the same he has shot off down the slope, gathering an uncanny momentum on such a crude vehicle. I try to follow, but feel stuck and afraid. I push with my feet and hands, but in the hope that I won't move too far too fast. Tommy's voice is tinny and distant now, and he is climbing back up holding his makeshift sledge. He smiles as he approaches, throws his cardboard down and climbs on to mine behind me. He puts his arms over my shoulders and grips the front edge of the cardboard, and suddenly we're away.

It is slow and bumpy at first. I try not to scream. Then, as we hit a ridge, we are tearing along: flying, soaring, whistling down to the hawthorns by the stream. I scream. He laughs. We come to a halt just inches from the branches.

After a while I become an expert with my cardboard. The more sheep shit it collects and the more journeys it makes, the shinier and more leathery it becomes. And the faster.

Resting up by the oak tree he signals me suddenly to listen.

Expecting the sound of footsteps, I hear nothing.

"Listen," he says again.

A soft cooing comes from the trees behind us.

"A bird?" I ask.

"Simon."

"Simon?"

"A tawny owl. He was a chick last year."

I crane my neck but can see nothing, and can't help being impressed that Tommy is on first-name terms with owls.

"You can't see him, but he can see you," says Tommy, looking up as well. "An owl can hear a mouse's heartbeat at thirty feet!"

"Thirty feet! A heartbeat!"

I put my hand to my own heart, and listen. This is a magical place, and no mistake.

"Will this really be ours one day?" I ask, wanting to hear him talk about our future together.

"Well, by rights, it won't ever belong to no one."

"I thought you said . . . after the war . . ."

"It'll be shared out, don't worry. Just you have to know: the land don't belong to us – not really. We belong to the land." He puts the palm of his hand on the grass and strokes it gently.

I watch him, out of my depth now. "Can we belong to this bit, then?"

"After the war I 'speck you'll be back with your mum and dad."

"You can come with us – I promise."

"Well . . . I'm building a farm right here."

I feel shut out. "When I'm grown up –"

"You in on it?"

"Yes!"

"Right!"

He lies back and puts his hands behind his head. He looks so thoughtful and competent, I am ecstatic to be included in his plans.

"We'll have sheep, shall we?" I suggest.

"An' cows. We'll have a dozen or so. We'll keep it small."

"How much do sheep cost?"

He props himself on an elbow. "What we need is a copy of the *Farmer and Stockbreeder*. Then we'll be able to work out all the costs." He looks excited. "I'll have to get some work first to save up for it all. But we need to work out costs."

"Where can we get a *Farmer and Stockbreeder* without any money?"

We both light up at the same moment. We jump up and start running, but by the time we reach the lane the cart has made its way back to the village hall shed, laden with newspapers and magazines.

Another group of children is sorting the paper into piles, and we volunteer to help.

It's not long before Tommy finds what we're looking for, but he says we must keep going. We need two or three farming journals at least if we're to sort out all the different stock. I feel so important leafing through the piles of paper, and so joyously mischievous.

Suddenly my contented grin droops at the sides. Tommy notices straight away and catches my eye. "What?"

I say nothing and show him what I have found.

"What is it?" he asks gently, still not understanding.

It is a painting of a knitting group. A masterpiece.

"I gave it to Aunty Joyce."

He takes the picture from me and looks at it. "It's lovely," he says kindly. And then, to make me feel better, he declares, "I've never seen anything like it!" I try to smile, but feel utterly winded and lifeless. Tommy looks at me anxiously, and then says more tenderly than I have ever heard him, "Please, can

I have it? I'd love to put it on the wall by my bed. It's the best picture I've ever seen. Honest."

I don't care what anyone says about him. I don't care what on earth he's supposed to have done. I love Tommy Glover and I always will.

You are my sunshine

In mid-August a parcel arrives for me. It is my ninth birthday, but I have never received a parcel before, and I dance around it after breakfast, hardly daring to break the string or spoil the thick brown paper.

"G'won – open it!" says Uncle Jack, full of curiosity himself. "It won't bite you!"

I can see from the writing on the label that it's from my mother, but if I open it, the parcel will be gone for ever, so I sit and stroke its crinkled pre-used paper, lift it up and smell it and weigh it and run my cheek along the knotted string, as if I might hear it speak to me.

"I might wait till dinnertime," I say.

Aunty Joyce sighs. "You're a funny old thing."

I smell it again, pushing my nose into the paper and inhaling deeply. "It's just I never had a parcel before . . ."

Uncle Jack raises an eyebrow thoughtfully at Aunty Joyce. "Well, whoever sent it wanted you to open it, I'm sure of that."

I take a deep breath and start to unknot the string. Then I unravel it and lay its yard length on the table, and Uncle Jack winds it up neatly and puts it in the pocket of his jacket which is hanging on the chair. Inside the brown paper is a box. More suspense. And inside the box is tissue paper, and under each piece of tissue paper is a red shoe. Two new red shoes with a bar and a buckle!

There are gasps and hoots all round as I try them on. I waltz up and down the room and feel like a film star. Uncle Jack and Aunty Joyce think I must be the luckiest girl alive, and I do too, although there is a little something niggling me.

At teatime there is a jam sponge cake with my name on and a candle, and Aunty Joyce and Uncle Jack sing 'Happy Birthday' to me and I feel like a queen.

But at the end of the day, after I've vainly worn my shoes in the lanes and spattered them with mud and risked scuffing them on stones, all for the joy of wearing them to the grocer's and the post office and round to Babs' house, I sit down on my bed and take them off and I know what the trouble is. At first there was just a hint of it, and I ignored it because I wanted to. But all through the day it has been getting worse, and now there is no escaping it: they are too small.

Aunty Joyce says I'm silly for wearing them out – we could easily have sent them back and my mum would've changed them. When I look wretched she apologizes because she thinks she has said the wrong thing. But that's not what I'm thinking at all. "See how fast you're growing!" she says, in an attempt to comfort me, but this is exactly what is tearing me apart. It seems that with every inch taller I grow, and every shoe size, I grow that much further away from my mother. My toes have been stinging all day and now they are red and raw and screaming out to me that I am growing so fast that by the time this war is over I shall have grown out of my childhood and out of my mother's arms and I will never fit back there again.

* * *

When we return to school towards the end of August I get caught up in the excitement of a new term. I will be in Standard Four now, but still taught, along with Standard Three, by Miss Hubble. Let them try keeping me away from her now! Ha!

But we're in for a surprise. It is not Miss Hubble's rosy face that greets us as we troop in, nor are there any jars of lavender and marigolds on the desk. It is a new teacher, Miss Priddle, who takes the register and appoints the ink and coke bucket monitors. She is pleasant enough in her pale rayon dress, and shows us how to defy Hitler by making nutritious meals from the school garden vegetables, but she is not Miss Hubble, and there are no clues as to why our smiley young teacher has left without at least a goodbye.

I have to wait till break time, when Betty Chudd tells Babs Sedgemoor who tells me: Miss Hubble 'got into trouble' and can't come back. Babs and I both imagine she's been arrested and spend the next few days plotting to rescue her from behind iron bars.

It's the knitting group which eventually disabuses me.

"Whatever she gonna do with a baby round 'ere?"

"Tiz such a shame to see our girls lettin' theirsels go so easy."

"Tiz awful."

"In my day we waited till we wuz married . . ."

"That's not what I 'erd . . ."

"Oooh! You devil you!"

"Tiz possible someone 'ad their wicked way against 'er wishes."

"There's no one'll 'ave 'er now, poor soul."

Then Lady Elmsleigh announces that she's staying with her for the time being. She has plenty of room up at the house. And everyone shuts up.

I have all the information I need, and I tell Babs. The prison rescue is hastily replaced by a plan to knit baby clothes in secret, but I can't help wondering how poor Miss Hubble can have allowed herself to be treated like that rabbit in the cage, and the image haunts me for the rest of the term.

No sooner has school started again than we're allowed time off for the harvest. This is a strange new experience for me, and like having a holiday all over again.

The fields around Sheepcote are difficult, sloping fields to harvest, and most of them were pasture before the war. Whole families I have never seen before seem to appear in the fields all of a sudden, along with soldiers and airmen off duty, land girls, prisoners of war, refugee Norwegian whalers and any of us children tall enough to stack a bale of corn.

Up in the field behind the house one of the land girls drives the tractor back and forth, put-putting loudly past our ears, then purring off into the distance. Thumper works the binder, and we crowd round it, heaving the sheaves to form stooks.

We work in pairs or threes, under a relentless sun, our legs streaked with stubble scratches and itching from head to toe with harvest bugs. There is something noble about our joint venture, something moving about the way the land girls sweat and toil and swig cider in exactly the same way as the prisoners and the soldiers and the refugees and the farmer and the gypsy children and the Heaven House boys and us evacuees.

I stack sheaves with a toothless old farm worker and a pretty land girl called Nancy. When we finish our stook, old Gum-face starts up another and Nancy and I bring the sheaves over from the binder, our fingers and palms burning from the binding twine, and resisting a desire to scratch every nook and cranny of our skin.

I catch sight of Tommy and he comes over to me. No one is here who will care, no one will tell on us.

"Meet us after?" he says.

"Okay then." But he is not looking at me all the time. He keeps stealing quick glances at Nancy, whose bra straps can be seen through her open blouse, whose milky cleavage is turning rapidly pink in the sun, whose breasts are speckled in tiny droplets of sweat. Nancy wipes her arm across her wet brow and seems unaware, but I know she knows, like all the land girls, just how explosive are their open-necked shirts and their bare bruised knees amidst the men and the stacking corn on hot, never-ending days like these. I long to be Nancy, and am angry with Tommy that I'm not.

"I'll see ya then," I say decisively.

"Yeah." He looks at me and Nancy. "One of the men in our lot's got some cider, look. Come over next break."

Nancy smiles. I put a sheath down in front of me and try hard not to pout. "Maybe."

When there's a break everyone slumps down in the shade of a corn stook or over by the oak tree. There are sandwiches and cider and extra rations distributed for the harvest. These don't amount to much, but make us feel important. Then there is a long soft lull of birdsong, voices that melt into silence, a quiet that is all the more intense after the noise of the binder and the tractor, a hush of bodies outstretched in the heat, all itching for one reason or another.

The harvest goes on for ever, days of gold and warmth and musty sweet smells that will always conjure up that summer in 1944 when I first began to learn the many secrets and surprises of creation and procreation. It was a time both enlightening and full of light: the yellow corn, the deep ochre of the stones scattered in the soil, the sky as blue and tran-quil as a picture book and, apart from the occasional miaow of one plane chasing another, barely a hint of a war.

A man and his dream

When harvest is over, the world begins to change, and I see Sheepcote as I haven't seen it before. First come the black-berries, a luscious surprise among brambles I have only seen as scratchy weeds until now. Then powdery black sloes appear in the yellowing blackthorn, shiny elderberries hang in upside-down bouquets and clusters of bright orange rowan-berries appear from nowhere. The hedgerows are full of fruit and colour, and the apples are swelling on the branches, ready for plucking.

Harvest Festival was just a phrase I heard before, some-where in the autumn. Now that I have taken part in a harvest I feel utterly overwhelmed by the service in church. Standing between Aunty Joyce and Uncle Jack in pews packed with children and villagers and land girls and refugees, I sing more passionately than ever before:

> "We plough the fields and scatter
> The good seed on the land,
> But it is fed and watered
> By God's almighty hand;
> He sends the snow in winter,
> The warmth to swell the grain,

The breezes and the sunshine,
And soft refreshing rain.
All good gifts . . ."

By the chorus I realize my eyes are filling with tears, but
thankfully no one notices.

"He only is the Maker
Of all things near and far,
He paints the wayside flower,
He lights the evening star . . ."

I can't imagine what has come over me, but I think that it
is around about now, in this little packed church with the
ancient thanks for the harvest ringing all around me, that I
feel I belong here. I am part of the scenery, along with the
sleepy cows and the stacks of corn, the frosty five bar gates,
lichen-covered stone and fruiting hedgerows; along with the
whispers of lovers in the barn and in the woods, the secret
sorrows of happy people, the longings and the joys of prisoners and evacuees and refugees, orphans and gypsies and
waiting mothers, the inflated importance of the Home Guard
and Mr Fairly and Uncle Jack, the gossip and giggles of the
knitting group; I, Kitty Green, am part of all this.

The early autumn is a time of plenty. We have stewed apple
every evening and often with cream. We start to eat the fruit
that was bottled in the late summer: damson, greengage,
strawberry, and we forget the hardships for a while.

The leaves turn bright orange and yellow and the copper
beeches turn dark pink. But the first heavy frost is followed
by gusty winds, which bring them swirling down into the
lanes, beautiful crimson carpets on which we walk regally to

school. The linesman has his work cut out now. He sweeps the leaves all day long into great ginger heaps by the side of the road, which we selfishly stamp our way through, sending them back in all directions.

Then the heavy rains start, and turn them all to mulch, and soon the lanes and roads and woodland paths are nothing but brown mashed potato, greasy leaves and thick mud sticking to every shoe and boot and making walking a heavy business.

By October Aunty Joyce is stuffing newspaper around the cracks in the windows and putting sacking across closed doors to keep out the cold winds. We keep our coats on in school and the coke is always running out. Sometimes we keep our coats on at home too, and everyone, young and old, has several layers of knitted garments, which stay on all day and often all night.

One November morning Tommy is overjoyed. Boss Harry announces the visit of an old boy, Jonathan Crocker. He reminds the school – although Tommy needs no reminding – that Jonny has been serving in the RAF, and they must all treat him with the utmost courtesy. If we are lucky, he might speak to Standards Four to Seven about his exploits over Germany. The wooden partition between the three classrooms is folded back for morning prayers, and I can see Tommy clearly from where I'm sitting. He can hardly contain himself, although perhaps irritated that he did not have more time to prepare for this bombshell. For Jonny Crocker has not fore-warned the headmaster of his arrival, having decided to come on a whim during some unexpected leave.

He comes after prayers, and I begin to panic. This is the man who will find a 'way in' for Tommy, which means a way out of Sheepcote. I am certain that by this evening, Tommy will be gone.

Everyone stands up when the RAF pilot enters. Boss Harry

is wearing his academic gown, which he reserves for parents' day, and some of the girls snigger.

I can see Tommy trying to catch Jonny Crocker's eye as he talks about aircraft designs, RAF training, and the advantages of youngsters joining the Air Training Corps. Then the children's hands shoot up with questions, and he gives impassive replies about missions over France escorting bombers, locating plots and chasing ME 110s, dodging anti-aircraft fire, flying blind at night and the differences between Spits and Hurris. I can see Tommy's hand is bolt upright, his face rigid and pink with desire to be chosen. I can tell his head is scrambled with questions, see the urgency in his eyes as Boss Harry slips his fingers into his waistcoat, removes his watch and looks at it. Tommy panics.

"Please, Mr Jonathan Crocker, sir," he blurts out, "how many Germans have you killed?"

There is a general murmur of excitement from the boys – who are clearly keen to get down to fundamentals – and a hiss of disapproval from Boss Harry, who scowls at Tommy and says, "Who asked you to ask a question? Were you asked?" Then he turns to the pilot and apologizes for the rudeness. But Jonny Crocker clears his throat and asks who asked the question.

When Tommy sees the pilot's eyes on him at last, he looks as though he's going to faint. All the blood goes from his face, and I wait for the moment when he will either pass out or Jonny Crocker will give him an expansive smile of recognition. But Jonny Crocker merely nods in his direction and speaks very soberly to the whole class.

"How many Germans have I killed?" He sighs, his face seems to cloud over and he looks suddenly not like a fighter pilot at all, but like a fourteen-year-old boy. "I don't know how many." He scratches his brow, and takes a deep breath, and starts again with a shaky voice.

"One thing I do know: they haven't just been men in uniforms with swastikas. I've escorted bombers that have killed women and children – children like you – and babies in their cradles and old people with walking sticks and people in hospital too ill to run for shelter. And I've killed German pilots too, blasted them to bits, young pilots with mothers at home like me. And I'm not proud of it, and I hate doing it, and every time we scramble my legs turn to jelly, and every time we come back I count the friends I've lost."

There is a silence. Only the squeak of a shoe. Boss Harry looks uncomfortable. We wonder if the pilot is going to cry, or is already crying, and we look down at our inkwells.

"So," continues the pilot, in possession of himself again, "don't be *too* keen to join up. Of course we have to do our bit for King and Country, and it is the right thing to do . . . I suppose. But there's no glamour in it – don't go away with that idea – there's no glamour in it at all," I catch Tommy's face, and it has collapsed, "only misery."

Boss Harry looks even more uncomfortable. We imagine he is unhappy about his pupils being given unpatriotic messages, and don't realize that he has squashed his mouth up, not in disapproval, but to choke a sob, and hung his head, not in shame, but to conceal his grief.

The silence is broken by a big forward girl in the front, none other than Mrs Chudd's daughter, Betty, who looks eighteen although she's only thirteen. "Please, sir, could I have your autograph?" She thrusts her exercise book under his nose and looks at him adoringly. The pilot smiles and sighs, and is then swamped with requests as children wave bits of paper at him while others rummage in their desks to find things for him to write on.

Tommy waits his turn. Maybe he has given up the cherished hope of a personal chat, but there is still time for confirmation of their agreement, a secret sign as he writes his name on the small cut-off exercise book.

To our surprise, Boss Harry allows the noise and moves to look out of the window, where he stands for some time with his back to the scramble.

At last there are only a couple of remaining books to sign, and Tommy wades in right at the very end. I am picking at my cardigan, rubbing little pieces of wool furiously into tiny balls between my fingertips, and dropping them on the floor. Tommy beams as he hands over his open book, and Jonny Crocker smiles wearily back. Tommy waits for him to write, but he continues to look at Tommy with a question in his face.

"Who shall I put?" he asks at last.

Tommy swallows. I stop picking at my cardigan.

"Tommy," he says lamely, and may have been about to add, "You remember me!" but the pilot is already head down over his pen. When he has finished scribbling he hands it back to Tommy without even looking at him, and looks instead at the clock on the back of the classroom wall.

The other children are admiring their autographs, momentarily losing interest in the visitor, and the headmaster is still staring at clouds, and Jonny Crocker is there, for a moment, unhindered.

He begins to rise from the front desk he was perched upon, and I can see Tommy is sick with disappointment. Jonny Crocker is just a film star to the others, a celebrity who can provide them with booty to show off at home. He is no more than a good film at the pictures – a weepie, perhaps. Maybe some of the girls will cry when they get home, and most of the boys will remember his words. But to Tommy he is something else. He is an escape route. And I see his dear face watching all hope being extinguished like a series of lights going out one by one, and he stands by, letting it happen, sunk like an ocean liner.

"Please!" he says suddenly, clutching the pilot's sleeve in despair. "Don't you remember me?"

The young man looks round at him, startled but curious. "Do I know you?"

By this time several of Tommy's classmates have noticed him and are watching, like me, in disbelief.

"I'm Tommy – Tommy Glover. You came last year – you remember? And you told me you'd get me in somehow. You said you'd make sure I got in when I left school."

The pilot looks blank.

"You did!" says Tommy desperately. "You . . . you –"

Billy Piggot, a tall boy whose pullover is too short by half, is laughing. Another boy joins in with a sneer: "Give it a rest, Tommy. You're living in cloud-cuckoo-land, you are! He don't know you from Adam, look!"

Perhaps moved by this sniggering, the pilot halts his move towards the door and turns right round to look at Tommy.

"I'm sorry," he says. "I said some cocky things when I'd just got my wings. I was probably showing off. I'm sorry." And he is joined by Boss Harry who, smiling apologetically at Tommy, ushers his visitor away.

(Not) In the mood

It is no fun to arrange meetings in this chilly, newly drab landscape; there is even a film of khaki moss on every tree trunk, as if the War Office has decided to put them in uniform. But I must see Tommy. I can't bear to let him loose with his feelings after the humiliation in class, and yet I didn't manage to catch up with him in the lane after school.

I'm told my dad's home on leave and is going to pay a visit. That might cheer him up a bit. They can talk about war and stuff, and I know Dad will let Tommy come and live with us after the war. I know he will.

After school on Friday I belt off home and still Tommy's managed to leave ahead of me. I run up the lane, panting through the stitch in my side.

"You coming up the farm, then, tomorrow?" I ask his back.

He turns slightly. "Might, then."

"My dad's coming! He's on leave and he's coming tomorrow!"

He slows down and watches me for a moment, as if hungry for some of my thrill, but then turns back and heads slowly down the lane towards the boys' home, kicking a stone and muttering something about seeing me some other time.

"Tommy!" I look after him but just catch the last of his

sullen profile as he turns his back on me. "Tom! Tommy!" His head is sunk so low in his shoulders that I reckon there are tears in his eyes. "You can meet him an' all! I want him to meet you!"

If he hears at all, it makes no impression on the dejected figure walking away from me. I want to run after him, but Aunty Joyce is already at the door up the lane and calling me in.

I am up at sunrise, combing my hair, pacing the room, running to look out of the window every time there's a noise. Downstairs Uncle Jack has polished my shoes. I am excused chores so that I can stay smart, and after breakfast Aunty Joyce gives me a newly ironed handkerchief with a rosebud on it.

At eleven o'clock he has not come. Dinner is delayed until one o'clock, but still he does not show up.

At teatime, I don't feel like the Apple Surprise with 'emergency cream' that Aunty Joyce has made specially, because my throat is too stiff. Uncle Jack finishes it off for me.

At six o'clock Tabby Chudd sends a boy up from the post office to say that my father has telephoned. His leave has been cut short so he's spending the day with my mum and the twins. He *hopes* to come and see me before he leaves tomorrow.

I don't sleep, of course, but take the rosebud handkerchief to bed with me and try not to blow my nose in it all night. In the morning it doesn't look so good.

After milking I sit down on a rusty old cart beside the barn and cry. Tommy finds me with my head in my arms.

"How'd it go, then?" His voice is unenthusiastic.

My shoulders are shaking but he doesn't comfort me. I lift

my head to see him shifting from foot to foot, looking coldly at the horizon, and I feel worse. "He didn't come."

The solace of my disappointment seems to soften him. He puts his arm around me and squeezes my bony limbs against his. Then I feel him tensing, and he catches his breath a little.

"It's my fault," he whispers. "I prayed for him not to come . . . and he hasn't!"

I look up at his face and see that it's blotchy. "Don't be daft! God don't answer prayers. I prayed for him to come. And he didn't."

We look at each other, confused by the Lord's meanderings. "Why didn't you want him to come?" I ask. His eyes are all pink. "And what are you crying for?"

He hangs his head very low, so low that it touches my forehead. Then, in a very shaky voice, he says, "I was afraid he'd take you away."

"Take me away! Wish he could, but he's got to go to the jungle!" I think he'll be impressed by this, and intend to elaborate with tigers and malaria and man-eating snakes, but he won't let go of his theme.

"But he'll take you away one day. After the war, he'll come and take you back 'ome."

I lift my face and watch his lips say the words. And as I watch him he seems a bit like Popeye, breathing little wisps of heat, barely hinting at the vast pistons of fury that are smouldering inside and could explode at any moment. I feel a jab of indignation that he hasn't revealed himself before, and a colossal sadness that I haven't seen the depths of his pain.

I clasp his huge white knuckles between my hands and look at his face. He is a child, a small lost boy, hungry for a family, spoiling for love.

"You can come and live with us. I know you can!"

He gives a little scoffing sound. "No one would have me."

"Why not?"

"No one would want me."

"Why not?"

"Mr Fairly says so. He says lots of people want to adopt children but they never want Heaven House boys because we're the bottom of the heap, and I'm the bottom of the bottom."

I pull my head back to look at him, furious. "Well, who's *he* when he's at home, I should like to know!"

"He knows my mother and father left me there . . . They left me there because they didn't want me. That's what he says." His voice has gone all high-pitched and breathy, and his eyes are flooding again.

"Well, that's just crap – I've told you before. He *would* say that, wouldn't he?"

"Well, why else would they leave me there? You've seen it. Would *you* leave a baby there?"

For the first time I think I imagine how he must feel: abandoned, unloved and cheated. I reach my head up to kiss him awkwardly on the side of his wet nose, and squeeze his knuckles tighter.

"Well, my Aunty Babs left a baby at the awfnidge. And d'you know why?"

"Why?"

"Because she wasn't married. That's why people leave their babies. And d'you know what?"

"What?"

"She never stopped crying about that baby, my mum says, and it'll ruin her life if she tries to get it back, because no one'll marry her, my grandad says, so she'll just have to put up with it."

He won't be consoled so easily. "Well, even Miss Hubble

is keeping her baby, and it's black, and it'll ruin her life for certain. The father was killed on Omaha beach. Fairly says no one'll marry her now." We are both quiet for a moment as we think about Miss Hubble. "You see, if you really love your baby, like Miss Hubble, you can't give it away . . ."

"Yes, but she knows. Miss Hubble knows they never let you see your baby – not ever again. My Aunty Babs thinks hers'll be going to a nice posh house where it'll have servants and things and be much better brought up than what she could've done with no husband nor nothink."

"But she's wrong."

"Yes. But who's going to tell her?"

"Who even knows she's wrong?"

"That's the thing, see. Only people what've seen awfnidges know. And you can be sure your mum is thinking of you just like Aunty Babs and I bet she blubbers every time she sees a pram and has to go to the pictures a lot so's she can cry in the dark and even her dishy boyfriend won't suspect there's anything wrong."

Tommy is silent. He scratches the side of his head.

"And you can bet your bottom dollar none of you lot at Heaven House was left there by your mum and dad. My mum reckons they're all Love Children at the awfnidge, that's what she told my Aunty Babs. They're called that because they've got only love to live on, and also because their mums love them so much they give them away so's they can have a better life. That's what you are, Tommy: you're a Love Child. Means you're loved more than anything."

"A love child?" He looks wistfully at the distant brow of the hill, as if he is aching for my words to be true, for there to be the remotest possibility that he isn't unlovable, and that somewhere out there, over the beechwood horizon, is a woman yearning to be his mother.

The sound of a motor makes us both look towards the

road. We make our way down the lane to investigate and see a thin young man in khakis leaping down from a truck.

"Daddy!"

He doesn't look much like my dad, with his leathery tan and white crow's feet, and he does things I have never seen him do before. For example, when I take him for a walk to show him about the place, he throws his arms up and gasps, "It's so fuckin' *green*!" and bursts into tears. I want to tell him it's not at all green compared to the summer, but don't see the use. There's something disturbing about seeing your old dad crying. They're supposed to swing you in somersaults, make their thumbs disappear, tweak your cheek and say, 'Bloody Nora, you've grown, gel!' But my dad looks away from me a lot, moved beyond words by gateposts and oak trees and Miss Lavish's tricycle, and when he does look at me, it is an intense look, gobbling me up with his eyes and holding my head in his hands as if I were a miracle.

All this leaves me with the uncomfortable feeling again that things have changed and that, even when this war is over, things might never return to normal as I know it. It is almost a relief to have Tommy lurking around, and I introduce him as my best friend who is going to join the RAF.

They get on well, my dad and Tommy, until he goes and says, "Listen, son! When you're old enough, you get yourself a job, mate. You don't want to go fighting in no war, believe you me. You stay here in these lovely green hills and get yourself a family, son. And don't you ever leave 'em. Not even for a war . . ." And then his eyes are all pink again, and Tommy doesn't know what to say, and neither do I.

Aunty Joyce is all ruffled because he doesn't stay long enough for a meal. He has to get to the station and hops on the truck after two cups of tea and the remains of the Apple Surprise.

125

Boogie-woogie bugle boy

It is December and the War Office has decided people need cheering up. There are parties everywhere, and it is generally felt that the war will come to an end at last.

The US signals base nearby throws a party for all the evacuees and Heaven House boys. We are each allocated a GI to take care of us all afternoon. Tommy is in seventh heaven because he was taken by jeep to the nearest airfield and got to sit in a Mustang: in the cockpit. I am given a ride on a motorbike and swung up on the shoulders of Ted Pearlman, a huge bear of a man from South Dakota, wherever that is. We eat cake and jam sandwiches, and at the end we are given an apple and sit watching a cine film on the History of the Modern Fighter Plane, followed by a Charlie Chaplin film, with the piano played by a giant GI.

I feel an excitement that is more than just party fever. I like being swung about by Ted Pearlman and I like the size of them all, their easy confidence and their smiles. The towns and villages are depleted of young men, yet here they all are, suddenly, in one big mass. Young men with as much energy each as the whole of Sheepcote can muster on a good day.

They drive us back to the village hall and when the

126

grown-ups come to take us home, Ted Pearlman gives me chewing gum and chocolate and bends down to whisper in my ear.

"Hey, Chipmunk, is that babe with the blonde hair your Aunty Joyce?"

I nod, and he whisks me up in his arms, takes me to his truck where he rummages in a box, and gives me a slim packet of nylons. "You give these to your Aunty Joyce from a secret admirer. Don't forget: a secret admirer."

"A secret admirer!" I whisper. "Do I get any?"

"No, Chippers, you get the chocs."

When I deliver the booty, Aunty Joyce beams uncharacteristically, and slips the nylons under some potatoes in her basket.

"You must never," she admonishes with no conviction whatsoever, "take presents from a stranger."

Just a few days later there is the Christmas party at the village hall. So many people want to come that it has to be changed to a new venue, and Lady Elmsleigh volunteers her large hall.

The Women's Institute have spent all afternoon making it look festive. Paper chains which have been used at so many previous events that they are crumpled and faded have been strewn from wall to wall, along with wads of ivy, mistletoe and holly.

The hall quickly fills with the whole of Sheepcote, a crowd of RAF, GIs and several husbands and sons home on leave. The music is provided by Ronnie's Razzlers (Ronald Tiffin is an ironmonger from Stroud who knows all the Glen Miller tunes) and the Sheepcote Sugar Quartet (a group of just three land girls singing in harmony).

At first people simply sway around, chatting and making sure they get their drink of cider or ginger beer. But as soon as the ash-baked potatoes and the upside-down pudding have been scoffed, the floor clears for the proper dancing.

The men change everything. There is real dancing — men with women — and the air is thick with sweat and musk. The daydream melodies develop a wolfishness I have never noticed when I hear them on the wireless, and people who usually sit quietly develop an unquenchable desire for movement. And it isn't the cider that turns the women pink — for most of them avoid the cider, which is 'like paint stripper' according to Tommy — it is some mix of longing and the thrill of the rhythm, along with the barely concealed hunger of lusty young men who are far, far too close for comfort.

Lady Elmsleigh is there too, wearing a paper hat. When Ronnie's Razzlers have a break from playing, she claps her hands and orders some chairs to be placed in the middle of the hall for musical chairs. A record player is wound up and there is a frenzied crush as children bump into each other and into chairs, but it all adds to the excitement as we hurl ourselves around the chairs in a great swarm, joined by every grown-up with a movable bone in their body. When the music starts we scream as we run, the butcher, the grocer, Face-like-a-spud and Baggie Aggie, Mrs Glass with the big fat arse and a GI, all of us squealing in delight to the drowned-out record player and the promise of a pile-up.

When it is established that the music has stopped, bodies are everywhere, pushing and nudging and sitting on top of each other, three to a seat. Because of the lack of chairs, each chair is allowed to hold two people, one on the lap of the other, and the pilots and GIs act swiftly to provide the laps, while the ladies fight feverishly to sit on them.

I find a place on Ted Pearlman, and Miss Lavish (hooting with laughter) is sitting next to me on a GI. The next time, I get to sit on the vicar, and Tommy (the person I was aiming for) is sitting on the lap of Aunty Joyce. I can smell her hot familiar body from underneath her short-sleeved sweater, and I want her to say something to him. I say, "Careful, Tommy, you're crushing Aunty Joyce!" He looks round, but she shows him her profile and her perfect jawline.

The music starts and stops again, and when I'm out I stand on a table at the back swigging ginger beer and watching. There are only eight chairs left and seventeen people. Ted and Aunty Joyce are still in, and he is shadowing her, determined to nestle her behind on his manly thighs. 'The Chattanooga Choo-Choo' keeps going for a tantalizingly long time, but Ted keeps up his position, and when the music comes to an abrupt halt, '. . . won't you choo-choo me –' he plonks himself right down in front of her. She makes to go for the next lap, but Miss Didbury is being snuggled by a farm labourer, and on the other side Betty Chudd is nuzzling a rakish Wing Commander. People start shouting, "In front of you! In front of you!" But Aunty Joyce stays rooted to the spot like someone who has seen a ghost, and Mrs Glass scampers round the whole circuit of chairs to beat her to it.

No one can make it out. People are laughing, calling Joyce dozy, a daydreamer. I feel a sudden pang of protectiveness. Some people in front of me whisper that she's lost it completely since her daughter died. Uncle Jack, standing by the door with the vicar, looks worried. But then I see it has nothing to do with what is going on: probably sorting out the numbers for the Sunday school party, and the vicar is nodding so vigorously that it is clear he couldn't care less.

I see Aunty Joyce heading for the kitchen. I know what she'll do there, and it's strange: of all these people who have known Aunty Joyce for years – even her own husband – not one of them knows why she didn't take the last place in musical chairs, but I know. I know for certain when I see her coming back out of the kitchen, wiping her hands on her skirt.

At first I think that she's just afraid of falling in love with Ted, or afraid that he might fall in love with her, or afraid that Uncle Jack might get jealous. But now I see it clearly, although I still don't understand quite how it works: Ted Pearlman is contaminated.

Gossip: The city charmer, the farmer, the man in the moon

It is the last knitting group before Christmas and Aunty Joyce cannot come. Instead I walk down to the village hall with Miss Lavish. I help her to carry the mince pies (except there is no mince so they are apple, and they're cold so we'll have to warm them on the stove at the back of the hall).

"Your Aunty Joyce all right, love?" asks Mrs Chudd.

"I think so," I say. "Just a bit busy."

"She looked a bit off colour at the party, that's all. Didn't seem quite herself."

It's aimed at me, but I say nothing.

"She a bit off colour round the house?"

"Not off colour – just odd," says Baggie Aggie. "Queer behaviour if ever there was."

"Did you see it an' all? In that musical chairs? Crumbs, she was daft as a brush, she was."

"She 'asn't been the same since . . . you know what."

There's a murmur of agreement. I'm not sure if I'm completely invisible yet, so I keep my head down, and pretend to count my ribbing.

"Still, we've all 'ad our grief," says Mrs Marsh with a twitch of her moustache, and she should know.

"And none so much as you, Dot. None so much as you."

131

"'Strue," agree the others.

Needles click quietly for a while.

"Still . . ." Mrs Chudd ventures, "Our Betty reckons she married the wrong man, and I must say I'm inclined to agree with her." She purses her lips, awaiting the reaction to her mischief.

"Oh! Jack Shepherd is a good man," says Miss Lavish.

"Ah, Lavinia, but good for what?"

Chortles.

"Perhaps not good for her," suggests Mrs Glass.

"I remember 'is father, Arthur Shepherd," says Tosser suddenly from her smelly corner. "Real tosser 'ee wuz."

But then she goes on to tell us about Arthur Shepherd, ably assisted by questions from the others, and I learn a lot about Uncle Jack. Seems he came from a strong Chapel family in Stroud, his father all hellfire and brimstone and preaching the evils of alcohol and lust. His mother was a compliant woman, a teetotal champion of needlepoint. Jack and his brothers were all brought up bent double with guilt. When Jack married Joyce, a Church girl, it was an extreme act of defiance. There were plenty of Chapel girls with no previous record of kissing, good girls with wide hips who could make pies. But no, he chose a church girl from Painswick who could floor a dozen men with a bat of her eyelashes. Whether it was because her generous lips and firm buttocks provoked feelings he preferred to deny or what, but Jack's father never forgave him. So Jack embraced the church instead (a little too tightly, maybe) while his father spent the first eight years of their marriage sulking and shovelling on the guilt, and the remaining years buried in it himself and wishing he had known his lost grand-daughter.

Joyce Stringer was not the woman her father-in-law made her out to be, neither did she have the strength he credited her with to bear his contempt.

"Lord, tiz awful."

"A tragedy."

"She 'ad plenty o' sweethearts, mind. But see 'er own father died in the Great War when she were – oh, barely four year old I'd say. 'Ee wuz just like God lookin' out of a photograph, 'ee wuz, an' they say she put men on a peddy stool. And Jack, she put 'im on a peddy stool an' all."

"Ah! There now, that could be true."

I can see why Tosser is so welcome in the knitting group now. But she only speaks if she chooses, and no one can make her.

"'Course 'er mother's side of the family wuz all inbred."

"*Never!*"

"Well! That explains it!"

"It explains a lot!"

I can't see how everything is made clear by the fact that all of Aunty Joyce's family were in the baking trade. But I listen intently.

"Joyce's mother seemed all right when we met her last Christmas, mind," says Aggie.

"Ah!" says Tosser. "She weren't inbred. Twuz 'er mother – Joyce's grandmother. An' 'course twuz what 'er uncles tried to do to poor Joyce's mother – Ivy . . . I've known Ivy when she wuz a littl'un. Not *well*. Tiz no wonder she's disgusted by you know what . . ."

"But Joyce's father, he would never've let that lot near his family . . ."

"No! No! 'Ee wuz Ivy's saviour 'ee wuz. But see that's Joyce's problem. When she were a littl'un, she asked 'er father why 'ee wuzn't in the war, so next thing Ivy knows 'er 'usband's gone and joined up. Well, she never saw 'im again. She 'an't never forgiven our Joyce for that. Not ever. Nor never will."

"Well I never!"

"Tiz cruel to make your own child feel bad like that."

"Dreadful!"

"That might explain why she's so —"

"Tiz a wonder she don't have more children, though."

"Perhaps he can't . . . you know what," suggests Mrs Chudd with a mischievous look.

"Ah, you know his trouble," says Mrs Glass. "All that Chapel lot. They want children but they want the Immaculate Conception. He wants a wife who's a virgin for ever!"

"Get away! Well, he won't find many virgins in Sheepcote!"

"Go on! There's always Lavinia."

Everyone looks at Miss Lavish, but she continues knitting without looking up, and says, "You presume too much."

People stop knitting and stare. Miss Lavish gets up, counts how many we are, and goes off to the kitchen to put the kettle on and prepare tea. As soon as the door has swung behind her, everyone looks at Tosser, who wipes her nose on her sleeve and decides to explain.

It seems Miss Lavish is a dark horse. She was once in the arms of a handsome young soldier who promised the earth in a whisper. Then he went and splattered his body over a field in France.

Had he married her before he went away, she could have been saved from a lifetime of the dreadful millstone named spinsterhood. But for one simple ceremony she was destined to face the world as a sad, unfulfilled Miss, instead of an aggrieved but worldly Missus. And to think it had been her own idea to wait until the war was over! It had been a foolish idea encouraged by her mother, who was afraid he would leave her widowed. This was before she realized that, in that infamous Great War, *everyone* came back in pieces, if they came back at all, and there would be no spare men to marry in his place.

But Miss Lavish is not what she seems at all. For one night, when he was home on leave, Jarvis Cooksley took her out walking up the woods near the school, and there, under the beeches, they made love.

I wonder how Tosser knows this, but then Tosser knows everything that happens under the stars in this little valley.

Miss Lavish comes in with a rickety trolley of tea things. But we all look at her differently. Sometimes, when children giggle at her tricycle, or when she sees beech-nut shells in the verges, or when she envies other women's domesticity, or when she hears them complain about their dull husbands, or when she senses a look of pity in their eyes, does she perhaps remember her night in the beechwood and think, "I, Lavinia Lavish, am not a virgin," and does she pedal faster and smile?

On the way home Miss Lavish takes my hand between the hedgerows and guides me through the pitch black.

"You know, you mustn't believe all they say about Uncle Jack and Aunty Joyce. They like to have something to gossip about."

"That's okay," I say, "I never really listen."

"Yes, I know. But they tried to draw you in today. I didn't like that. They've no right to ask you questions. None of their business."

We walk on into the total darkness.

"Lavinia . . ."

"Yes?"

"Why do you think they're so horrible to each other, Uncle Jack and Aunty Joyce?"

"Oh, I'm sure they're not."

"They are."

A bit of elder bush swipes me in the face and she beats it out of the way.

"Well . . . sometimes, I think, things can go so wrong that it's hard for people to show their feelings for each other."

"Oh, they know how to show their feelings all right. They're just rotten to each other."

Miss Lavish swaps places with me and walks on the inside, to protect me from stray twigs and branches.

"You know how sometimes at school the boys tease the girls and pull their hair?"

"Yes . . ." I say, unsure why she's changed the subject.

"Well, what they're really doing, of course, is flirting."

"Flirting?"

"They'd really like to kiss them."

"Really?"

"Yes. It's just a way of making contact."

I think this through. She could be right.

"And sometimes, when people are so badly upset that they don't know how to be affectionate, well . . . they hurt each other instead."

"Why?"

"Making each other feel guilty – hurting each other – it may be all they can manage. But it's a way of making contact."

Grown-ups are all a bit confusing.

"I know they love each other really," I say.

"I expect they do."

"Oh, they *do*!" I insist.

"What makes you say that?"

"Well . . . it's just . . . she always warms his socks on the range for him. And he . . . he cleans her shoes every night. Scrapes all the mud off with a knife and a rag, and polishes them. He leaves them in the hall."

Our eyes have become accustomed to the dark, and we can see the dark outline of Weaver's Terrace next to us. Miss Lavish stops and holds both my hands in hers and whispers, "You know, Kitty, you're the best thing that could've happened to them." Then she opens our little creaking gate and kisses me goodbye.

People will say we're in love

The next morning after milking Tommy lies in wait for me and pulls me aside as I'm about to head back down the lane. "Follow me."

I expect him to lead me across the fields to an adventure, but he scrambles up some large stones behind the cart at the side of the barn and beckons to me, putting his finger to his lips to stop me asking questions. Although the barn is made of Cotswold stone, its top half has been renovated with corrugated iron, and in it is a rusted gap which Tommy now puts his cheek to. "Come on!" he whispers. "Look!"

I look. We press our faces on the cracked iron and watch. There is nothing to see. Three POWs are heaving milk churns on to the cart. And there is Aunty Joyce pouring the milk pails into the churns. She wears brown corduroys and wellingtons. Her blonde hair curls out from under a red headscarf, tied gypsy-like at the back of her neck.

"What are we looking at?" I whisper.

"Keep looking."

So we do. Aunty Joyce continues to pour milk from the pails, and the three men continue to shift it. The horse lifts its tail and does a poo. I whisper a laugh, thinking this is it. But Tommy is still pressed up hard against the rusted iron, concentrating, and I can hear his breath next to my ear.

Then I see something. It is only a small difference, so slight I wonder if I'm on to the right thing at all. But I'm intrigued.

As Heinrich bends down to pick up the churn next to Aunty Joyce, their eyes meet. She flushes, and continues to look at him for a moment, then reaches for the next pail. As he lifts the churn on to the cart we can see her steal a glance at him, then look down quickly.

"She's in love!" I whisper.

"Ssssh," Tommy whispers gently, putting a hand on my arm.

I pull away from the spy-hole and look at Tommy's hand on me, then I look up at him, trying to recreate some of Aunty Joyce's drama for myself. But Tommy is too busy spying to notice me.

We hear the two other POWs leave the barn and walk, chattering, up to the farm. Tommy beckons me to look with him again.

Aunty Joyce is gathering the empty pails and Heinrich walks over to her. He stands in front of her for a moment, then enfolds her pink knuckles in his giant hands. She stands there looking at him, as if waiting for something.

"Joyce!" he says. "I luf you!"

Suddenly Aunty Joyce has shaken her hands free and is walking towards the barn door. She turns to look at him, bright red and shaking, and says quietly, with a note of apology, "I'm a married woman!" Then she gathers her tray of tea things with wobbly hands, clunking cups all over the place. "And I love my husband."

She is out of the barn door and coming this way, so we duck down behind the old cart until she's passed us.

"Golly! D'you think Uncle Jack knows?"

"'Course he don't."

We sit quietly for a moment on the cold stones, each pondering what we've seen. Much as I like Heinrich, I find I'm not at all happy about this turn of events. I want things to be as they should be: wives with their husbands, children with their mothers, fathers tumbling about with their children and not crying when they see a tree.

"Tommy . . ."

"Yeah?"

"Why doesn't Aunty Joyce have another baby?"

He shrugs. "Dunno. P'raps Jack can't get it up."

I frown and say, "Oh, right."

"Like the rabbit," Tommy explains. "The rabbit *could* get it up, Jack *can't*. I 'speck. Dunno for certain."

Ever so briefly I picture Uncle Jack in a cage with Aunty Joyce. "Still, she did say no to Heinrich. She did say no, didn't she? She said she loves Uncle Jack, didn't she?"

Tommy looks thoughtful. "Yes, she did."

We get to our feet and amble down the farm lane.

"You wanna meet my mum? She's coming Boxing Day."

He shrugs.

"I want you to meet her." He kicks at the muddy stones, so I add, "So's we can arrange for you to come an' live with us, after the war."

"I . . . I . . ."

"I, yi, yi, yi, yi I like you very much!" I say, attempting an exotic accent like Carmen Miranda.

He tries to look indifferent, but smiles at the bare hedgerows, and then at me. "Okay, then."

On the last morning of term I have a sudden urge to ask Aunty Joyce a question as she sees me out of the door.

"Can I have a cuddle?"

"Pardon?"

"Will you give me a cuddle?" I look up at her earnestly. "I haven't had one in ages."

She stops tying my ribbon for a moment, and with a look of mild exasperation she kneels down and puts her arms around me. I cling on as tightly as I can. I can smell the soap in her housecoat and the deeper woman-smell, and I can feel her softness. I squeeze and squeeze and just can't bring myself to let go. She is a familiar scent to me now, and I want more of it. Eventually Aunty Joyce wrenches herself free and begins to do up my shoelaces, which I usually do up myself. She is biting her lip and fumbling furiously with them.

Then she packs me off to school, and when I turn to wave I see her sheltering her eyes with one hand, and I could swear she is crying. But she couldn't be, because Aunty Joyce never cries.

I'm gonna see my baby

On Christmas Eve the church is full. Whole families with grandparents and children and soldiers home on leave squash into the pews, and babies' heads pop up between shoulders. Candles have been lit in all the windows. The organist is playing a medley of carols at a lethargic pace as the last few people arrive and say their silent prayers.

I wait with the Sunday school and older children at the back of the church ready to process forward at the sign of the vicar. I wanted to be a lamb or an angel, but Miss Didbury made me a donkey. I'm wearing cardboard ears, attached to a donkey head made out of a cardboard box. An old grey woollen skirt (that belonged to Aunty Joyce's mother), slit at the seam, makes a tent-like cloak tied above my head, upon which the donkey-effect head perches precariously. I keep peaking out from the slit in my cloak. I want to see the look on Uncle Jack and Aunty Joyce's faces when I arrive with Mary and Joseph. I find, inexplicably, that I want them to be proud of me.

Everyone seems to have arrived now. A tune ends, and as the organist pauses a gust of wind comes from the porch at the back of the church as the outer door is opened again. Heads begin to turn to see the latecomer. It is Miss Hubble, carrying her baby close to her chest.

A low murmur begins.

Peeping out from my cloak I can see Uncle Jack's drained face turned towards Miss Hubble. He looks at Aunty Joyce who looks back at him with a frown. Then Uncle Jack rises to his feet and walks slowly towards Miss Hubble, head bowed. He is going to find a seat for her, and I begin to feel little pangs of pride. With an avuncular arm around her shoulder, he steers the young mother back towards the door, and all the shepherds and angels and farm animals distinctly hear him say, "This isn't the place for you," for all the world as if she were an infant who had mistakenly wandered into the senior school.

I am furious. I look at the lantern-holder next to me – who is Tommy – and I can tell he feels the same, only Tommy is so used to the unfairness of everything that it only just surfaces on the rigid set of his mouth. I don't know if he slips out for a fag stub with the older boys or what, but at about that moment he seems to disappear.

Uncle Jack returns to his seat, the self-appointed do-gooder applauded by the quiet relief of the treacherous congregation. The organist begins to play, pulling out all the stops, as we process to the crib at the front of the church carrying candles and lanterns. After depositing our lights around the manger, we disappear into the vestry, where Lady Elmsleigh has offered to help 'backstage' despite her lack of belief, and where Tommy is miraculously waiting for us by a little external door for the vicar's use only.

When the music stops the vicar welcomes everyone and says a prayer. It is accompanied by rustling and giggles from the vestry as shepherds struggle to secure their blankets' safety pins and wise men run about looking for their tobacco tins of frankincense and myrrh.

At last an innkeeper emerges and stands under the pulpit, with Mary and Joseph hobbling after him.

"Is there any room at the inn?" asks Joseph in a soprano voice, lifting his head a little to reveal a beard of boot polish.

"I'm sorry," says the innkeeper, "we're packed like sardines in 'ere."

"You sure? My wife is with child." He nods at Babs Sedgemoor who is wearing a blue candlewick bedcover.

"Sorry. Nothink 'ere, Joseph."

The parishioners smile, babies shriek and sing from the depths of the pews and the vestry continues to bubble with noise.

After two more innkeepers, Tommy eventually takes pity on the pair.

"Well, I've no more rooms left," says Tommy, "but if you're really desperate like, I've got a stable you can 'ave."

"That's very kind. My wife's . . . with child."

"Oh, is she? I'll get some fresh straw." He heaps some more straw on a hay bale set out for Mary to sit on, and takes her hand to help her.

Then the prisoners of war stand and face the congregation. They sing 'Silent Night', and their voices are beautiful. Some of the women have to wipe tears from their eyes, ashamed and confused at how they can be so moved by their enemy. Aunty Joyce does not take her eyes off them, and even her eyes are glistening when the song is over.

While Betty Chudd reads the first lesson, it is my job to fetch the baby Jesus doll from the vestry door, secrete him under my cloak, and hand him miraculously to Mary.

"Thanks be to –"

A small blanketed figure in the central aisle cries out before Betty Chudd can complete her last word: "It be a cold night, me masters!"

The shepherds all give an exaggerated shiver and exclaim at the brightness of the clouds. Iris Holland tiptoes up in a sheet with a paper plate perched on her head, and everyone sings 'While shepherds watched their flocks by night'.

A short reading by Mr Fairly heralds the arrival of the wise men, who deliver their gifts with suitable awe at the baby Jesus. Then as the entire assemblage of Sunday school and other children sing 'Away in a manger', shepherds, wise men, cattle and innkeepers all crane to see the holy infant.

During the hymn the baby begins to cry, and a few members of the congregation look uneasy.

> *"The cattle are lowing,*
> *The baby awakes,*
> *But little Lord Jesus*
> *No crying he makes . . ."*

At this, the Lord Jesus does indeed fall silent. A lamb takes an unwarranted interest in him, and the innkeeper gazes at the donkey with a fond look of complicity.

Joyce and Jack eye the exchange with curiosity, then sit open-jawed with the rest of the congregation as the holy infant raises a chubby arm towards the bosom of the virgin mother.

The verse ends, and in the slight pause the silence is filled with glances and gasps. In the confusion we children continue, primed to sing our song to the end. The vicar, now in his pulpit, can see better than anyone that Jesus is what everyone has suddenly noticed he is: a real, live brown baby.

> *"Bless all the dear children*
> *In thy tender care,*
> *And fit us for heaven*
> *To live with thee there."*

Say something sweet to
your sweetheart

After the service Miss Lavish offers Miss Hubble a cup of tea in the vestry, lighting a little camper gas ring in the corner, and the vicar offers her a cigarette. Miss Hubble accepts both, and I get to cuddle the baby, who is a beautiful coffee-colour and called Jerome like his father.

As soon as we have changed we are all ushered back through the church and out to where the grown-ups are waiting for us by the gravestones along the church path. But just before we reach them a group of POWs have lined up by the porch and are handing out presents to us. They are all gifts they have made: little baskets of bark with flowers and moss, ships and dolls made out of sticks or even carved from wood, corn dollies, miniature toys made out of match boxes or acorn cups. Heinrich hands me a small piece of wood and wraps my hands around it, as though I must not show it to anyone else. I take a peek and see that it is an intricately carved cat.

"Boomer!" I whisper. I am so overcome that I throw my arms around him, all churned up and eyes full to bursting.

Uncle Jack comes over and pulls me away. "Come on, you've caused enough trouble already," he hisses.

I am saved from a bollocking on the way home by Miss

Lavish, who catches up with us and trills about the lovely service as we climb the sunken lane towards the terrace. But as soon as we sit down for our Ovaltine, Uncle Jack switches off the wireless that Aunty Joyce has turned on. To my surprise he starts off with her.

"I couldn't help noticing in church that you're wearing nylons."

Aunty Joyce cups her mug in her hands and does not look at him. "So I am."

He flares his nostrils slightly and bangs his pipe on the hearth.

"Are you going to tell me where you got them? . . . Or should I ask *how* you got them?"

He is beginning to turn pink, and I feel I should help her out. "I gave her them, Uncle Jack. It was when we was up at the American base. My GI guide gave them to me."

"A GI!" He spreads his hands flat on the chair arms as if he is about to get up, but just breathes heavily instead. "And I'm supposed to just sit here and do nothing while my wife goes round like a *slut* wearing the nylons some *American* has given her? What do you think everyone has made of it, hmm? You tell me that!" He points a finger at Joyce, and his spite makes me angry.

"That's not how it was!" I protest from my position at the table. "*All* the GIs were giving treats out to the children for them to take home to their families and friends."

"And what was *your* GI called?"

"Ted."

"So, a GI called Ted gives my wife stockings and I don't know about it?"

Joyce stares vacantly from her armchair towards the table-cloth. Heinrich's carved cat is sitting there: it really is very good.

I thought she was in a defiant mood, but now she just

seems to have given up. I wish she would say something, but she doesn't.

"Look, I wish I'd just saved them for my own mum," I say. "She wouldn't have worried where they came from and neither would my dad. He'd just've been pleased to see a smile on her face. And he'd have trusted her enough to know she wasn't no slut."

Uncle Jack twitches a bit and begins to stuff his pipe with tobacco. Aunty Joyce shoots me what might be a grateful glance. Then he starts on me.

"There's no need for rude language like that," he says, forgetting that he'd just used it himself. He lights the tobacco and takes one or two puffs, filling the air with vanilla. It seems to soften him a little, for he leans forward and says in a much gentler voice, "You know what you did in church was very wrong, don't you, Kitty?"

"I'm sorry, Uncle Jack, but I just don't understand."

"Well . . ." He puts his elbows on his knees in a thoughtful manner. "You may not understand it all yet, but . . . having a baby outside marriage is a wicked thing to do. And people do have a choice, it doesn't just happen."

I assume a bewildered look. "Are you saying Miss Hubble is wicked, then?"

"Well! I know you liked Miss Hubble, Kitty, but we must all respect the teachings of Christ, and I'm afraid . . . it was wrong of her to bring the fruits of her sin to church – to a family service as well!"

Now I am bewildered. It wasn't fruit that Miss Hubble brought in at all. I want to get back to the point, and why Uncle Jack is wrong about Miss Hubble. I think for a moment about what he did in church, and I can't let it go. I have tried hard to understand the bible stories I've heard in Sunday school and church to please Uncle Jack, but this just doesn't add up.

"But Uncle Jack, 'Whoever receives a child in my name is really being nice to me.'"

There is a sharp intake of breath. "Don't quote the Bible at me, young lady!"

"But Uncle Jack, aren't you afraid of the millstone?"

"What millstone?"

"The one that you have to wear round your neck if you're horrid to one of God's . . . you know . . . little ones." I'm on uncertain ground here. There's a millstone in the field behind the school and it doesn't look like the sort of thing you could hang round your neck at all.

He begins to turn pink. I scratch my nose and say in a singsong voice, "I'm only saying . . . that's all."

"Upstairs NOW! You'd better watch out you don't get cinders in your stocking!"

But Father Christmas doesn't leave me cinders. When I awake in the morning my stocking is full, with an apple, a biscuit, a small colouring book, a pencil and an intricately knitted doll. The doll has long black hair in plaits with a red skirt, and if you turn her upside down she becomes a lady with blonde plaits, and a blue skirt. Each doll has little ribbons, one has a handbag, which opens, and the other has an apron, which comes off if you want.

I have never had anything like this before. I am so thrilled I can't wait to tell everyone. Not only was God on my side over the Miss Hubble incident (because he didn't tell Father Christmas to leave me cinders), but I have the most amazing present I have ever known (apart from Heinrich's cat).

"Look! Look! Look at my beautiful doll! Look!"

When I come hurtling down the stairs to show Aunty Joyce, she gives me a smile so tender I can hardly believe it, and pours us all porridge.

Poor hurt people

At around half past nine on Christmas morning, Aunty Joyce's mother turns up in a horse and cart, driven by a neighbour from Painswick who is also visiting relatives.

"I'll be back this afternoon!" shouts the man at the reins. "I want to be home before dark, look."

In she comes with a blast of cold air, carrying a carpet bag full of knitting.

She has the same features as Aunty Joyce, but more extreme. The eyes are paler and bluer, the cheekbones more widely spaced. But the full lips have collapsed a little with age and the hair is almost white, the curls piled on top like Queen Mary's. As soon as she comes in, the house is different.

She refuses a comfortable chair by the range and takes a seat at the table, from where she can watch us preparing vegetables.

"I see you got the littl'un working," she says, sucking the side of her cheek.

I smile from my carrot scraping, but Aunty Joyce just looks flustered.

"You're doing a good job there, love," she says to me. Then, under her breath, she mutters, "You wanna watch she don't pack you off fishing."

Aunty Joyce slams down her potato knife and glares at her mother. There is a silence in which Mrs Stringer carries on knitting with eyebrows raised in total innocence, and in which Aunty Joyce is clearly deliberating about something.

"What did you say?"

Mrs Stringer looks up a little surprised and tugs at her wool. I am about to repeat what she said for Aunty Joyce – because I heard it quite clearly – when I realize that this is something grown-up and unpredictable, and I had better keep my mouth shut.

I am relieved when Uncle Jack comes in from the back with a scuttle full of coal.

"You're looking well!" he says, smiling at his mother-in-law. "Journey all right?"

"Not so bad. That horse of Gill's've seen better days, mind. Bump, bump, bump all the way!"

The kettle whistles on the range, and Uncle Jack pours some water into the teapot. There is a silence even louder than the ones I'm used to at the tea-table here, and the sounds of the water going into the pot and the scraping of vegetables seem to thunder through the whole room.

"'Twill be bump, bump, bump all the way back an' all," she says at last.

"I'll sort out something soft for you to sit on," says Uncle Jack.

Aunty Joyce is chopping my carrots, aggressively, with a mouth clamped very shut.

"I 'ope you're not doin' them all like that. Great fat slabs o'carrot. You know I like mine fine."

There is a silence again, just the shuffle of coals as Uncle Jack stokes the fire.

"Sorry," says Aunty Joyce and, to my amazement, she starts to cut carefully, producing delicate rounds of carrot without a trace of malice.

151

At first I think it is a little battle between the two of them, but soon I see there is only one winner. As Uncle Jack pours the tea, Mrs Stringer pipes up: "You got him well trained then!" And she just can't seem to help herself from adding, "Always did know how to twist a man round your little finger!" And then she just can't resist patting his hand: "You watch she don't pack you off to the war, Jack."

Aunty Joyce does not rise to it. She carries on, subdued, wrestling with the carrots and potatoes, her pretty mouth beginning to lose the radiance it had at breakfast.

At dinnertime we bring out a beautifully roasted half of chicken. Miss Lavish has had the other half and taken it down to the school house, where she, Miss Miller and Boss Harry are having their Christmas meal together.

"I 'ope this isn't one of yours," says Mrs Stringer.

"Certainly is," says Jack, smiling. "Only we couldn't bring ourselves to do it, so we got Thumper in on it."

"Well, all I can say is what a waste! All them eggs it could lay for you every week and you throw it all away on one meal!"

Aunty Joyce starts to carve it reluctantly, but Uncle Jack takes over. "Here, let me." I can't work out if he is cross or not. But if he is, it is certainly not with Aunty Joyce, and he is hiding it very well.

"The war will be over soon, and what on earth will we do with all these chickens then?" He smiles at me, and I smile back.

"They said that last year, and look what 'appened," she says.

"Breast?" Uncle Jack holds up the best meat, poised above the tablecloth, and his mother-in-law nods.

"No need to use disgusting words like that," she adds.

The food is dished out with the quiet clinking of cutlery. We munch and hear each other munching.

"No holly on the table this year, then?" asks the old goat.

Aunty Joyce puts a hand to her mouth. "I'm sorry!" She sounds devastated. "Oh hang, I completely forgot! I've got some out the back —"

"Sit down," says Uncle Jack calmly. "Enjoy the meal."

More munching.

"Sprouts are a bit crunchy," Mrs Stringer observes. "'Ow long you do them for, then?"

"Twelve minutes."

"Twelve minutes? I always do mine for fourteen. Like bloody rock they are otherwise."

Aunty Joyce apologizes again. "Everything else all right for you?"

"Oh yes. Yes . . . tiz lovely . . ." Mrs Stringer sucks her cheeks a little. "Mind . . . the gravy's dreadful thin — you never could make gravy, though, Joyce." Joyce looks down at her plate and seems almost to shrink.

"No . . ." continues her mother, "never could make gravy for tuppence."

I don't recognize the Aunty Joyce I see before me: shrunken, defeated, utterly wrong-footed at every turn.

"I think it's a *lovely* meal," I say suddenly. "I've never tasted a meal like it!" I smile at Aunty Joyce, desperate to raise her spirits. She looks at me and smiles weakly, but full of gratitude.

'Well, 'course you would say that, wouldn't you, my darlin'? Don't 'spose you eat food like this back in London, do you? Lucky to get bread up there, I 'speck."

"Well, I —"

"Now you make sure our Joyce takes care of you." She smiles at me mischievously. "She tends to be a bit careless with little girls, do our Joyce."

Now, you'd expect Aunty Joyce to throw the rest of the gravy at her mother, or the bread sauce, or the delicious Brussels sprouts she has been growing for months in the back garden. But no, she just puts the carefully prepared food into her mouth and eats it painfully slowly, as if the meal she has planned with such love and foresight is making her nauseous, and as if she is unworthy of every mouthful.

I am glad when the horse and trap comes to take Mrs Stringer away, but she has left Aunty Joyce crippled with bad feelings way beyond my reach. As soon as she is gone the washing starts. Not just the washing up, which I help her with while Uncle Jack lights his pipe and listens to the wireless, but washing the taps, washing her arms, washing her clothes, washing her face, washing the taps again, cleaning her shoes, scrubbing her nails, washing the door handles, washing her hands again and again and again . . .

Dumbo

My mother was supposed to come at Christmas, but she didn't and no one says a thing about it. Two days after Boxing Day Aunty Joyce tells me to put on my coat, she gives me mittens, straightens my woollen bonnet and takes me off to the bus stop.

The battering winds have strewn the lanes with twigs and branches, and the sad hedgerows, empty of leaves, show the old nests of song thrushes, blackbirds and warblers, all trilling indignantly at their secret haunts laid bare. The leaves of autumn are now a thin brown paste spread over the road. We tread crisply along the stony patches, avoiding the yellow puddles near the verge.

When the bus comes no one gets off, but we get on. The bus conductress comes over breathing smoke and winds us tickets with blue fingers. One and a half return to Cheltenham. She shakes her leather bag and the coins shuffle richly.

"Shoppin' then?"

"Yes," says Aunty Joyce.

She takes me to Ward's and lets me choose half a yard of ribbon for my hair. When we buy it the money is put in a tube which is sent rocketing down a chute like magic, only to return with the exact change.

We go up in a lift and down in a lift. We giggle at the stiff snooty models and feel all the fabrics. We go into Cavendish House and put Shalimar on our wrists, try on hats and pop the handbags open and shut. We listen to the Salvation Army playing carols, put a penny in their tin, and then walk up to Suffolk Parade to queue up outside the Daffodil where Dumbo is showing.

I have never seen anything like it. I laugh and laugh at the stork letting the baby elephant slip through the clouds, and Aunty Joyce laughs too. I hum to the music of the little train, and she looks at me in the flashing shadows and smiles. We all stop breathing when the circus tent comes down, and we all say "Aaah!" when Mother Elephant gets locked in a prison caravan.

Later, there is a scene where Dumbo goes to see his mum and they get to touch trunks. She puts her trunk out through the bars of her prison and he reaches his trunk up to meet it. My face and neck ache with grief, and when Mother Elephant starts to rock her baby on her trunk and sings 'Baby of Mine' I feel the tears messing up my cheeks.

But Aunty Joyce is laughing. I can't believe it. I can hear her laughing next to me. Other mother animals are rocking their babies to sleep – giraffes, tigers, monkeys, even hyenas – and I am all choked up trying not to burst and Aunty Joyce is laughing.

Then I glance at her, and see that her hand is clutched over her mouth not to stifle giggles but wails of despair. I stare at her pale face flickering in the dark. She is sobbing loudly now, and I have no idea what to do.

I grab the free hand in her lap, and squeeze it gently.

On the way home she says nothing of the little episode, and she is chattier than usual, perhaps to make sure I don't refer to it either. But when the bus gets out into the country-side, and the dark is so dark the driver could not drive unless he knew the road from childhood, then I take her hand again and give it a squeeze. Let her think I am afraid of the dark. Let her think what she likes. It felt good to hold her hand in the cinema, so I'm doing it again. And she lets me.

It is a freezing night. I wake up a couple of times as I turn in bed, trying to shift a hot-water bottle cold as a slab of haddock.

Just before the call-boy comes I awake in a delicious cocoon of warmth. Behind me and all around me is a body; I am wrapped up like a baby in its mother's arms, like Dumbo in Mother Elephant's trunk. I lie very still, afraid that if I move it will all disappear. This is not a dream. The bedclothes send up a deep musky smell of grown-up. I am in heaven.

With the rapping on the door Joyce gets up quickly and I turn to see her. She informs me matter-of-factly that I went into their room for a cuddle because I was cold, and that she came to warm me up and must have fallen asleep.

Too many details. And anyway, I know she is lying, because I haven't ventured out of bed all night. She talks in that crisp tone of hers, as if cuddling me were a complete mistake, which she won't make again.

My mother does turn up, but the day before New Year's Eve, and she has to dash back because she's helping to organize the New Year's Eve party at the munitions factory. She comes without the twins, though, so at least I have her to myself. She has stopped breastfeeding so her friend Dot is looking after them, and she did the same for Dot's kiddie yesterday.

Somehow it isn't the day I wanted it to be. My mother

spends ages admiring Aunty Joyce's needlepoint and her crockery and her pies and her rug and her smocked apron and her chickens and her home-made jam. I wanted to be proud of her, but instead I am ever so slightly ashamed of her rough language and her daft accent and her adulation of everything that isn't hers. I have no idea that it is she who has the very thing Joyce wants most in all the world.

I want her to show Uncle Jack and Aunty Joyce what real loving is, but she just witters on and on and doesn't seem to appreciate the gravity of any situation at all. She gives me a few sound hugs and the rest of the time plays the guest. Uncle Jack is kind, and makes her a cup of tea, which he never does for Aunty Joyce.

She brings me two presents: a bar of chocolate and a woollen tam-o'-shanter. I could've knitted one better myself, but I say nothing and look delighted. I take her for a walk to the farm in an effort to get her alone, but it all backfires in the mud and muck.

"Gawd! What ya trying to do to me? These are the only decent blinkin' stockings I got!"

So she goes, paying Joyce and Jack far more attention than they deserve, and telling me how grown-up I am. And I am left in an ugly torment, wondering if I will ever be little girl enough to get my fair share of cuddles again. I throw the tam-o'-shanter in the hall, shut myself in my room and play disloyally with the knitted doll instead, turning her back and forth from one woman to the other.

No one bothers to wonder what Uncle Jack makes of it all. He is a man and probably doesn't have feelings, but he cleans the mud off my little shoes and leaves them polished in the hall like he always does.

The way you look tonight

I have not seen Tommy to speak to since the nativity play, and I miss him. As I plod down the lane to the village hall I see Heaven House in the distance and wonder which window he might be sitting at, wonder if he is lonely or sad, or having exciting adventures with the other boys, which I would not be allowed to join in with. The grey-golden walls of that handsome house begin to thrill me every time I walk by. The sorcery of the ivy-clad balconies, the tantalizing studded green door, the knowledge that he is in there somewhere: I start to feel excited just catching a glimpse of it.

The mud has gone today, and the lane is hard, every footprint and hoof print filled with ice. There is no knitting group as such, but we have sorting to do, because so many of Our Boys will be home for New Year and they are all to receive knitted comforts to warm them in foreign lands and remind them of home. Personally, I can't imagine anywhere foreign can be as cold as Sheepcote. Even in the village hall we breathe smoke. But conversation soon perks us all up, and we forget about our numb fingers as we contemplate the New Year's Eve party.

"Tiz very kind of Lady Elmsleigh to have it up the 'ouse again," says Mrs Glass.

"Oh yes!"

"Yes."

"Well," says Mrs Chudd, "I don't know. It was her behind all that prisoners in church stuff last week, and you can say what you like, but our boys shouldn't have to mix with the enemy like that, not while they're home. She's got some funny new-fangled ideas, she 'ave, an' I don't like it."

"'Strue."

"Well, there is that."

"Oh, Tabs," says Mrs Glass, "but it is kind of her. We'd never be able to fit much of a party in here. And if it's her house, she can have who she likes."

"That's it though, she don't think about how it feels for people what've lost loved ones at the hands of these people." Mrs Chudd purses her lips decisively and matches two socks.

"I think you're forgetting something," says dear Miss Lavish. "She's lost a husband and a son at the hands of 'these people', and what's more she has a second son missing. Which one of us would feel like throwing a party for the world and his dog – two parties – if we were in that position?"

"She's right, you know."

"There is that . . ."

"Come to think of it . . ."

"I'm only saying," says Chudd, sick with defeat, and whispering under her breath, "it don't seem right to me, Germans in our church." But she won't give up. "This year we get a brown baby as Jesus, next year it'll be doing a Nazi salute!"

"Oh, Tabby!" There are giggles.

Then Mrs Marsh picks up a pullover and holds it against her chest, ready to fold. "All I can say is, if it were your son taken prisoner, how would you want him to be treated by the locals?" There is a respectful hush. We would all like to think some kind German gave each of Mrs Marsh's sons a slice of cake and a cup of tea before they passed away.

160

Conversation moves on to soap and stain removal.

"Anyone tried Rinso? Supposed to cut out the need for boiling."

"Aunty Joyce has," I venture, because it's true. "She tried it on the nappies in the summer. I think it worked."

"Nappies?"

"*Nappies?*"

I have to explain about the twins, and Aunty Joyce sending the nappies by post, but I have opened a can of worms.

"For a moment there . . ."

"D'you think she'd ever . . ."

"She'd suit another baby . . ."

"How was she?" demands Mrs Chudd. "With your little'uns?"

"Fine," I say.

And then, even more dangerously, "Do you think she might ever have another herself?"

I shrug.

"Don't she ever talk about it?"

"Tabs," says Miss Lavish.

"P'raps he can't get it up."

"*Tabs!*" says Miss Lavish, and this shuts her up.

"Only wondering . . ." she tapers off, disgruntled.

But it starts me thinking, and I think it would be a very good idea. After all, the war is nearly over – everyone says so – and I won't be here to keep them company much longer. And when I go, what will they have to do? I make a plan.

Lady Elmsleigh's New Year party is much like Lady Elmsleigh's Christmas party: an excuse for some merriment and expertly organized. This time the children have their own rooms, with a magician laid on (he is actually Mr Tugwell, but we all pretend not to notice), and a room full of mattresses and cushions for the very small children to fall asleep. I am not a very small child, and I sneak into the large hall to execute my plan.

Aunty Joyce is having an orange passed to her from the butcher's chin. Mr Glass is deliberately making a hash of it so he can nuzzle her neck as long as possible, but Uncle Jack is talking to the vicar again and doesn't seem to notice. Then she has to pass the orange to Ted Pearlman, the GI, and I watch with interest as he stoops gently to receive the fruit. Very briefly, she puts a hand on his arm to steady herself, but it is hastily withdrawn and the whole orange delivery is over more speedily than most. Their team has won, whilst Miss Lavish is still struggling with Thumper in the next team, and Aunty Joyce conceals the slight flush to her cheeks with a grin of victory.

The music starts, and Ted Pearlman asks me to dance. I feel very grown up.

"You come here often?" he jokes, as we waltz around. "I asked myself, 'Who is that babe with the cute face and no partner?'"

I am very, very happy dancing with Ted, even if I am perched on his toes. Uncle Jack is looking at me now and, although he doesn't look exactly cross, he is not looking at Aunty Joyce, and that is simply not good enough.

When the music stops, Ted bows melodramatically, and I curtsey.

I notice Nancy, the land girl, is leading Uncle Jack by the hand on to the dance floor. I blow the air up my face in exasperation. This was not supposed to happen.

Now Uncle Jack is being foxtrotted around at a merry old pace by the very pretty Nancy, who knows how to handle a tractor and certainly knows how to handle a man. To my surprise he seems to be enjoying it. His face is all smiles, and he does cut quite a dash with her, I must admit. Of course,

162

he glances over at his wife – to check her reaction, maybe – and she looks down at the tiled floor and scratches her nose.

I tug at Ted's sleeve and stand on tiptoe. "Why don't you dance with Aunty Joyce?" I whisper.

"You think she'd let me?" he whispers back.

"Try it!"

He does, and she accepts. Even I am surprised. A full-blooded man, heavily contaminated, and she agrees to touch him and be touched.

Now I am quite pleased that Uncle Jack is dancing with Nancy. She can get any engine going, and she can get any man going too. His face is pink with excitement, so pink and so excited that he looks for Joyce again (to check that she's looking? To check that she isn't?) and can't find her. Back and forth they go, she so expertly weaving him about that he has the happy illusion of being a fine dancer.

This will do nicely. I lean back against the wall and snaffle a paste sandwich.

Ted is so tall next to Aunty Joyce. She turns her face up to his now and then, and looks so pretty I wonder he can stop himself kissing her. He has his large hand firmly on her back with the fingers spread wide, and he is holding her very close as they sway quickly to the rhythm. Her lips are very red tonight, and her cheeks quite pink, but as the dance wears on I watch them grow an even deeper pink.

At one point Nancy almost hurls Uncle Jack into them, for she is going quite wild now, whirling him all over the shop and getting dangerously close to his cheek. But he has seen his wife, and the smile loosens a little round the edges, and he keeps looking over.

The dance ends, Aunty Joyce gives a nervous little 'thank you' with her head hung low, and Ted gives a nod before returning to the sandwiches.

The next dance is a fast one, and Nancy looks for all the

world like she might make another grab for Uncle Jack. But I step in fast.

I take Uncle Jack's hand and pull him away.

"Oh no!" he says, laughing. "No more dancing, Kitty!"

But I keep pulling him, and lead him over to Aunty Joyce. He looks at her and raises his eyebrows like a naughty boy waiting to be scolded. I take Aunty Joyce's hand, place it in his, and give them a good shove towards the dancing. They both look at me in exasperation, and Aunty Joyce rolls her eyes.

"I can't jitterbug!" protests Uncle Jack.

"Then do something else!" I say firmly. "Go on!"

They sort of shrug and sort of smile, and to my utter delight, they dance.

Chattanooga choo choo

Just before term starts Uncle Jack announces that he is taking the bus to work for a change, and he is taking me with him. I help Aunty Joyce pack sandwiches, and we set off on the seven-thirty to Gloucester through the cold January morning.

At first I think I must have done something wrong, and that he is trying to keep me out of mischief. But it soon becomes clear that this is Uncle Jack's treat, and I begin to get very excited as he tells me about the train we will ride and the fireman I will meet, how the coal fires the steam and all about the signals. It occurs to me that Aunty Joyce and Uncle Jack seem to be falling over themselves to give me treats at the moment – almost competing with each other – but I am too busy enjoying myself to pay it too much attention.

The engine shed is a bewitching place, full of strange new smells and echoing metallic sounds. I have always marvelled at the size of trains when they come into the station, their impossible power, the blaze of glory in which they steam to a princely halt. But here, standing on the ground beside it without the platform to diminish it, I look up to see the engine is a colossus. It towers above me, dark and smelly and mysterious. Even the steps up to the footplate are mountainous.

"So this is the new driver!" says a friendly face, peering down from way up high.

"This is Kitty," says Uncle Jack, lifting me in the air so that I can reach the first step.

The fireman grabs me under the armpits and pulls me up, smiling. "I'm George, your fireman. I 'ope you don't make me work too 'ard."

I smile, and Uncle Jack skips up the steps with impressive ease and is beside me. There is something about the way he is with me today that makes me feel he is almost proud of me. But this can't be, because I am a wicked, disrespectful and foul-mouthed girl and always letting him down.

We soon get the engine up to steam, and set off along the track to who knows where in the late morning winter sunshine. There is an almost frightening energy in the pulsing of the pistons, and the way the footplate sways from side to side, rocking us about on our feet, makes it feel that we are riding some giant, untamed animal.

George opens a round oven door from time to time and shovels in the coal from the bunker behind. He stands on the left, and Uncle Jack on the right, and I sit on a wooden seat that pulls down from the side. Every time we approach a bridge someone waves to us from it, and the steam is pushed back from the chimney into our faces so that we drive blind for a few seconds when we come out the other side. Tunnels are even more fun, and we emerge in a huge blanket of steam as if we are in the clouds.

Uncle Jack lifts me up to see through the portholes at the front, then he sets me down and gives me his hat, and I stand in the driver's position for the rest of the journey.

"When you get home you can tell your friends you drove a seventy-seven class tank engine," says Uncle Jack.

We are carrying freight, and when we reach our destination Jack goes off to the lav while George and I tuck into our sandwiches.

"You're doin' well," says George, his mouth full of bread. "You'll make a good driver, you will."

I tilt my head right back to smile at him under my driver's hat. "I didn't know I was coming today."

"Didn't you?"

"Uncle Jack never said."

George shovels some more sandwich in before speaking. " 'Ee always says 'ee'll bring you down one day. Always talking about you, 'ee is."

"About me?"

"Oh yes! Talks about nothin' else! Thinks the world of you, 'ee does!" Then he adds with a wink, "An' I don't blame 'im." He takes a shovel and wipes it with a cloth, then balances the shovel on the coals and breaks an egg on it from his lunchbox. "Miss Lavish — never-been-ravished!" He laughs, loudly. "You're priceless, you are!"

"But how . . . ?"

Uncle Jack comes back, and they talk for a while before George goes off to the station lav. "You want to go?" Uncle Jack asks. "George'll show you where it is."

"No, ta," I say. "Got a bladder like an elephant, me."

They both laugh, and George goes off, leaving me alone with Uncle Jack and our cheese and Flag Sauce sandwiches. I consider now might be a good time to broach things.

"Uncle Jack . . . ?"

"Yes?"

"Why don't you and Aunty Joyce have another baby?"

He stops munching for a second, and then continues with an exaggerated nonchalance.

"Just one of those things, I s'pose . . . and not for you to go worrying about."

167

I frown under my hat. "Why do grown-ups say things like 'just one of those things' when it obviously isn't? You can have one if you *want* one, can't you?"

He says nothing, and a blackbird trills furiously from a tree on the other side of the track.

"Is it because you don't like children?"

"Don't *like* children?" He turns to look at me, confused. "Do you think I don't *like* children?"

He looks a little hurt, so I quickly take it back. "No, no. It's just . . . I don't see why you don't have another. You'd be a good father. In fact, I think you'd be a very good father."

He gives a modest smile. "It's not as easy as just wanting one, Kitty."

Of course I can't just shut up and wait for him to speak, I have to keep goading him. "Aunty Joyce wants one."

This is not a clever thing to say, for I don't strictly know if it's true, but it gets him going.

"Does she? Who said that? Did *she* say that? What's she been saying?"

I scratch the side of my face hastily. "Well . . . it's not that she said it *as such*, but I reckon she would be on for it. I can tell these things."

Uncle Jack sighs. In disappointment? In relief? There is a long silence with just the rustle of paper bags, the crunch of apples, and the crotchety blackbird throwing another tantrum.

This is not good enough. I have to set things in motion.

"Or is it that you can't get it up?"

There is a clatter as he drops his sandwich tin on the footplate. He leans both hands flat on his knees and glares at me. "Who . . . ? What . . . ? Wherever did you hear that? Who's been saying that?"

"No one . . ." I wing it. "It's just this friend at school, she's got rabbits, and the daddy rabbit can't have babies because he can't get it up. That's what her mum said."

Uncle Jack rolls his eyes, and heaves a sigh.

"Well! Look, I don't want you to repeat that expression, all right?"

"Is it rude, then?"

"Yes, it's rude."

"But is it true? Is that your problem?"

"NO!" He bangs his fist on the bunker and a piece of coal topples down. "Has anyone said that about me?"

I shrug. "I don't think so." Then I add mischievously, "Still . . . if they *had*, you could always prove them wrong . . ."

George has come back and is up beside me, winking. "Where to next, Driver?"

Uncle Jack lets me work the lever, and the pistons steam like a giant angry bull.

When we get back it is bitterly cold, and he walks me all the way home from the bus stop holding my hand. It is a giant, brown, warm engine driver's hand, and it completely covers my own. He is as pleased as Punch to tell everyone we meet that I have driven a seventy-seven tank engine, and I am as pleased as Punch to be wearing his driver's hat, even if I can only see the road.

More secrets revealed

Back at school we go out to play in the numbing wind, almost longing for the bell so that we can huddle again around the schoolroom stove. A crowd of us are playing dub-dub, and I stand at the dubbing post staring up at the sky and the hills. The bare trees are mouse brown on the humps and hollows, making Sheepcote woods like the secret hair of a woman.

A few twitters of joy go up as the first snowflakes fall on us, soft as thistledown, but melt to nothing on the old tarmac.

I venture from the post, trying to spot people hiding, and see Tommy standing with the big boys. These days they rarely bother with the schoolyard, and spend their playtimes in the lanes smoking or checking rabbit traps in the wood.

I'm sure he is cross with me because I didn't introduce my mum to him like I promised. He probably spent all of Christmas Day and Boxing Day hanging around the farm waiting for me to bring her to see him.

"Hiya!" I say.

"Oh . . . hi, Kitty!" He smiles at me, then returns to his conversation with Will Capper and Eddie Wragg as if I were invisible. I hang about for a while, then pretend to kick a stone which isn't there, and hum to myself as I wander away.

"Dub-dub in!" scream Babs and Iris together.

"You've lost, Kitty! You're out!"

I wonder if Tommy knows how much I've missed him, and that it wasn't my fault I couldn't get to see him. I wonder if I've lost him for ever.

I am nervous at the first knitting group after the holidays, anxious they might ask me questions again like Miss Lavish warned me. I stick to Miss Lavish and stare intently at her thick wool stockings and lace-up shoes, hoping to become invisible once more.

I need not worry, however, for on this particular day Lady Elmsleigh turns up and shows us all the photographs that were taken at her house during the Christmas and New Year's parties.

We gather round and gawp, trying to spot each other in the crowd.

"And I brought this along as well," says Lady Elmsleigh, holding up a large, framed photograph. "It's a summer fête at Elmsleigh – the last time we had one, it seems – in 1929. I thought we could revive the tradition this year – what do you think?"

There are murmurs of agreement, and already the women are planning what stalls they could have, who could play the music, entertain the children. She gives the picture to Miss Lavish, and one or two of us lean over to see it.

"Oh, look!" says Miss Lavish. "That's me when I was younger! My goodness, look at my hair! What *was* I thinking?"

I giggle, and she points out some other people I would know: Mrs Chudd and Mrs Glass in their teens with low-waisted dresses and bobbed hair; Mrs Marsh carrying a toddler with another little boy in tow. Baggie Aggie Tugwell in a hat standing next to a young man and both laughing at something together. I am intrigued by the photograph. It is undeniable evidence that old people were young once, that they are just like me, that we really are all alike; and I find this both deeply reassuring and astonishing.

Soon everyone is craning to see it, and Miss Lavish yields up the photograph to Mrs Spud, and there are whoops and cries of wonderment for the next five minutes.

"Who's that then?" asks Mrs Big-fat-arse, pointing at the picture.

"Dunno. Looks familiar."

"Never seen 'er."

"Who's that, then, Annie?"

Tosser takes the picture and sucks in her cheeks, then chews on something imaginary in her mouth. "Where am I, then?" she says. "Oh aye. There I am. Ha! An' there's Tilda . . . See that? We looked smart then, didn't we? Heh!"

"Yes, but who are these two over here?" Mrs Arse points at two women on the edge of the photograph.

"You remember them! That's Mrs Shorecross and her daughter – only stayed a while. Now she was related to my neighbour Tilda, that's why she come over to Sheepcote, when 'er husband died."

"I can't remember no Mrs Shorecross."

"Oh! Tiz a tragedy about 'er, it is. Now, this'll make you think twice about that tosser Fairly. You listen to this . . ." Tosser is enjoying the attention. "Well, she had three children, only one boy died of scarlet fever and the other one died of . . . diphtheria I think twuz, and she only had the daughter left . . . Kath, she was called. Lovely girl. Well . . . oh, it breaks your heart, honest, she was engaged to a lovely young man an' they wuz about to be married an' off 'ee went to a TB sanatorium. Too brave for 'is own good 'ee wuz. 'Course, 'ee fought very young in the Great War – got all kinds of medals, 'ee did, but the mustard gas messed up 'is lungs good and proper, didn't it? Never come back from the sanatorium . . .

An' there wuz that lovely girl with a baby on the way . . ."

"Never!"

"Whatever happened to her?"

"Well . . . Mrs Shorecross, she didn't 'ave a penny to 'er name, so she goes an' works at Heaven House an' takes Kath with 'er. But 'twuzn't Mr Fairly then, 'twuz old Mr Northwood, remember 'im? Dear old soul, 'ee wuz, an' 'ee took 'em in an' gives 'er time off with the baby – ooh! She *doted* on that baby, she did. An't would've gone on well enough, but *trouble* wuz round the corner . . ."

"What happened?"

"What trouble?"

"Well . . . Mr Northwood died, an' Mrs Northwood went into a 'ome, an' Mr Fairly come along, remember?"

"Oh yes!"

"He made some changes."

"Smartened it up a bit, didn't he?"

"*Well* . . . Mrs Northwood made 'im promise to look after the two women like before, but . . ."

"What?"

"*Well* . . . young Kath got taken poorly, an' she died. An' then 'ee made poor old Mrs Shorecross go too, an' she died of a broken heart. All 'er family gone before 'er. S'enough to break anyone's heart, that is."

"Mr *Fairly* did that?"

"Yes . . . tosser!"

"Mr *Fairly*? You sure?"

"Oh yes. Some do say 'ee 'ad 'is wicked way with the girl, too!"

"Never!"

"Annie Galloway! Listen to you!"

"I'm not saying tiz true. Only some do say . . ."

"What happened to the baby?"

"Oh, 'ee stayed there."

"There's no Shorecross boy, is there?"

"Kath made 'im take 'is father's name, seeing as they wuz about to be married. Glover. Edwin Glover wuz 'er young man."

Everyone looks at each other. People who haven't been listening look up. Lady Elmsleigh goes over to Tosser and leans over her, pointing at the photograph. "You mean this young girl is Tommy Glover's mother?"

"That's the one. Kathleen Shorecross. Barely stayed six months. If that."

Now everyone is letting out gasps of amazement, but they are not really bothered – not like I am. Before long they are knitting again, and wittering on about pork rinds and tripe, and I am so churned up I wonder I'm not sick.

Still, I have something to tell Tommy now, and he will have to take notice of me.

Paper doll to call my own

It is so cold on Saturday morning that Aunty Joyce suggests I stay in by the range and do some colouring, but it is my only chance to see Tommy, so I climb the frozen lane to the milksheds with her.

The cows are steaming in the cold, and we rest our cheeks against them, glad of their warm twitching hides. I wait until Aunty Joyce has popped into the farmhouse before I go down the line of cows and find Tommy. "Wait for me behind the barn!" I hiss. "*Really* important news. *Really* important!" He looks unmoved, as though he perhaps thinks I'm going to tell him my mother is coming or something, so I add, "About your parents!" and dash back to my cow.

He does wait for me, of course, and I draw him back down the lane to be out of earshot of everyone. As we lean on an old wooden gate I feel heady with power. I tell him everything as I remember it, and he hangs on my every word, making me repeat things over and over. When I see his face light up with completely new expressions of joy, I feel I have worked the magic all myself.

"*Doted* on me, you said. Are you sure those were her exact words?"

"She *doted* on you. That's what Tosser said. You can ask her."

I take him to the village hall and we push open the door tentatively. There is no one there, but the picture is hanging by the noticeboard, where Lady Elmsleigh left it.

"Which one do you think she is?" I ask, overcome with my own importance.

"She's *here*? In this picture?"

"And her mother."

Tommy lets out a whistle and swallows in anticipation as he looks along the rows of Sheepcote villagers in their outlandish hats and hairstyles.

"Tell me! Tell me!"

I savour the moment. Raising my hand I point slowly to the smiling dark-haired girl and her mother standing by the flowerbed at the edge of the picture.

He seems to stop breathing. He puts his finger on her face and strokes it, over and over.

I thought I was in control, but now I see that I'm not. He doesn't speak or answer me for a long time, and when he moves it is his shoulders, which are shaking, and tears, so powerful I know he is wishing I wasn't there. I am way out of my depth. I try to think of something funny to say to snap him out of it, because I think that's what he'll want me to do. But nothing comes to me. So I just push my head into his chest and give him a hug. He wraps his arms around me and squeezes me for dear life, as if I was his dead mother come back to him.

Shagging in the barn

All through January and February the winds tear at the bushes, wrenching them this way and that, and huge trees are pulled about like seaweed underwater. These are winds so bitterly cold that no one wants to venture out. They slam doors shut, rattle bolts and loosen catches, and they flatten trousers and skirts against us so that every contour of our legs is visible. Still it doesn't snow, but on the highest slopes and Sheepcote woods there is a scattering of white.

The sheep are brought in from the fields and penned up for lambing. Three barns are now full of them, divided according to how many lambs each is carrying. They are due the last weekend in February, and all our efforts concentrate on getting them well provided for with bales of straw, making space in the barns, fixing pens.

Heinrich comes into his own now. He was a sheep farmer in Germany, and knows exactly what's going on. Thumper says he's his best worker and is quite happy to let him take over a little, and you would think he was an old friend of Thumper's and not a German at all.

"Three lems," says Heinrich, nodding at one pen. "And over here, two lems, and there one lem each." I am impressed that he can tell what's inside these great woolly boulders, and

I smile, taking his hand between mine for warmth. He smiles back. "You will have one, I sink, to hold and feed."

I run up to the barns every day after school, hoping the lambs have started. The sheep stare at me in that funny way they do, always smiling no matter what I say to them. They are gigantic barrels on twig-like, knock-kneed legs, and it is a wonder they can remain standing at all.

Then, at the very end of February, we hear bleating on the way home from school. I run up to the barns with some other children to see that four lambs have been born in the big barn and the mothers are in separate little pens with them. Thumper takes the children off to see the lambs in the next barn, but Heinrich sits me on a straw bale and lifts out a lamb for me to hold. It bleats a little, then sits very still, as still as me. I am shocked by it being there in my lap, alive, newly born and smelling of hay. I am surprised by the feel of it, like tough carpet, not soft at all. I close my arms more confidently around it, and it bleats and rests its chin on my arm. I can feel its warm tummy moving in and out under my hand, smell the rich, maizy lamb-smell, and I sit immobile, mesmerized by the miracle under my nose.

Its mother honks loudly a few feet away, so Heinrich lifts the lamb and places it gently back by its mother's side. Aunty Joyce comes in with a tray of tea, and Heinrich takes a cup, smiling.

"Watch this one now," he says, and we both look at a ewe who is lying at the front of the pen. She is rolling her eyes back and her top lip rolls back too.

"Is she all right?" I ask.

"Fine," he says. "Watch."

The ewe continues to roll her lip back every now and then, and makes an uncharacteristic sigh or two. Heinrich checks her back legs and takes a piece of cord from his pocket. He puts a little lasso over some hooves which are protruding from the ewe's behind, and tugs gently. With a rush of liquid a lamb shoots out on to the straw. He swings it by the legs and puts it in front of the ewe, who seems to lick life into it.

Aunty Joyce is sitting on a hay bale next to me, and I jump up to loll over the pen and ogle the newly born lamb. I am so busy marvelling at it that I don't see Heinrich sit down beside Aunty Joyce and put his arm around her.

"Is it a boy or a girl?" I ask, but when I turn there are tears in her eyes, and Heinrich is comforting her. I frown. "What is it, Aunty Joyce?"

Heinrich looks across at me. "It can be very moving, I sink, to see a lem borning."

I nod sagely, but I have no idea what he is talking about.

That same night I am woken in the early hours by Uncle Jack getting up for his shift. I don't usually wake up, and soon realize there are voices. Aunty Joyce has got up too, and they are moving about downstairs and talking. I hear the front door go, and then footsteps on the stairs. My door creaks open.

"Kitty? You awake?"

"Yes."

"I'm just going to do teas for the lambers. I won't be two ticks. Stay in bed till I get back."

I hear the front door close again, but I can't stay in bed. I'm awake now, and I can hear lambs bleating. I lie in bed for a while then look out of my window and see glints of a brazier or an oil lamp glowing inside one of the barns despite the blackout. I want to see more lambs being born. I want to hold one again. I have no intention of missing any of it.

* * *

When I get to the lane I head towards the cracks of light escaping from the broken corrugated iron and slatted wooden doors of the barns. As I draw near, there is no sound at all, except the occasional rustle of sheep's hooves on straw, and an owl in the trees beyond the farmhouse. Barns two and three are pitch black, and there is an eerie movement now and then, which turns out to be a ewe getting to her feet or sitting down. The big barn is shut, and I have never known the door shut before but guess it is because of the light. It is too heavy to open, so I peep through the broken door and am relieved to see Heinrich and Aunty Joyce standing in the glow of a hanging oil lamp. He looks tired, and I suspect he has been up all night lambing. But just as I am about to call out to them to let me in, something happens.

Aunty Joyce puts a hand on his arm, then takes it away again. They stand looking at each other and saying nothing. And there is something about the way they say nothing that stops me from opening my mouth. It is a very telling nothing they are saying. He is a little bit closer than he needs to be, and she is not at all intending to step back. I can see her face clearly from where I am, but not all of his. She is very flushed and looks down at the floor then up again, each time holding his gaze a little longer.

The next thing I know he has put his hand on her hair, and is stroking the back of her head. She leans into him and rests her head on his chest. I am freezing cold, but I can't bring myself to interrupt. Something tells me this is a significant moment, and I might learn something.

She lifts her head for an instant and he takes it between his two giant hands. He is leaning forward . . . is he kissing her? . . . I think he is! I stop shifting my weight from one wellington boot to the other and stare. Heinrich is kissing Aunty Joyce on the lips, and she is letting him!

He runs his hands up and down her back, and then, to my

180

amazement, he passes them over her hips and her bottom. She has taken his neck in one hand and is pulling his face down towards her, pushing her lips on to his like they do at the pictures, only a bit more hungrily. Now he is pushing up her skirt with his hand, and I can hardly believe it of Heinrich. He seems such a gentle shepherd-like person and here he is doing rude things to Aunty Joyce. But she doesn't seem to mind a jot.

I want to interrupt, to tell them to stop, but I find I can't. I am too intent on what is happening to call it to a halt, and so I go on watching.

Now he has buried his hand deep inside the undergrowth of her skirts, and she is crying. In fact, no – she is not crying: she is making little groans, little sighs. He is whispering things I can't make out, and moving his hands gently, and the effect is to make her give little 'oh's' and sobs and sighs, but she is definitely not crying.

Now he is leading her to the back of the barn and is laying her down on some stacked hay bales and there, amidst the lambing ewes and the air rich with the smell of birth, he lies on top of her.

My view has disintegrated with this move, and I can just make out the tops of Aunty Joyce's stockings, her knees bent, and Heinrich's strange nudging movements against her. It is like nothing I've seen before, except perhaps the caged bunnies. This is it then. This is shagging, and it's ever so rude! One of the ewes bellows angrily, but they continue to move against each other, obscured by straw and shadows and the limit of my chink in the wood. Her sighs turn to soft wails, and she seems to be in pain. Just as I am about to go to her rescue, it stops. There is no sound, no more movement, except one or two indignant ewes kicking the straw and bellowing as though they are well and truly hacked off. Heinrich and Joyce seem to be smiling now, laughing at the sheep and brushing down their clothes. I dash off back down the lane. I can't wait to tell Tommy. In the big barn I have seen birth and I have seen shagging, all within the space of a day and a night. Two of the great mysteries of life revealed under one roof.

Don't sit under the apple tree with anyone else but me

Tommy is set to leave school at Easter when he's fourteen. The Top Class children do practically nothing, and Boss Harry seems to turn a blind eye to them. The boys stalk the streets at dinnertime, loaf about with half-smoked Woodbines tucked behind their ears and talk about ambushing girls. The girls, on the other hand, have transformed themselves from the adventurous minxes they were in Standards One and Two. They no longer show all for a Victory V or allow themselves to be examined in a harvest stook surgery with tufts of barley. They are all buttoned up now, soaped and curled and saving themselves for the men they marry. And the boys, bursting with lust, full-grown and aimless, are so tormented by a coy look or a swinging hip that they plot violation.

Only one or two girls can be counted on to break ranks, and in so doing they probably save the virtue of many others. One is Betty Chudd – mother's pride and joy – who is rumoured to have gone all the way with Leslie Capper.

Since Leslie is a couple of years older than anyone at school and works at the sawmill, no one can really verify it, although his younger brother Will is convinced. And anyway, everyone can testify to Betty's loose ways – except for her mother who can't see the wood for the trees – and it is Betty who becomes the trophy that lures them on, even if it is the lowered lashes of some other girl that really fuels their frenzy.

I can't imagine that Tommy will be affected by anything so daft (especially now that I know what it entails). Even so, he does seem to grow in height each time I see him, and his voice – a varying reedy-rusty-bray when I met him – now seems to have settled to a deep, liquidy bass which I adore. And then one day something happens to threaten the easy friendship we have, threatens to change things for ever.

It is the weekend, and I have spent the morning stone-picking up at the farm, and the afternoon daydreaming with Tommy amongst the snowdrops, which have appeared slyly in the woods. Tommy and I are wandering back home across the fields, a little wary of being seen together, but too busy chatting about Aunty Joyce and Heinrich to care. As we reach the lane that links the village to the farm, Betty Chudd comes out of nowhere like a fox, leaning suddenly on a gatepost beside us, and twisting her toffee-coloured curls around her fingers.

"Comin' up the lane then, you?"

Tommy turns from my strong protector into a clumsy oaf. His arms and legs seem suddenly not to fit his body, and his head seems too heavy to hold up straight on his neck. It lolls hopelessly, rolling from one shoulder to the next, as his eyes take in the panorama from the gatepost to his boots.

"Might then," he mumbles.

"When?" she presses, wrapping both arms backwards over the five bar gate, so that her breasts stick out and pull at her dress buttons.

I assume he is just being nice, using the 'maybe' as a means of escape. So now I wait for something that will send her politely packing. But he folds his lips, then glances at her briefly, and says, "When 'er's gone."

I am horrified. There is no doubting, from the slight nod of his head in my direction, that ''er' is me. I simply can't believe Tommy can do this, and I plant my wellingtoned feet in front of him and stare for an explanation. His avoidance of my eyes confirms my worst fears: he is putting *her* before *me*. But there is worse to come.

"G'won then. Wunt wait f'rever."

She's up to something, in my opinion. Her cardigan has fallen completely open and, apart from her brown buckled shoes, her legs are entirely bare, as though imitating stockings. A daft thing to do in February. She looks like she'll catch her death of cold, if you ask me.

"I'll walk 'er back, then I'll be up."

"The little'un can walk 'erself back, can't she?"

"Wunt be long, look."

"What, you 'er lover or summut?"

He exhales as if desperate, then swallows earnestly. I am beside myself. Not only are they talking about me as the 'little'un' and 'er', but *worse*: they are talking about me *as if I'm not there*. I should stomp off, I suppose, and leave him to the Sheepcote trophy he is longing to grab. But I let him walk me back and say goodbye, shooting him a wounded look, hoping to stop him. All I do, possibly, is inhibit his pleasure as he races back up the lane in the growing shadows of a late February afternoon.

It is a savage lesson to me; for all our intimacy and mutual security, there is a huge, burgeoning, crucial part of him that I cannot share. Not yet, at least.

The days slip bleakly into March. The skies are a blank grey-white and the lanes full of mud. There is nothing to look forward to, now that Tommy is lost to me. I don't know if it is jealousy, fear or just plain callousness that fuels my cunning, but I have a way to make him notice me. A way, at least – as Miss Lavish would say – to make contact.

"I need to ask you something in private," I say, as I catch up with him in the lane one morning, with some other big boys.

"What's up then?" he asks, tousling my hair, but still walking.

"In private!" I hiss.

He grins at his mates and stops for a while. "What?"

I watch until they are out of earshot. I glance at the hedgerow and then at him, doing my best to adopt a pained, confused look. "What does 'have his wicked way' mean?"

He breathes a laugh.

"Who's havin' their wicked way, then?"

"No one."

"Where d'you hear it, then?"

I shrug innocently.

"Oh . . . it's nothing . . . just someone said Mr Fairly had his wicked way with your mum."

His face turns ghostly. Now I have his full attention, but it's not what I expected.

"Who said that?"

"Just someone."

"Who?"

I swallow, uncertain: "Tosser . . ."

He looks up to the sky then bends almost at the waist, burying his head in his arms as if it is all too bright for him. "No! No! Please God, NO!"

I am aghast at what I've done, and not sure how to undo it.

"She only said, 'Some folks say . . .' It may not be true . . ."

But Tommy is making strange grunts of pain, wails of misery. "You don't understand, do you? You're too young to see what this means!" He turns away from me, not towards the boys, but towards a gate, and he runs like a hare across the fields.

I am the person who makes Tommy decide to run away from Sheepcote. So what happens next is all my fault.

Moonlight cocktail

The clump and thud of Uncle Jack leaving wakes me up, and I can hear Aunty Joyce clattering about downstairs although it is still dark. She pops her head round the bedroom door and whispers, "Kitty?"

To her probable disappointment I show that I am awake. "What time is it?"

"Early. Go back to sleep. I'm just off to do some teas."

But I can't go back to sleep now. I don't like being in bed when the house is empty. As soon as she's gone I get dressed and go downstairs. It is four thirty in the morning, and I'm suspicious. Lambing finished last week and there won't be anyone up all night waiting for Aunty Joyce to bring them a cuppa.

I give her a ten-minute start, then set off and turn into the dark lane that leads to the barns up behind the house. The light is flickering from behind the broken slats as before, but when I peek inside there is only Thumper and the farmer, talking about some ewe that seems to have been in difficulty overnight. I have to step back quickly as they make their way to the barn door, cover the oil lamp, and head across the yard. Their voices trail off towards the farm door, and when it opens I can see Aunty Joyce for a moment, holding a kettle and bathed in the kitchen lamplight, until the door clatters shut and they have all three disappeared behind it.

The lane behind me is so black I don't want to go back home, but I can think of nothing else to do. Slowly, I pick my way along the hedgerow, wishing there were a moon.

Suddenly I hear footsteps. They are coming towards me. I stand stock-still and stare into the dark, but can see nothing. Then I hear breath and I try to hold mine. The footsteps get nearer and nearer until they are almost next to me, and I can make out a tall, dark figure.

I must catch my breath or something, because it stops.

"Who is it?" I ask.

There is no answer, but the dark figure moves in closer towards me. I can no longer keep the panic out of my voice, and I ask again in a high-pitched whisper, "Who is it?"

"Kitty!"

"Tommy?"

"Kitty! What you doing 'ere?"

"What . . . ? Oh, God! You gave me such a fright. Christ alive!" I take deep breaths of relief. "What on earth are you doing so early?"

Tommy puts his arm on my shoulder and whispers urgently, "Listen! I'm running away. Whatever you do, don't say you saw me, okay?"

"But you can't! What about me? Where are you going?"

He sighs, as if he knew I wouldn't understand. My eyes are accustomed to the dark now, and I can see the outline of his face. "Look, Kitty. I have to go. I can't explain it now, but I'll write to you."

"What d'you mean, you *have* to go? Who's making you?"

"Fairly's my bloody father, isn't he?"

"Of course he's not! How d'you make that out?"

"You wouldn't understand. I've got to go. Just believe me."

"Are you going for ever?"

"Yes."

"But . . . you mean I won't see you again? Not ever?"

He sighs again. "I'll write."

I'm horrified. I hold on to him tight, as if I can keep him here by force. "You can't go without me! I'm coming too!"

"Don't be daft. I'm going to sea."

"I'm coming! If you go now, you'll never see me again. Don't you mind? Don't you care about me at all?"

"Of course I'll see you, one day."

I am beside myself with frustration. I feel so powerless and confused I want to shriek.

"Tommy! Listen to me! The war'll be over soon, my mum said, and I might be gone from here and never get your letter! Who knows where I'll be? And then you can't come and live with us, can you? She said you could, I asked her, my mum said you could."

"She didn't even want to meet me."

"That's not true! She came unexpectedly. Look! We can go there now – she'll give us somewhere to hide at least. An' she'll give you money for a ticket – she earns lots at the factory. Honest she will. Let me come with you!"

I'm pulling at his coat sleeve and jumping up and down. He keeps sighing.

"If you come with me an' we're found, I'm as good as dead. They'll all reckon I kidnapped you."

"Well, I'll say you haven't."

"You don't know what they say about me. There's rumours . . ."

"I know."

"You do?"

"We won't have to be found, then, will we?"

He sighs again.

"Five minutes. You got five minutes, okay? Get summut

190

warm to wear an' food – an' a blanket. Five minutes an' I'm off."

I dart into the blackness of the lane, turn on to the road and into Weaver's Cottage. I find an old canvas bag of Uncle Jack's under the stairs and grab the remains of a loaf of bread and a tin of meat from the shelf. I run upstairs for a blanket, but decide against taking one as it's sure to be noticed straight away. I go back to the cupboard under the stairs and unhook an old oilskin and sou'wester from underneath a heavy coat. It will have to do. I roll it up and stuff it in the bag, and run out of the house and back up the lane in dread that Aunty Joyce might come back home before I leave.

The sky is turning from black to royal blue. We don't go through the farm fields in the end. We let the March wind blow us down the lanes in search of escape. By the time the sky has turned pale we are beyond the woods. With a canvas bag of bread and Spam, a rolled-up blanket of Tommy's, socks and the old sou'wester, we make our bid for freedom: two specks bobbing along the budding hedgerows into the verdant, wood-fringed horizon of the wolds.

Tommy's secret

I have always known that Tommy has a secret. I have always known that he will tell me one day, and that when he does it will uncover some much deeper mystery, something vast.

He is the one person I haven't been able to badger with my constant curiosity. He will tell me when he is ready, and I feel certain it is going to be now, on this journey.

He is like a wild animal, testing the ground, wary of sudden movement, biding his time. And I have waited, motionless, letting him get the scent of me. Beneath all my laughter and endless babble I know I am marking time, inching closer.

Do I realize what I'm doing, running away with someone who is thought to be a killer? Have I any idea, as we turn off from the hedgerows into the secret smells of the woods, what dramatic train of events I have set in motion? The sun ducks in and out of the wind-blown trees, lighting up the spikes of dog's mercury that are beginning to carpet the ground. There are hints of cow parsley, along with the first fierce green arrows of arum leaves unfurling along our sappy woodland path. Spring is on its way, and it is unstoppable.

When the sun goes down on our first day, we make our bed on a blanket of sorrel waiting to flower, and spread the oilskin beneath a leafing canopy of hazel branches.

As light fails, Tommy pulls his blanket around us and begins to point out birdsong. The yellowhammer, mistle thrush and chaffinch sing their last notes, while the blackbird goes on way into dusk before it falls silent.

We wait.

Then the song thrush gives a tuneful nocturne, then the robin. And when at last, from deep within the woods, the tawny owl gives its first tentative hoot, Tommy is ready to tell his story to the darkness.

It had been a hot day in June seven years ago when Tommy and Rosemary took their nets to go fishing. Their hopes were pinned on minnows, nothing more. If there was a leader, it was Tommy, but only because he knew the stream so well, and because Rosemary was quiet and more inclined to follow. Otherwise they were two peas in a pod, two seven-year-olds with time on their hands and a summer afternoon to explore.

They padded down the valley towards the willows, heading downstream. They talked of sticklebacks, but didn't extend their hopes that far. Identification was their joy. If they could see beneath the dark surface those creatures who were meant to be there, they would go home happy, satisfied that all was right with the world, and just as it said it was in Rosemary's *What to Look For in the River*. Although neither of them said as much, fish spotting was much more fun than fish catching, because they never really knew what to do with the ugly blobs they took back in jam jars, and there was always an awkwardness as the day went on and they were still there, dying or dead.

For Tommy, the pleasure of outings like these was going back to Joyce and Jack's for tea. Not the home-made sponge cake or the gooseberry jam, but the tender look from Joyce, and the smell of a home.

They had been by the bank for an hour, and must have dozed off in the shade of a willow, when a noise startled Rosemary. She stared at two figures wrestling much further up the grassy bank some fifty yards off. She nudged Tommy, without taking her eyes off the writhing figures, who were performing something she had only ever seen done by animals.

Tommy looked up, his face dotted in sweat, his head swimming with sleep. Rosemary was sitting up with her mouth open.

There, in the long grass of a hollow, shaded by a willow, was a man, holding down a small boy of eight or nine. The boy was crying, and the man seemed to be hurting him. Rosemary gasped in horror, and Tommy, suddenly panicking, pushed her down into the grass. But the wrestling stopped. The man sat up.

Rosemary began to whisper, barely able to breathe under Tommy's grip. "Let me go!" she hissed.

The man had stood up, and hastily buttoned his trousers. He had seen them, although Tommy was hopeful he might not have recognized them at a distance.

"Come on! Quick!" Tommy yanked Rosemary to her feet, but she just stood there, gawping in horror.

"Mr Fairly!" she breathed, not loud enough for him to hear, but directly enough for the man to know that he had been spotted by the Shepherd girl, who sat in the third pew at church.

"Run!" screamed Tommy, grabbing her away. "Run, Rosie! Come on! RUN!"

And they ran – they both did – and Mr Fairly ran after them, leaving a bundle of a boy in the grass.

Back along the stream they went, Tommy leading, Rosemary just yards behind. And Tommy could think of only one thing as he ran, and that was the punishment he would receive for witnessing this dreadful act. Not for what he had seen – for he had seen it all before – but for allowing Rosemary, an outsider, to see it. Mr Fairly would never live it down. No one knew about his secret except people who were too terrified of him to betray it. But Rosemary Shepherd would tell her parents and Tommy would be punished for the rest of his days. He would have to run away. He would have to run, run, run . . .

"Run, Rosemary, RUN!" he screamed, and Rosemary ran, and the dry grass rustled, and the stingers burnt, and the mud and the cowpats were rock hard and bumpy. The air was thick with pollen and summer smells, acrid and heavy.

They put a good distance between themselves and the panting ogre, and Tommy was hopeful that he hadn't been recognized after all. But as he made for some undergrowth he heard a scream several yards behind him. Rosemary had slipped and fallen into the stream.

If he stopped for her, he would be caught. There was no point going back. Mr Fairly would probably grovel to Rosemary, make up some excuse. He might not even see her if she lay low, for the banks were quite steep here.

But Rosemary was calling out.

"Tommy! Tommy! Help!"

Why did she have to use his name?

"Tommy! Tommy! I'm stuck!"

Was it deep enough to drown there? It could only have been a couple of feet at most. But anyway, Fairly had arrived. Tommy crouched until he heard that Rosemary would be safe.

"Mr Fairly! Help me! I can't get out!"

He watched Mr Fairly go down to the water's edge, and then he began to run again. He ran like a hare, and he didn't turn round until he was a safe distance away and could hide behind a cluster of hawthorn. And there, turning back, he saw Rosemary's face as she clutched at the side of the bank, and there, as he watched, was Mr Fairly's boot in her face, pushing her back again. And again. And then no more.

In the stillness Mr Fairly turned and looked about, and Tommy ducked behind the hawthorn where he crouched, sobbing and shaking with terror, until dusk and the first beams of torches from villagers.

It was the next morning they found Rosemary, hooked on some low branches a mile downstream. Tommy was questioned for hours, but knew nothing. Someone had made certain of that. Mr Fairly was relieved that Joyce and Jack Shepherd cut off all links with the boy, in case he was ever tempted to blurt out the truth. But that was unlikely. Mr Fairly had ways of keeping boys' mouths shut. He'd had plenty of practice. In fact, Mr Fairly actively encouraged the odd rumour about Tommy, both because it helped transfer suspicion and because it emphasized his own charity in keeping the boy on.

When he finishes speaking, Tommy does not look at me, but gazes up at the hazel branches. A creeping chill makes me shiver, and we wait for the tawny owl to give its wavering hoot from the heart of the dark woods.

Baby, it's cold outside

The injustice of it all smarts like the icy cold of the night. I cling on to Tommy for warmth and to give him comfort, trying to take it all in, make all the connections, but I feel overwhelmed. I burrow into his pullover, feel his chest heaving suddenly, and I know he is crying.

His tears terrify me. Aunty Joyce I can handle, but Tommy, Tommy is my rock. This isn't supposed to happen, and I don't know what to do except cling on tight and hope it will pass.

At some point I notice that the shaking is no longer crying, but shivering, and I venture to speak.

"Why now? Why run away now though, Tommy? You'll be fourteen this month, won't you? You can go off and find work."

He puts his hands over his face and groans. "Oh . . . that's what I wuz going to do. Only when you said that about my mum an' Fairly . . . Oh God! It all makes sense . . . see, I think I'm his son! I'm that . . . thing's *son* . . . an' I can't bear it . . . I can't –"

"No you're not."

"Why else would they say he had his wicked way with 'er? See, Kitty, what it means, is Fairly and my mum . . . it means . . ."

197

Tommy frowns at me curiously. Then he reaches into his own canvas bag, rifles around, and brings out a tube and a torch. Carefully he pulls out a little scroll of paper and unravels the photograph Lady Elmsleigh had put on the wall of the village hall.

"You stole it!"

"I 'ad to."

The photograph is unruly, constantly springing back into its new rolled shape. We hold it open together, and he strokes her face again.

"Look," I say, "she's expecting a baby."

"Me!" he sobs.

"Yes! You. And look, over here . . ." I point to a little collection of boys with identical trousers and jackets, "these are the Heaven House boys, aren't they?"

"I suppose . . ."

"And this old man, see? He's Mr Northwood, and that's his wife."

"I know."

"*Well* then!"

"Well then what?"

"Tosser said Mr Fairly didn't come until after Mr Northwood died. So if that's you in that tummy . . . well . . . you're already there . . ."

He looks at the photograph and begins to wipe his face, smiling. He looks at me and laughs. "Ha!" Then he lets out a huge sigh and hugs me.

"So . . . my father *wuz* Edwin Glover. Ha!" His breaths are tumbling over themselves with excitement. "Tell me what Tosser said about him again."

"She told it all to you."

"I know, but what did she say the first time? What were her *exact* words when she told the whole knitting group?"

"She said he was gentle and kind . . ." I see an opportunity to please him, and I just can't help myself: "She said he was the kindest, bravest and most handsome man you could ever hope to meet." Although, given the way Tommy turned out, he probably was.

He is smiling wistfully across the torchlight into the night.

"You might have cousins," I say.

"No . . . her brothers died, remember?"

"Or second cousins."

He lets go of his side of the photograph and it spins into a roll.

"Second cousins!" he breathes, and I realize what a strange and lonely place he has been living in to see such treasure in such remote kinship.

"It's facking cold!" I say.

"Yes, it fuckin' is."

"Shall we go home?"

"No! We can't do that. It's like I said, they'll kill me. And you must never, *never* tell no one what I told you. If 'ee thinks I've told anyone, I might as well be dead."

I think about this. After what Tommy has told me about Mr Fairly, I don't want him to have to be punished in any way.

"Well, okay. But can we find a farmhouse?"

"That's how I got found last time. No. We've got to stay hidden."

But after an hour or so even Tommy gives up, and we go in search of shelter. We find an old lambing barn and settle down in the hay with a couple of fat sheep. There isn't much warmth here either and we spend a sleepless night, shivering and whispering to each other.

"You will still marry me, won't you?" I ask.

"What?"

"If you go to sea. You'll still come back and marry me?"

"You're *eight*!"

"Nine! Anyway, when I'm sixteen you'll be . . . nineteen, twenty, twenty-one! That's all right, isn't it?"

He chuckles.

"I will marry you, Tommy."

He tells me to stop making so much noise, but I put my head under his pullover and lie in a cocoon with him, and he lets me.

I cannot sleep. I doze from time to time, but true sleep will not come. I keep thinking of what Tommy has told me, and the burden of secrets he has had to carry for so long. And I can't stop thinking of Aunty Joyce and Uncle Jack, and how it all makes sense now, their distrust of Tommy, their inability even to smile at the boy they once loved so much they were willing to adopt him.

But one thing still does not add up at all. If I can understand their behaviour towards Tommy, I cannot make out their behaviour towards each other. I can't imagine why Uncle Jack is so cold towards Aunty Joyce. Why would he punish her for something which wasn't her fault, and after all these years? I know that she isn't the Jezebel he makes her out to be. I sense that the incident with Heinrich was the first time she has betrayed him, and I'm sure he doesn't know about it. I've seen the way she pushes all men away – I've seen it, watched it over a year – the way she punishes herself and lets him do the same.

There is some other mystery, something she is keeping to herself, but it will be a good eleven years before I discover Aunty Joyce's secret.

Aunty Joyce's secret

What Joyce Shepherd had told no one was what she was doing on the day Rosemary went missing.

More than seven years had passed since the birth of their daughter, Rosemary, and in all that time she and Jack had tried hard to keep their romance alive. She remembered how he had come home when they first married, bathed by the fire, eyes wide with tenderness. And she had ached each evening for his return, every part of her sprung like an arrow.

It had been such a gift when Rosemary befriended the lovely Tommy. Sweet, gentle Tommy from the boys' home, two dreamy souls delighting in each other's company. And they had welcomed him — oh, how they had welcomed him! How good it had looked in the church to bestow so much love on an orphan boy, and how dearly they had grown to love him like one of their own.

What a delight — that day when Tommy and Rosemary went fishing — to spend some time together, just Joyce and Jack, lovers again. It had been her idea, and that was the pity of it now. But Jack had been keen too — oh, yes — he had been very keen! He had gone upstairs while she made sandwiches, and he had fiddled breathlessly in a cupboard for a blanket.

They had set off hard on Rosemary's heels to give themselves plenty of time, and they had chosen a spot well hidden by willow trees a mile or so downstream, knowing that the children were heading upstream. It was their own special spot, where once ten years before Jack had first told her that he loved her more than any man ever loved a woman. And in accordance with

God's holy law, they had gone forth and been fruitful, and it was those care-free days of galloping blood that Joyce hoped to recapture on that modest outing in June.

It was all there, just as they remembered it. The willows dipping their leaves into the dark water, the blue dragonflies, the soft grass reeking of pollen. They lay down and made love to the smells of a full-blown summer.

They both heard it. At first it sounded like a human scream, but they dismissed it as a bird without interrupting their kissing. Then it came again, and again: a kind of squawk, the scream of a bird or the scream of a child.

Jack had stopped. "Listen!" he'd said, and propped himself on an elbow. It came again, an angry, frightened bird-scream.

"It's only a bird," she had whispered huskily, and then (oh, shame!) she had rolled him in the grass and pinned him down. "A bird, Jack. No one's coming. And you're going nowhere!" She had planted her naked breasts on his chest and sunk her lips on to his hot face. He had succumbed.

So it had all been her doing, hers, that they went home with their Marmite sandwiches uneaten, unaware that they had listened to their only child drown and felt nothing but lust.

Slow boat to China

We are on the move at the first sound of voices, and set off across the fields.

We make our way through the sodden edges of the ploughed furrows, collecting mud on our boots and adding to the weight of our steps. We head for the road to relieve our feet, and the biting wind makes a clearing in the clouds, so that we are bathed in sunshine for a while.

The hedgerows are speckled with green now, little hawthorn buds and elder leaves pushing their way into spring. It is hard to believe that in a few weeks' time this will be the heaving, leaf-clad world that greeted me last year.

When we can, we take cover in woods, plodding on soggy paths through drifts of snowdrops, having lost the purpose of our escape, but unable to turn back.

By mid-afternoon we seem to have been walking for ever. My feet are so sore I can barely keep up. I'm still wearing the large wellingtons I slipped on to go up to see Aunty Joyce, and they seem to stay on the ground when I lift my feet. Most of the food has gone now, and we sit down on the roadside until teatime, weary and aimless.

A horse and cart clops along, and the driver stops to give us a lift. He sets us in the back with his sheepdog.

"You local?"

"No. We're from London," says Tommy in his local burr. "Stayin' with relatives."

"I see." The driver is chewing on something green in his mouth – a leaf, perhaps. "Where's that, then?"

"Er . . . Bristol . . . well . . . near Bristol . . . past Stroud – you wouldn't know it."

The driver carries on chewing, his back to us. "You're a fuck of a long way off, then."

"Yes . . . well . . ."

"We got bikes," I suggest. "Only, they got punctures."

There is a silence. I feel uncomfortable that we can't see his face. He makes clicking noises to his horse.

"You want me to find someone to drop you 'ome, then?"

"No! No, that's all right. Thanks ever so much. Take us wherever you're going. That'll do us."

The driver clicks to his horse again. "What about your old irons?"

"We'll get my Aunty Agatha to pick them up tomorrow in the car," I say, affecting a much posher accent than I did the first time I spoke.

The driver turns and looks at us, still chewing. Then he turns his back on us again.

"Right you are."

He takes us home to his farm where his wife feeds us fried bread and eggs and makes us sit by the fire. Then she puts us to bed in an old musty room in the loft, end-to-end in a single bed.

In the morning, with the trilling of a skylark rising over a ploughed field outside, Mr Fairly comes for us.

Ain't misbehavin'

On my return, I am not sent to my room as I expect, but wrapped in a blanket and given a mug of Ovaltine beside the range. It is an overwhelming welcome, and I'm confused. I can hear Mr Fairly talking in the front room with Uncle Jack, and I'm afraid for Tommy. Aunty Joyce watches me closely as I take each sip. When the mug is empty she takes it and, to my amazement, she kneels down on the floor in front of me and throws her arms around me.

"Oh, Lord above, we've been that worried! Whatever possessed you? Have we been so awful?" She buries her face in my blanket and begins to cry. "Oh, my Lord! Oh, I'm so sorry! What have we done to you?"

I sit bewildered, then lift a hand to stroke her hair. "Please don't cry, Aunty Joyce."

This makes her cry even louder. She lifts up a blotched face and whispers, "Am I so terrible?"

I try to wipe the tears with my own fingers. "It's not that, honest. I thought you didn't love me, it's true . . ." (more sobs) " . . . but Tommy had to leave, and I love him. He *had* to go. He couldn't stay, you see . . ."

Aunty Joyce recomposes her face. "So it *is* him, is it? Jack said it was all down to him, but I —"

"No! No, it's not his fault. It's Mr Fairly. Don't you realize what he's doing to them?"

"Kitty," she sniffs, sitting back on her heels, "you mustn't listen to Tommy. You mustn't – " She breaks off suddenly and clambers to her feet, smiling. Mr Fairly has come into the parlour with Uncle Jack and Tommy.

"What have you got to say for yourself, boy?" Mr Fairly pronounces the words slowly, savouring each one.

Tommy raises his eyelids tentatively and looks at Uncle Jack and Aunty Joyce in turn, remembering perhaps the last time he was in this room, eating sponge cake. "I'm . . . sorry. I'm really sorry."

"Go on!" he is prodded.

"I . . . I wuz wrong to run away an' wrong to take Kitty with me. She's only small an' she might've got 'urt." He looks across at me and I try to send him a little cuddle in my eyes.

"At least she's safe," says Aunty Joyce crisply, "and there's no harm done."

Uncle Jack looks at her, perhaps surprised by her easy acceptance. "Yes," he says. "That's the main thing. We've been worried sick, but at least she's safe."

We are all five of us standing around the parlour table, as if in reverence to a pot of tea and a jar of marmalade that are standing upon it. I feel anything but safe.

"No!" blunders Mr Fairly. "It is not all right, I'm afraid. You see, you haven't considered, have you, whether Kitty is . . . well . . ." he assumes a gentler tone together with a look of mild disgust, " . . . intact?"

"*What?*" whisper Aunty Joyce and Uncle Jack in unison.

Mr Fairly looks pleased at this reaction, and nods sadly. "Yes, I think you know what I mean."

"But Kitty's only nine! For goodness' sake!"

Mr Fairly gives a shrug of a look. "I know. Exactly. But you see, you don't know Tommy." He leaves a meaningful gap for them to digest this horror. "And I do."

Uncle Jack scratches his neck. "You're not suggesting . . . that Tommy has defiled our Kitty in some way? . . . Are you?"

It is the first time I have ever been 'our Kitty' before, and it gives me an odd feeling. Everything is different from usual today. Even though Uncle Jack is still trying to use his posh voice, something significant has changed since the last time Mr Fairly visited – and not just because I know what I know: it has something to do with us standing at the uncleared breakfast table, and something to do with being 'their' Kitty.

I notice the muscles in Tommy's cheeks flinch, and I realize with terror what Mr Fairly is capable of and what he would be capable of if he found out that Tommy had told his secret. I have already almost broken my promise, and the five of us stand around the table oozing secrets about each other, each in the thinnest of bubbles that could burst at any moment.

"Well, let's ask Kitty, shall we?" smiles Mr Fairly. "Where did you sleep during your little holiday with Thomas here?"

My throat is knotted in panic. "In a barn, sir."

"And with whom?"

"With Tommy."

"And at the farm?"

"In a bed, in the attic."

"And with whom?"

"With Tommy – but it wasn't like that, it –"

"Did he cuddle you?"

I see Tommy's face: bright red and cringing.

"Yes, but –"

"Did he . . . touch you?"

"Yes, but –"

"Oh, stop, for heaven's sake!" cries Aunty Joyce, surprising everyone. "She's only a child. She doesn't know what you're driving at."

"I do!" I pipe up, grateful for a moment to gather my thoughts. "What you mean, Mr Fairly, is did he shag me, isn't it?"

Everyone falls silent.

Aunty Joyce speaks first. "She doesn't know what it means."

"I do!"

Uncle Jack clears his throat. "We need to talk about this sensitively. What Mr Fairly is suggesting, Kitty, is —"

"I know!"

Tommy covers his face.

"Kitty, don't be silly," says Aunty Joyce. "You're only nine."

"And I bloody *do* know what shagging is!"

"Kitty, you don't seem to —"

"It's what you were doing in the barn with Heinrich!"

My head fills with blood. I think I even hear a little pop. We are still all here, standing around the breakfast remains, but I have silenced them all. One, two, three grown-ups and Tommy, and I have shut them all up. I am screaming inside for someone else to speak. It isn't right that I should have this power. I don't want it. I shudder, trying to shake off the ugly omnipotence that has suddenly stranded me in this household. All I want is to go home and be insignificant again.

I chance a look at Uncle Jack's face, but it has crumpled like waste paper and distorted all the features. In Mr Fairly, I detect the faintest smile on his heavy lips before he clamps Tommy on the shoulder and says, "I think we'll return to this another time."

As he goes out he looks Aunty Joyce full in the eyes, a trace of smugness creeping into his own.

Filth

I wish it had been a desire to protect Tommy that made me blurt out my revelation. I wish I could say I only wanted to save his reputation. But the truth is, it was nothing more than childish vanity. I wanted so much to prove I was a grown-up and understood grown-up things. After all the trouble language had got me into, I wanted to show off the fact that I wouldn't be caught out by it again. But here I am, watching the world of 1 Weaver's Terrace collapse around me, and it is all my fault.

As soon as they have left, Jack gathers up his half-made sandwiches and clamps the lid of his sandwich tin shut. He hovers for a moment to look his wife in the eyes. But it isn't a look of contempt or even hurt. He looks more like a trapped animal than anything else, cornered and frightened and unsure where to move next.

Then he is gone. He slams out of the back door and wheels his bicycle through the side gate on to Farm Lane. I feel he ought to say something, although I don't know what. He can't leave without a proper reaction, it's all wrong. At least he could show us how angry he is. So I follow him outside.

"Uncle Jack!" I call over the gate.

"What?" He does not look at me, but throws his leg over the cross bar.

"She loves you. She told him that an' all."

He blows out a sudden puff of air contemptuously through his nose.

"She does! She loves you!" I insist desperately. I have to make amends for my treachery, but I'm afraid I'm making matters worse. He ignores me and starts to cycle off down the lane, and I don't know what to do for the best.

"She loves you!" I shout. "Everyone knows it!"

He turns into Church Road, cycling fast without looking back.

I am packed off to school with a note. It rains all day. Babs Sedgemoor and all the others want to know what happened, but I find it surprisingly easy to keep my mouth shut, because I never want to open it again.

The rain never stops, and I plod home along a muddy, puddle-filled road, with new leaves glistening above me and dripping down my neck. Tea is a silent affair with the two of us, after which Aunty Joyce washes herself to the bone – over and over: her hands, her arms, her face, her entire drawer of underwear.

I go to bed early, but can't sleep. She and I are both still waiting for him to come home, but there is no sign of him. Then at some stage in the night, after I must have dozed off, I hear their voices – so loud I can hear it all.

It seems Uncle Jack can't live with her because she has made him a laughing stock, and Joyce can't live with him because he has become a cold fish. There is sobbing and silence and more loud exchanges. On and on. All sorts of strange stuff. She doesn't think she's had enough to eat, he thinks she has an unnatural appetite, but she is convinced she's starved. I want to intervene and tell them to stick to the subject. All right, there may be something a bit unnatural about Aunty Joyce's love of offal, but no one starves in this house and no one is greedy. Now he is telling her she's rubbed his nose in the dirt. This is Aunty Joyce we're talking about. She doesn't rub anything in dirt.

My ravenous curiosity is defeated by sleep. When I awake it is to door-slamming, and Uncle Jack goes off far earlier than he needs to, leaving me alone on a Saturday with Aunty Joyce.

I find her sitting in front of her dressing table, staring into the three-way mirror.

"You all right, Aunty Joyce?" I venture after a while.

She doesn't turn to look at me, but keeps on staring.

"I'm sorry," I murmur.

"It's not your fault." She covers her face with her hands for a moment. "I brought it on myself."

I want to put it all back together for her, I want to make things right because I've made everything go so wrong.

"He does love you, you know."

She turns her pale face to me and tries to smile. "No," she says, "I've ruined it all."

I stand for a moment, wondering if she wants me to go, but I don't know where to go.

"Aren't you coming up the farm to do the teas?"

"How can I?" Her lips are trembling. "I can't show my face again. They'll all be talking."

"Why should they? They don't know anything."

Her eyes are fixed and empty.

"It's only a matter of time."

"Well, Tommy won't say anything, I know he won't. And Mr Fairly won't, will he?"

"Oh God!" She covers her face again. "Oh God! To think

that he knows! Whatever must he think of me? Oh God!"

"Well, he can't talk, can he? After everything he's been up to."

"What do you mean? Whatever's Tommy been telling you?" She lets out a huge sigh. "Oh, that boy! It's all his bloody fault! If only we'd never set eyes on him!"

"If only you knew what I know, you'd . . . you'd . . ." Here I go again. "If you knew what Mr Fairly did to Rosemary, you wouldn't be so cruel to poor Tommy! He never killed Rosemary! It wasn't Tommy! Don't you see –"

"What do you know?" She grabs me by the shoulders, her eyes darting now. She has turned white. "What do you know? Tell me! Tell me!"

"I can't – it's a secret. I promised Tommy." I wish to God I hadn't fed her these clues.

Aunty Joyce tightens her grip and shakes me. "TELL ME!"

So I tell her.

She disappears for the rest of the day. I don't know where to start looking for her, so I go up the farm and stay there doing odd jobs.

At around five o'clock, when I'm helping to bring the cows in for milking, she turns up. Her face is blotchy and her hair is all tatty and frizzy with rain. "Time for tea!" she calls breezily. She is not carrying a tray. She is calling me home. "Come on, Kitty! We'll be late for Uncle Jack!"

I wonder if she is scared to go home without me, but I'm flummoxed by the lightness in her voice. I follow her across the mire, my wellingtons sinking six or seven inches into the mud. The cows are swishing their tails, moving slowly into the cow barn. Aunty Joyce has plain shoes on, and she places a hand on a cow's back to steady herself through the slime. The cow moves forward suddenly, and she slips. She falls on her bottom, and sits bolt upright in a sea of wet cow dung.

The prisoners are inside the barn and have already started milking. One of the land girls spots her and asks, giggling, if she needs a hand. Aunty Joyce says no, she doesn't, and then does something really quite odd.

She sits back in the dung, then lies back. She stretches her arms wide and sinks her fingers into the muck. It is frothy and green and running with fresh cow's piss. And she giggles. She giggles like the land girl, but at the sky. Then she turns her head from side to side, covering her hair in the filth. I reach over to give her a hand, and she takes it, sitting up. As she climbs to her feet she falls over again, and laughs.

"Aunty Joyce! You're covered in it!"

"Yes!"

Her dress is like brown leather and her hair and hands are dripping with the reeking sludge. My own hand is covered in it too, and I lead her out on to the lane home. As soon as we start walking, Uncle Jack appears, coming up the lane to look for us.

"You're right, I'm filthy!" she shouts. "Absolutely filthy!" But then instead of laughing, she kneels down in the lane and sobs like a child.

Sheepcote blitzkrieg

In the morning the church bells remind us that it's a Sunday. We breakfast in almost total silence, with the occasional word from me. I feel uncomfortable without a bit of talking. But I soon see I don't know the rules to this game, and I shut up.

Then Uncle Jack rises from the table and starts to put on his coat. "Church," he says. We put our coats on too, and our gloves and hats. Just as we are about to go out of the door, Aunty Joyce unhooks a brush from the hall wall and brushes Uncle Jack's coat collar. This is what she always does, but today I feel a huge relief that he lets her do it.

As soon as we arrive at our place in the third pew from the front, we all kneel down to pray briefly. I've become used to doing this with them, although I usually just say, "Blah, blah, tits and bums. Our men," in my head for a few seconds, whereas I'm sure they are saying something more meaningful.

Today I imagine Uncle Jack is saying, "Please God, let it not be true" about Aunty Joyce, but I can't imagine what she is saying. I'm cross with her, actually, for not believing me about Mr Fairly. She obviously hasn't said anything to Uncle Jack. And now she's happy to sit behind Fairly, without so much as hitting him over the head with her Book of Common Prayer.

It is morning service, and to top it all, Mr Fairly is giving the sermon as a lay preacher. He stands at the golden eagle because he has been quoting from the Bible.

"We have endured a long and taxing war," he begins, gripping the sides of the eagle. "Everyone has had hardship, and some . . ." he affects a dolorous pause, " . . . more . . . than others." He looks genuinely grief-stricken for those who have lost loved ones. "And it is not surprising that we wish to enjoy ourselves, to eke out every last bit of pleasure we can from these days of shortage, of grief, of loneliness." He looks around at the faces in the congregation, like a reproachful headmaster. Aunty Joyce looks down at her prayer cushion, and Uncle Jack adjusts his hymn book.

"LUST!" cries Mr Fairly suddenly, seizing the golden eagle by the wings as if it might take off. "We must all soar above it! Look around at what it has done to our community! Look around at the relaxation of values we used to hold dear! Where were your daughters last night? And where . . ." he looks around again, over his reading spectacles, ". . . were your wives? Oh, yes! It's easy to think that anything goes in times of crisis, but while our young men are away fighting, what favours are we doing them if they come back home to find their wives and daughters and fiancées the victims of unhealthy matches made in the heat of the moment, born out of a loss of self-control, born out of lust?"

I'm not too sure about 'lust', but I get the gist of it. I can feel Aunty Joyce shrinking on my left, and on my right Uncle Jack rearranges his hymn book, re-counts his collection money and furiously brushes dust from his trousers that does not exist.

"No one knows more than I do, in charge of Heaven House, what the fruits of such slack self-control can be. Oh, yes! Be in no doubt, that lust will find you out! Even those of you who come to church every Sunday and sit there with your collection money in your spotless Sunday best, not even you . . ." (here he looks directly at Aunty Joyce and Uncle Jack, and I see her begin to tremble) ". . . can escape the *weakness* of the flesh! And I say to you – I say to you all – confess your sins, and God will forgive you. Put Satan behind you, arrest your slide down the shameful slippery slope . . ."

I feel a sudden movement on my left, and realize that Aunty Joyce has stood up.

People don't turn round, as such, since she is standing in the third pew from the front; they merely divert their attention from the preacher and land it, with intense curiosity, on Aunty Joyce. They are curious perhaps about whether her sudden stance means she objects, has left a pie in the oven, or is merely busting for a wee. But interest turns to surprise when the blonde enigma of Weaver's Cottage squares up to Mr Fairly and opens her mouth to speak. Since few but me, Uncle Jack and Mr Fairly can see the look of defiant rage on her face, it is not until the words come out that the shivers of awe go bristling round the nave.

"How DARE you! HOW DARE YOU!"

People brace themselves. This is going to be a good one.

"You! You stand there and preach to us about lust! YOU!" (Mr Fairly's face alters slightly, but only a twitch betrays the nerves behind his composure.) "You, who have betrayed the whole neighbourhood with your lust for young boys –" A sharp collective intake of breath makes her turn towards the congregation: "Yes! While we've been falling over ourselves to admire this . . . pillar of the community, Mr Fairly here has been satisfying his own warped pleasure with the orphans in his care –"

"That is utterly –" he begins.

"Don't even think about denying it, you . . . you self-righteous little . . ." She looks up at the ceiling for help.

"Bully!" I supply in a whisper.

". . . bully!"

"Joyce!" hisses Uncle Jack, leaning across me and trying to tug his wife inconspicuously back to her seat. "Joyce!"

Mr Fairly musters a half-smile at Joyce. "Well, I think we all know why my sermon got *you* worked up, don't we?"

It is a powerful counter-attack, and one which makes Uncle Jack cover his face with his hands. But Mr Fairly has underestimated Aunty Joyce. She rounds on him with such venom that children grip their mothers, and ladies dig ridges into their handbags with their nails.

"You evil, slimy little BASTARD!"

Nice one, Aunty Joyce. She raises her arm and points one of her beautiful fingers at him. "*You* murdered my daughter!" Her voice begins to wail: "You killed my little girl!" She sobs. Then she takes a great breath and rallies, turning to the congregation again. "Yes! He killed Rosemary. *He* did! Because my little girl saw him at it one day! He watched her drown! He kicked her and kicked her and watched her *die!* And she screamed . . . oh God . . . I know she screamed . . . and he didn't . . . and he . . ."

She is heaving with rage and tears, and Uncle Jack, now horrified and confused at the revelation, looks at Mr Fairly for a clue, along with the rest of the congregation.

And it is all there: the anger in his face, as he smarts with fury, betrays a far less kindly pillar of the community than they have seen before. This is a new face, with narrow eyes and flared nostrils, and only to the front two pews – the Heaven House boys – is it utterly familiar.

I find myself taking Aunty Joyce's hand, and she clings on to me, sobbing. Uncle Jack puts his arm around both of us. Whether instinctively, or to keep up appearances, I don't know, but it's a good move. I'm so proud of him I could cry.

The gasp at Aunty Joyce's revelation makes the church seem full of whispers, and people exchange glances for support and direction. Mr Fairly makes one last bid for his good character, slamming shut the heavy Bible in front of him and striding down the side aisle, snarling, "You'll be very sorry for this, Joyce Shepherd. *Very* sorry!" The fierce words are interspersed with his heavy clop clop on the stone floor, and just before his exit he beckons roughly to his wife, who rises and shuffles after him, her hand clasped over her mouth.

Run, rabbit, run

If anyone was confused by all the goings-on, Mr Fairly's sudden change of character convinces them. And before long the fact that he is 'not frum round 'ere' – whereas Joyce Shepherd was born and bred not two miles away – becomes a significant factor too.

I have never seen Uncle Jack in such turmoil. He has watched as his wife's treachery was so nearly revealed to the world, braced himself for perpetual humiliation, and all of a sudden the plot has changed. And it is much darker than before. It is as though he were sentenced to death, but now he's let off the hook, only to be told that the world might explode at any moment.

The church service disintegrates. People hang around the churchyard for ages afterwards, but we go home as soon as we can. Miss Lavish takes me next door into her house for some reason, and I'm most put out. I try to hear noises coming through the wall, try to work out if the wails and sobs and silences are shared grief or not. But Miss Lavish spots my game and puts the radio on.

"When April showers . . ."

I try to turn it down and stand next to the wall while she puts the kettle on, but she turns it back up again.

> "So when it's raining, have no regrets,
> Because it isn't raining rain, you know—
> It's raining violets . . ."

She tells me Aunty Joyce and Uncle Jack need some time on their own together, and she gives me a nice cup of tea.

At teatime Aunty Joyce calls me back, although none of us has the stomach for eating. We sit at the table, Uncle Jack, Aunty Joyce and I, fiddling with a jar of last summer's green-gage jam and pushing slices of bread around our plates. Uncle Jack wants me to repeat the whole story again, to tell him exactly what I told Aunty Joyce. I have never been allowed to speak so much at table, but my words put such a torment into his face that the telling of it makes me feel sick.

They talk more than they've ever talked in front of me.

"If it's true . . . what a fool I've been!"

"It is true," says Aunty Joyce. "Look at the way he behaved in church!"

"Of course it is! It all makes sense!"

"What have we done to that poor boy? Poor, poor Tommy!"

"Yes, poor Tommy." He closes his eyes as if to block out the sight of it all. "What wretches we are!"

"To think that . . . bastard pretended to be our friend!" Aunty Joyce speaks through gritted teeth, her eyes still red with hours of crying.

Uncle Jack hears the swear word and lets it go. Free as you please. And uses one of his own: "If I ever get my hands on that monster, I'll . . . bloody well tear him limb from limb!" His mouth is turned down and rigid, as if trying to stop itself doing anything reckless, like crying, perhaps. "I bloody well will!"

She puts her hand across the table and lightly presses his fingers into the cloth.

"Jack!"

It is half pleading, half comforting. It is a hand stretched out, that is all. But I look at the raw pink knuckles of her pretty hand, the hand that's made do and mended for seven long years, and realize that I haven't seen it there before, touching his. I am invisible again, and glad to be.

There is a knock on the door, and Lady Elmsleigh comes straight through to the back kitchen, resisting all attempts to show her into the front room.

"Mr Fairly has been arrested," she says. "I thought you would like to know."

It seems that after the church service, Tommy took all the boys to Lady Elmsleigh's, all twenty-one of them, and Lady Elmsleigh heard their story and telephoned for the police. "He's been taken to Gloucester, and let's hope that's the last we'll see of him." She stands up and goes over to Aunty Joyce, taking her hand in both of her own. "You've had such a *dreadful* time of it, Joyce! I don't know how I can help, but you must let me do anything I can."

She doesn't stay long, but I'm shooed off to bed, and I can just hear Uncle Jack's gratitude as she leaves, and mention of Tommy. So it all seems to have turned out for the best, my betrayal of Tommy's secret. I shouldn't have done it – I promised I wouldn't tell, but now there are twenty-one happy boys and the monster is where he should be.

But, I should have known, nothing is quite that simple.

The following day, a Monday, Tommy is not at school, and neither are any of the other Heaven House boys. I am the centre of attention, of course, and everyone flocks around me, thirsty for more of the bad news they heard in church. I play my part happily enough, but when Tommy doesn't appear on Tuesday either, I begin to feel uneasy.

It is on the last leg of my journey home, the bit I do on my own between the Heaven House path and Weaver's Terrace, that I see him. He is suddenly there, fox-like, in the hedgerow. He emerges from behind an ivy-clad tree so silently I don't see him until I am almost upon him.

"Tommy!"

"Listen!" He looks around and lowers his voice. "I'm leaving this evening. This time you can't come with me. I'll be out the back of your house to say goodbye at eight o'clock, if you want."

I laugh in disbelief. "*Again*? But why? Fairly's locked up. You don't *have* to go now."

"Oh, I do all right!"

"No, you can stay and work on the farm. Or go on to study till you're old enough to be a proper pilot."

"He'll be out again soon."

I'm not smiling now, because I can see that he's serious. He really is going to go, and I don't think I can stop him.

"It'll be *years* before he's out. You'll be a proper pilot by then."

"No." He leads me off the lane and behind the tree, still looking in all directions. Then he takes me by the shoulders and looks as if he must make me understand something I am too young to grasp. "It's like I told you, Kitty. If I say anything, I'm a dead man. Even if they put him away, he'll find me. And if they don't – and he's a clever man with friends in the right places – if they don't, I'm as good as dead. I'm the only witness, see. He'll be after me. I'm not saying nothing. I'm just gonna go."

"But then he'll go free!"

222

"Yes — and I'm gonna be out of here!"

"But what about the others? Don't you care about the others?"

He draws his hand over his face slowly. "Of course I care. Lady Elmsleigh'll take care of things. I know she will. And any road, any one of them boys could put him away if they wanted. Let them do it. I said I saw nothing. And I'm saying nothing."

I can't understand his wish not to tell. It goes against one of my greatest childish instincts: to tell on someone who's done wrong, to save my own skin. Sunday school may have taught us to turn the other cheek and so forth, but if Tommy's being godly then I want to thump him. I can't imagine what strange force is holding him back. The thought of this odd resignation makes me so angry with him I want to shake him into telling the truth to the world.

"Where'll you go?"

"To sea," he says, confidently.

"You can't — you're not old enough."

But one look from those anxious conker-coloured eyes reminds me it was I who betrayed his trust in the first place, who dug him this terrible dark ditch.

At eight o'clock I say goodnight and slip out of the house to the lav. Up the back of the garden I hover behind the newly creosoted shed and see his dark figure waiting for me. I put my hand out to touch his gabardine coat, to get the feel of him.

"I'm sorry," I say. "I'm sorry I broke my promise. Facky Nell. I've ruined everything, haven't I?"

He gives me a huge, deep bear hug, holding me against him so tightly I know he forgives me. He puts his nose in my hair and I nuzzle mine into his neck. We smell each other like sheep sniff their lambs. Even now a whiff of creosote brings back the smell of parting and the oily wool of his pullover, and a longing that seems to grow as each year passes.

"I'll write," he says, and picks up his bag to go.

"Behave," I say, remembering my father's words to me when I left. "And no fackin' swearing."

Then, as though this is wholly inadequate, he puts it down again, holds me again. "You're the most precious thing in the world to me," he says. I cling on to him, aware at last that this is no game, and that in a few moments he will be gone. "Don't ever forget that. Wait for me. I'll find you."

We hold hands, and then just fingertips. I feel like a film star, but before I can really take it all in, he has gone: halfway across the field with no moon.

When I go back in the house no one notices the state I'm in because Lady Elmsleigh is there, sitting in the parlour again in Uncle Jack's armchair.

"Out?" breathes Aunty Joyce. "Free?"

"I'm so sorry," says Lady Elmsleigh. "Tommy wouldn't repeat his story – even though he'd told me – so there was no case to answer for."

"What about the other case – the other boys?"

"None of them will speak out."

"Not one?"

"Not one."

"What are they playing at?" Uncle Jack is cross.

Lady Elmsleigh frowns sadly. "It makes you wonder what on earth they've been through. They're all so very frightened. Tommy is the oldest, and he was fourteen yesterday, so he's free to go. Perhaps if we all work on Tommy . . ." She turns to me. "Kitty, perhaps you could persuade him how important it is to tell his story – to get this monster locked away . . ."

"And we could do something," whispers Aunty Joyce. "We could welcome him back into our house." She fiddles with the neck of her housecoat. "We've been so unkind. He needs to feel safe." She puts her hand to her mouth and looks so full of sorrow that Lady Elmsleigh insists it is not her fault.

"That man must not be allowed back near any of those boys. I'll keep them with me if needs be."

I want to go home now. There's no point me being here without Tommy, so I say one of the boys can have my room. But all the grown-ups agree there are still V2s over London, and I must stop here for the time being.

I want to scream, I want to smash everything. I can't believe Tommy was fourteen yesterday, and I forgot. I can't believe I am being charged with setting the world to rights just moments after I have let the possibility slip through my fingers for ever. I feel all the wretchedness of being only nine.

Try a little tenderness

I mix the ink at school, and its camphoric smell reminds me of writing, and the letter I'm still waiting for. I am something of a celebrity, of course, the centre of a murder mystery, a mystery that has hung over this village for years. And every face, at every inkwell I fill, looks at me in that searching way they did when I first arrived: trying to read me for some clue.

The Heaven House boys are back in school today, so they have taken some of the pressure off me. It seems some man from the council came round to Lady Elmsleigh's and told her she had to return them all to the boys' home, or else. Mr Fairly was a free man, because all charges had been dropped. Of course everyone wants to know if it's true – what he's supposed to have done – and all the boys are saying it is, but it didn't happen to them personally. And no one can find anyone it did happen to, or exactly what 'it' is, although there are all sorts of interesting stories of Nazi-style torture. It is not long before Mr Fairly becomes a Nazi, after all, and not a child molester: it's just that the police can't see it. By home time he is Hitler's right-hand man, and we are all immensely sorry for the Heaven House boys, having to go home to him for tea.

*   *   *

In the days that follow there are strange goings-on in the Shepherd household. My first suspicion that something different is afoot comes with a peculiar little ritual just before Aunty Joyce makes our Ovaltine one evening. She thinks I can't see her, because I am deep in a comic, but I do.

She takes a very bright white towel from a pile of laundry and lays it on Uncle Jack's knees. Then she kneels before him, takes his hands and lays them on it, stroking his hands on the towel and, as he watches incredulously, she lifts his hands and turns them over, and strokes the back of them against the towel too. He says not a word, but lets her continue, laying her own hands on the towel where his have been, and performs the same ritual. "Now I'm clean," she whispers, leaning back on her heels and closing her eyes in relief.

When I look up officially from my comic, Aunty Joyce has a definite spring in her step as she puts on the milk to boil.

The following evening it happens again, only this time, something even stranger happens after I've gone to bed.

I'm woken in the night by a curious whimpering noise. I get up and open my door carefully, but it becomes clear that the noise is not coming from their bedroom, but from downstairs. I tread very gently on the landing and lean just far enough forward to see over the banister into the parlour.

There, in front of the range, Aunty Joyce is sitting in the bath, her slender back towards me. Her shoulders are shaking, and I can tell she is crying. And that's not all — I can barely believe what I see — Uncle Jack is kneeling beside her, sponging her down. He dips the sponge in the lightly steaming water and squeezes it gently over her shoulders. And this is the oddest thing: his eyes are full of tears. And he keeps saying the same thing over and over in a voice high-pitched with sorrow: "Not dirty, Joyce . . . not dirty . . ."

* * *

March turns to April, and still no letter. The school holiday is short and barely noticeable. There is blackthorn blossom appearing above the hedges and, from my bedroom window, the evening sun slants low over the back field, giving every blade its own blaze of green and shadow. The wireless hums sad love songs downstairs and competes with the frenzied twitter of a few excited birds.

The evenings are getting lighter now, and this mock summer sunset reminds me so much of last summer that I ache with grief at the thought of empty sunny days to come.

A couple of giant rabbits are on the back field. The largest one circles the other and then quite suddenly leaps into the air on long, outstretched legs. He continues to make wide circles, then goes for another wild leap, and I realize that it is not a rabbit at all, but a hare. My first mad March hare – and in April. I envy its joyous bounding into spring. For some reason it gives me a nauseous memory of Betty Chudd with her tight blouse, and Nancy the land girl with her loose one. At the same time there is something exciting – almost dangerous – about this crazy energy that appears from nowhere and races off into the undergrowth without a trace.

In the middle of April I get a letter, written in Tommy's unmistakably neat hand.

HMT *Alexandrina*
April 16th 1945

Dear Kitty,

I am in the Merchant Navy! Today is my first day as a galley boy! It's all very different to Sheepcote, and I'm treated like one of the men!

This morning we had sardines on toast for breakfast! I haven't been seasick once!

Who knows when I'll be back? Promise you will write soon! You can give your letters to Lady Elmslee and she will send them on.

Promise you won't give up on me! Even if we lose each other in this war, I will find you!

Write soon! Lots of love,

Tommy

I am thrilled. Apart from those from my mother, it is the first letter I have received in my life, addressed solely to me. I parade it around school, I show it to Aunty Joyce, I read it to Babs Sedgemoor, and she reads it back to me.

I write back straight away. Some silly mushy stuff about love and marriage that probably makes him tear it up the moment he gets it. At any rate he's not in a hurry to reply. The days stretch on uneventfully. The countryside slyly unfurls its greenery when we are none of us looking, so that all of a sudden a green mantle appears on every stem and bough, and those mighty green tunnels sweep me off my feet again like they did when I first arrived.

I get out last year's old flattened cardboard and Babs and I go sliding down the slope in the buttercup fields. It hasn't rained for two days and the grass is just right for sliding. We race and tumble all the way to the bottom, sending sheep bleating in all directions. As we scramble back up to the top, inspecting our vehicles for sheep shit, Babs sings "Tommy Glover's gone to sea, Silver buckles on his knee, He'll come back and marry me – "

"Neville Adlard's gone to sea," I start, teasing her about the boy she likes in our class. "Neville Adlard's done a wee . . ." We are giggling so much we can hardly stand up, when someone comes walking up to us.

"Hello, Kitty."

It is Mr Fairly.

We both stop giggling, and say nothing in reply. It's an odd place for him to come walking.

"I'm glad I found you here. You heard from Tommy, I hear?"

I swallow hard, and look at Babs.

"Yes," I say. I can't imagine why I feel the need to reply to him. Because he is a grown-up, I suppose. There is something imposing about him, and neither of us could dare to be rude to him, although we would like to be.

He smiles and scratches the corner of his mouth. "I wondered if you might give me his address."

I feel cornered.

"She can't," says Babs. "He's gone to sea."

"Ah yes!" He nods, as if he knew this already, then takes out of his top pocket a slim bar of Cadbury's chocolate. Babs and I stare at it. "He told me . . . what was the name of the ship again . . . ?"

"I can't remember," I say nervously.

He fingers the chocolate bar and we both look at it longingly. "HMS *Charlotte*, wasn't it?"

"No – HMT – A –" I clap my hand over my mouth.

Mr Fairly smiles, "Ah, Merchant Navy," and hands over the chocolate.

"I don't want it, thank you," I mutter.

"I'll 'ave it!" says Babs.

I'm shaking by the time we reach the lane, although the sun is out and there's hardly any breeze. To my shame, I scoff half of the chocolate with Babs, but afterwards I feel like retching.

Victory polka

Hitler is dead, and the war has been as good as over for ages. Everyone says so. I really can't see why I have to stay here now.

Then on the first of May everything changes.

I'm woken, along with everyone else in Sheepcote, by a bugle call. It turns out to be Mr Tugwell, who played his bugle in the last war. But this time he is signalling the beginning of May. At school there are flowers everywhere, and at play-time we are all ushered out to line the main street and cheer a motley procession of children who have been practising for some weeks. But then again, they have been practising with Miss Miller . . .

They spill out of the school porch and skip or run towards the school gate: little girls in long-discarded bridesmaid dresses with rumpled skirts and boys in grubby tennis shoes. Miss Miller organizes them into two raggedy lines behind Mr Marsh's milk cart festooned with flowers. They fidget with excitement as the May Queen emerges from the school entrance hall, accompanied by her two maids-in-waiting, and processes towards the waiting cart. The May Queen is huge: tall and plump with widely spaced grey teeth, a full bosom, and a white 1920s dress several sizes too small, swathed in tiers of torn and crumpled chiffon. She carries a posy of forget-me-nots and may blossom, and on her head she wears what appears to be an entire basket of flowers.

The small crowd cheers and putters out a dry clap as she clambers into the back of the cart ('Sheepcote Dairy: Fresh Every Day') assisted by two far prettier maids-in-waiting with wild flowers woven in their hair.

At first the horse fails to move and the two lines of children, primed for movement in a forward direction, collide with each other and skip back to their places. A concertina, which has started up, fizzles out. Miss Miller looks unperturbed and rallies them all again, trying to achieve two lines from a clump of giggling children now all practising their own steps on the spot.

As the cart moves off, the children start a ranting step behind it, clattering cymbals and triangles, but soon lapse into running, skipping, and movements all their own. The queen is now revealed in her full splendour, her fat, white-socked feet in brown sandals and her knees squatly apart. It is Betty Chudd. When we all reach the village green Mr Marsh stops the cart and Boxer lifts his tail and does a giant dollop of poo. The dancing children come to a halt and chant, "We come to greet you, O Queen of the May!" and watch as she steps down from the cart, assisted by her two pretty maids. The children skip on to take positions around the maypole, while the queen steps in the horse dung.

"Ah, fuckit!" she cries.

Miss Miller urgently orders some music, and eight children skip around the maypole at a colossal speed to a lone concertina. The pole lists violently to right and left, and the ribbons are woven into an impossible tangle. We all roll about giggling, and even Boss Harry has to cover his face. Babs and I laugh so much we almost cry.

* * *

It is a day when I swell with pride for my little village, and the day when I learn I must leave.

When I get home for dinner (blossom stuck all over the place in my hair and in my cardigan buttonholes), I find Aunty Joyce and Uncle Jack in the back garden, hugging. She is pink-faced with crying, and he seems to be almost in tears too. I catch words like 'poor thing' and 'not fair' and 'Burma'. Or else it could be 'Birmingham'. Burma and Birmingham are pretty interchangeable to me, and it is not until much later that it makes any sense.

When they see me, they hurry in.

"We had a letter today," says Uncle Jack. "From your mother."

I notice an opened letter on the green baize tablecloth, and reach out for it. Aunty Joyce snatches it away and puts it high up on the dresser.

"Yes . . . you're going home! Your mother's coming next week – a week tomorrow!" There is a fake breeziness about her tone, and I vainly take this to mean that she doesn't really want me to go. "Aren't you pleased?"

The truth is, I'm not sure if I am. After all this longing for it, I'm not sure where home is now. There is only a pile of rubble waiting for us in London. And all my friends are here. All except Tommy.

"Is Dad coming home too?"

Aunty Joyce swallows hard and glances at Uncle Jack. "You'll have to ask your mother about that, poppet."

So I'm a poppet, now. I should have guessed something was up.

"How are we going to get there? By train?"

Uncle Jack reaches out his big brown hand and wraps it over mine. "First Class. I'll make sure of it."

* * *

Over the next few days everyone starts to save up their sugar rations. There is a feverish excitement about the end of the war. They are saying it down the grocer's, at knitting group, at school. The war is as good as over. But I'm not sure what to get excited about. I've never known life without 'the war' so I can't picture what it will be like. It seems that something huge is about to happen – something like a volcanic eruption or a tornado – but no one can tell me exactly what. The war will be over and there will be jelly to eat and street parties, and we'll all go back home to live in houses that aren't there. Babs says the shops will be full of sweets and ladies will wear lace again. But I think she says this to cheer herself up, because, unlike the rest of us, she can't look forward to seeing her parents again.

Lots of the evacuees say they don't want to go home. You can see a sort of panic in some of them at the thought that lives they had grown used to will suddenly be turned upside down. All over again.

There is an air of holiday about school on Monday. Outside the smell of baking and warm sugar fills the air. Girls and boys have replaced their shoelaces with red, white and blue tape; anything remotely like a Union Jack has been hung from the ceilings; Boss Harry announces every hour that the news of victory is due in the next hour. We are still waiting when we go home, clutching our hastily drawn paper flags down by our sides.

In the evening the wireless tells us that the Germans have surrendered to the Allies, but that it will not officially be VE day until tomorrow. By pub closing time it is clear that a group of soldiers and airmen stationed nearby have decided to celebrate anyway. A couple of home-made explosives go off. A few rowdy whoops and shouts can be heard right up the lane well into the early hours. But most of us wait until

Tuesday, when the cakes have cooled down, the toffee is rock hard and the jellies are well and truly set.

We wake up to the sound of a bugle – Mr Tugwell again, competing with the dawn chorus. By breakfast time the streets are already buzzing, and Aunty Joyce and I add an urgency to our colouring as we finish some home-made bunting. Even then, we wait until eleven when Uncle Jack finishes his shift.

We are standing by the front door, the three of us laden with baked goodies, when Uncle Jack turns to Aunty Joyce and says, "Go and put your best dress on – the one with the pink flowers."

She looks at him quizzically.

"G'won!" he says, without smiling. "Quick though."

She looks like a schoolgirl who has just won a prize, and she scampers upstairs to change.

The street party must be like millions all over the country: makeshift tables all along the green outside the pub; all the WVS women running about with more cakes and sweet stuff than any of us could dream of; men who should be working bringing booze out of the pub; servicemen still drunk from the night before; someone hammering out all the sentimental tunes they can think of on the pub piano with half the village joining in.

At three o'clock a portable wireless is brought out and turned up very loud, so that we all hear the official announcement. Then all hell breaks loose. Someone starts up a human chain that snakes around the tables, someone else wheels the piano out of the pub and starts to play 'Roll Out the Barrel', moving seamlessly into 'Pack Up Your Troubles' and 'Tipperary'.

The entire village seems to have joined in. I'm clutching on to Babs (who's dressed as Maid Marian for a fancy dress competition) and she's clutching on to Neville Adlard (who's miraculously dressed as Robin Hood – so she's happy). Behind me a Norwegian refugee is holding my waist and singing at the top of his voice. Will Capper climbs on to the last war memorial and waves a flag and a bottle of beer. Then everyone starts linking arms and swaying back and forth to 'Bless 'Em All.'

I notice Uncle Jack standing with his arms folded, looking on disapprovingly. Aunty Joyce is trying to tidy the mess on the tables, and is pushing chairs in so that no one will fall over.

Suddenly a jeep full of land girls arrives, all dressed in their civvies. The piano changes to 'In the Mood', a couple of trumpets join in, and every girl is grabbed by a man as soon as she sets foot on the road.

Then the music stops mid-tune.

First the piano, then the wind section, which has grown to the size of a small rhythm band. Everyone looks about. Through the noises of bewilderment some shouting penetrates.

"Stop! Stop! Stop!" It is Uncle Jack. "This is a disgrace! Listen to yourselves!" People go quiet to listen. I shrink into my dance chain. For a moment I can't bear anyone to know that he is in any way connected to me. "There are plenty of people in this village who have lost loved ones – some only recently – and here you all are making a rowdy mockery of their suffering. This is meant to be a thanksgiving for victory, not a riot! Have you no shame? Have you no respect? You might as well dance on their graves!"

There is a split second of total confusion, and then Mrs Marsh pipes up: "I've lost two sons in this war, Mr Shepherd – and maybe three! I respect what you're saying, and it's very good of you to think of us, but I say, let's thank God no more of our young men will be killed now! Let's have a bit of joy for once! All these young people fought the same war as my sons and they deserve it! We all deserve it!" She turns to the piano. "Come on! Get playing!"

Well! He doesn't know which way to turn. I wriggle out of my dance chain and go to him. Aunty Joyce is there too, looking awkward. I feel suddenly sorry for Uncle Jack. I'm sure it was people like Mrs Marsh he was trying to protect, and now he feels a right Charlie. I take his hand and oddly he looks down at me as if he might cry.

"Go on," I say, putting his hand on Aunty Joyce's pink-flowered waist, "you heard what she said!"

I start to push them around to the music, which is now 'When April Showers . . .', and they begrudgingly shuffle around with me holding on. A couple of bystanders cheer, and when it comes to "It isn't raining rain, you know . . ." I look directly at Aunty Joyce, and she smiles, and we both sing "It's raining violets!" and everyone else shouts it out too.

I fondly imagine that the little red rings around Uncle Jack's eyes are on account of how moved he is that I have fixed things for him and Aunty Joyce, and I feel dead pleased with myself. Are those tears glistening in the lower lids? – Yes, they are. He is looking at me as if he is about to burst with love, and it is all because of me.

Then I leave them, and watch them holding on to each other, swaying gently in an afternoon that reeks of beer and spring and new beginnings.

Wish me luck as you wave me goodbye

Aunty Joyce is in such a flap, tearing through the rooms and rebuking herself for not having packed everything earlier.

"Just look at all this I've got to do! They'll be here straight after dinner and it's nearly eleven now! It's all my fault — I should've sorted this out last week!"

I try to point out that then I wouldn't have had anything to wear, but she is intent on bearing the full burden of guilt for it and nothing will stop her. Since I came without a bag or suitcase, I do not have one to leave with. But my belongings seem to have multiplied tenfold. Aunty Joyce wraps all my woollens in brown paper and string, and marks the parcel "Kitty Green, Paddington station". Since there are only soft cardigans to support the paper, her pencil goes right through and she starts to fret even more. "Now I've broken the ruddy paper! What am I going to do now?"

Uncle Jack comes through the door after his night shift and does not even tell her off for bad language. Instead he clonks around upstairs for a bit and comes down with a dusty old brown suitcase.

"There!" he says, putting it on the table. "We never go anywhere."

"Oh, thank you!" says Aunty Joyce, as if giving away their

only suitcase were a gift from the gods. "Now we can really get things going."

I suddenly take a notion to fling myself at Aunty Joyce and give her a great long hug. "I'm going to miss you two so much!"

She's a little taken aback, but holds me too.

Uncle Jack chuckles when I go and give him a hug too. "What were we then?"

I look at him quizzically.

"You know . . . Miss Lavish, never been ravished, Mrs Marsh with the small moustache . . . what were *we*?"

I shrug. "I never had one for you."

"Go on!"

"I didn't."

"Well, if you had to, then . . ."

"Hmm. Aunty Joyce without a voice. Uncle Jack . . . with God on his back!"

"Am I like that?" she asks. "Don't I speak?"

"I just made it up – off the top of my head. It's only because it rhymes."

At about that moment there is a knock on the door. I go to answer it, and a telegraph boy holds out a small brown envelope.

"Miss Kitty Green?"

"That's me."

He hands it to me, and waits while I read it, in case I need to reply. It is typed, and brief, so I don't take long to work it out:

"*The captain of HMT Alexandrina regrets to inform you that Thomas Stuart Glover was drowned at sea.*"

My first thought is that they must have got it wrong. Perhaps there is another Tommy Glover who calls himself Thomas, or perhaps he just decided to swim ashore. Then I see the telegraph boy's face: the sad, sympathetic squeeze of the eyebrows. "Bad news, eh?"

I feel a great rush and everything starts to gallop inside me.

"Any reply, miss?"

I must have shaken my head, for he walks to the front gate and throws his leg over his bicycle, and I loathe him for having the audacity to ride up here, bold as brass – whistling probably – and hand me his skinny little envelope from his efficient little bag and turn my world upside down.

I put the telegram on the kitchen table next to the open suitcase.

"It's my fault," I whisper, as Uncle Jack picks it up and reads it silently, handing it ashen-faced to Aunty Joyce. "It must be a punishment. What have I done wrong?" I'm shouting now. I lift my red face to them both and implore them: "Tell me! TELL ME!"

Uncle Jack perches on the wooden arm of the fireside chair and covers his face with his hands. Then he reaches out a hand to my trembling shoulder.

"This isn't a punishment, littl'un." He stops and swallows hard, as if searching desperately through the Bible in his head for an answer. "God is a kind God . . . it may be hard to see it now, but this is a *challenge*, not a punishment. Through it you will gain a strength you never knew, an understanding and – "

I run to the bottom of the stairs. I already have a bone to pick with God and he's not going to be wheeled out now to piss me off. I harness all my anger and fling it at the pair of them.

"If that's true, then why can't *you* see it as well? Why can't you see that Rosemary's death wasn't a punishment, and stop blaming each other! Stop it! STOP IT!" I am screaming now, my face aching, prepared to deliver any cruelty in the reckless hope that it might soothe my pain.

Uncle Jack and Aunty Joyce look across at me from the

240

table like two lost children, but I just keep going. "Her death wasn't a punishment — it was a fackin' *challenge!*" My fury knows no bounds. I ignore their pathetic, beseeching faces. "And just look at you! You've fackin' failed it, haven't you? Just look what you've done to each other!"

I can't shout any louder, and my whole head is aching. I stomp off upstairs and slam the door to my room. A corn dolly falls off the wall. Jesus stays resolutely in place, looking intently over my shoulder from underneath his halo. Then I lie face down and wail out my hot anguish to the bed springs, raising my head only to lob contempt at the one available face. "And *you* can stop looking at me like that!" I scream. I thwack Jesus of Nazareth with a flying copy of *Farmer and Stockbreeder* and he falls face down off the wall.

They have both come up the stairs to speak to me, and when they open the door, I dash past them and down to the back door. I run up the garden path sending the hens chuckling in all directions, and I scale the low back wall into the field. I run and run and don't stop until I get to the oak tree. I kick the old furrowed bark and wail and wail and it does not mind. But I can't sit down, can't stop. I run towards the farm, down the lane, across the road and over the five bar gate. I run and run and don't stop until I reach the buttercup field, and Boomer's grave, and all the valley spread out before me, which Tommy said one day would be ours. I let out what is meant to be a huge scream, but it comes out as a whimper. I sit down on the spot where Tommy once told me, in his coy way, that I was his idea of heaven. I rip up handfuls of buttercups. Rip, rip, rip. I pummel the ground with my fists and send up wafts of wretched sweet grass, and I sink into it, spread-eagled tummy down, and let the anger give way to tears, and I hold the earth like a mother and cry and cry until my face stings with tears and snot.

* * *

It is Uncle Jack who finds me eventually. He picks me up and carries me home, saying nothing but "Poor lamb" from time to time. I find it comforting to be carried, and to hear him justify my behaviour with his soft words, and I nuzzle into that old blue jacket and smell the coal smoke of a thousand train journeys and the vanilla of his tobacco for the last time.

My mother arrives at three o'clock, although she said she would arrive at two. She rolls up in a Ford motor car with her own driver. She is dolled up to the nines, with stockings and lipstick and a hat with a feather in it matching her dress. All beams, she is, as she comes up the path, walking two little toddlers in their Sunday best.

"This is Maurice!" she says valiantly, before she reaches the door, "Maurice Trigg. He's my foreman where I work and he's kindly offered me a lift and he's going to drive us to the station. Isn't that kind, Kitty?"

Maurice, all teeth and moustache behind her, tips his hat at us.

"He's dead!" I mutter, from the doorway. Uncle Jack and Aunty Joyce are poised in the hallway to shake hands, but now they hold back.

My mother stops in her tracks and looks at me, shocked.

"I just got a telegram," I say tearfully.

She lets go of Shirley and Peter and rushes at me with her arms outstretched. "Oh, my darlin'!" she says, kneeling down to my height at the front door. "Oh, my poor darlin'! I didn't know you'd had a telegram! I thought . . . Listen! It only says 'missing in action', you never know . . . he might still be alive . . . you never know . . ."

"No, it says 'drowned at sea'."

"Drowned? How can he be drowned? *Mine* didn't say nothing about him being *drowned*!"

242

She pulls back from me, and I pull back from her. As we look at each other, and as we hear Aunty Joyce say, "Mrs Green, I think . . ." we both understand there has been a mistake.

"Oh, my Lord!"

"You don't mean Tommy, do you?"

Peter and Shirley have toddled off into the garden and are in danger of following Kemble back out of the gate into the road. Aunty Joyce squeezes past my shoulder to go after them, and Lady Elmsleigh arrives.

"I've some news," she says at the gate.

"Lady Elmsleigh – oh, dear. I'm afraid this isn't a very good time . . ." Aunty Joyce drops her voice a little, but I can hear it – I can clearly hear it say: " You see, Kitty's just heard that her father is missing, presumed . . ." – and this she whispers – " . . . dead."

"I'm so sorry. I'm *so* sorry. I'll call back later. I don't want to miss her before she goes."

And that's how I know. Did they all know? When were they planning to tell me?

It is deemed appropriate to invite my mother and her beau in for an hour or so to break the journey, and this is an hour I can barely recall. There seems no point left to anything at all. I am a dead girl walking. I am food for worms.

I resent it when my mother dips a biscuit in her cup of tea, and when Maurice Trigg smiles at something I loathe him. I don't want my mother's erratic sympathy, her sudden smothering hugs. There is nothing nor anyone who can console me, but I find myself going over to where Aunty Joyce is sitting, and silently wrapping my arms around her until it is time to go.

* * *

243

The door knocker goes a good few times during that hour, and Uncle Jack turns people away. When we come out of the house I see a little group of people waiting to see me off. There is Mrs Marsh with Babs, Mrs Glass, Mrs Chudd, Aggie Tugwell, Tosser, Miss Lavish, Miss Hubble and even Thumper, who is carrying a basket.

There isn't time to speak to them all. I am ushered into the car by my mother, who dumps Shirley in my arms before I can bid anyone a proper farewell. I sit on the springy leather of the back seat and turn to look out of the window. There they all are, the faces that studied me so curiously when I arrived, gazing at me all forlorn.

Everything is happening too quickly. I want some time to say goodbye. It is all wrong, and inside I can't help blaming my mother with her fancy new man and her blundering bad news and her poor time-keeping and this wretched posh car.

Uncle Jack leans in the front door and hands my mother some tickets.

"First Class!" she squeals. "Ooh! Ooh . . . you shouldn't have!"

By way of response, Uncle Jack explains which platform we'll need to get on. Meanwhile Aunty Joyce leans in the back door and gives me a basket with a lid. "Just a little going-away present from me." She gives me a quick peck, strokes my hair sadly, and we are off. Out of the back window I see them all waving, and Lady Elmsleigh running up, panting, shouting "Kitty! Kitty!" and then flopping her arms by her side.

I am so bereft, so all at sea, and I thank God for Aunty Joyce's gift. For the sound of frightened mewing makes me lift the lid to see a black and white kitten – the spitting image of Boomer – just crying out to be cuddled.

Sentimental journey
(Late April, 1956)

I don't know how much of all this I told them, and how much just came drifting back as I was talking: there can only have been time to tell them the bare bones of it all. I'm sure I was careful not to use surnames – they could've been those of the little faces peering up at me – and I'd called Jack and Joyce by different names. But when the bell went it was as though I were being lifted out of a trance. And the oddest thing is, I felt physically sick. I looked around and saw that the boys in the back row had already got up to go or were shuffling in their desks. Those were the same ones who had fidgeted for the first half-hour and had swapped things under the desks. I didn't tell them off then, because I wanted to be liked, and I was afraid they might turn on me and I wouldn't know what to do. Then they had all gone quiet as mice when I got to the killing of Rosemary by the stream. They all knew that stream, had pirated galleons on it, been shipwrecked on its fallen branches and scored their names into the hawthorn bark with knives. There had been such a hush then, and it had lasted until playtime, when everything fell apart and they were out of the door with a great clatter and thud before I realized what was happening.

After playtime Miss Pegler still hadn't returned and I was

terrified as they began to thunder back in. I gave them all some paper to draw their ideal picture of the new school at Heaven House, and while they were drawing they started asking questions, wanted more of the story. I told them about going back to London, and how when we got back to Maurice's mother's house – where we were going to be living with him and his daughter when they joined us later – it too had been hit and was like an open doll's house, but with everything looted and crumbling. But I didn't mention that when I opened my suitcase I saw that Aunty Joyce had mounted Tommy's sketch of me in a frame I recognized as belonging once to Jesus of Nazareth, and she had packed all the things that remotely fitted me from Rosemary's wardrobe.

I did write to them once, but then I forgot to put my address on the letter – partly because we didn't have one for a while, and partly because you forget these things when you're nine.

"Miss, you 'aven't done the register, miss. You 'aven't." A girl with a chest smaller than her tummy looked earnestly up at me from the front row.

"Right . . . I'll um . . . stay where you are! I'll just . . ." I found it on Miss Pegler's neat desk, clearly labelled with a hurriedly written note: 'Essential: take register'. Even at speed her writing was classically neat. "I'll be quick – surnames only . . . Ardlan . . . Bunting . . . Capper . . . Chudd . . . Fletcher . . . Glass . . . Hubble-Schmidt . . ." I looked up and murmured the name again, searching to see who said yes. "Could you put your hands up as well as saying yes, please?"

"Yes."

I gazed at the beautiful brown face of a boy who probably didn't know he once played Jesus, and couldn't help a little smile of triumph. They were all there, the same twisted noses and heavy brows and pointed chins, the same big ears and buck teeth and blocked sinuses, passed on from generation to generation. Nothing had changed dramatically, but everything had changed a little. A slight shift in the combination of genes, and there was a whole new set of possibilities. ". . . Rutter . . . Shepherd . . ." I looked up like a startled fox. She was a little version of Joyce, with Jack's dark curls.

"Miss, yes, miss," she said tentatively for the second time, because I failed to continue.

". . . Tugwell . . . White."

Miss Pegler came in as I was finishing off, and made them all stand in silence before letting them go home for dinner, row by row.

She was full of apologies. The architect hadn't been on the first train so she'd felt obliged to wait for the second, but he'd not been on that one either, and so on. She invited me home for some dinner, but I made my excuses: I wanted to stretch my legs and explore a bit. Before I closed the register I glanced at it again to check the Shepherd girl's name. It was Kitty.

Long ago and far away

Off I went into Sheepcote with my briefcase and my new red-print dirndl skirt, not sure if I was a grown-up transformed into an eight-year-old, or an eight-year-old pretending to be a grown-up.

And this time I felt like a giant. There were familiar hedges and fences which used to block out the world, but which I could now see over; five bar gates I could lean on if I wanted, without having to climb up them; and drystone walls no higher than my waist.

I hadn't smelt hedgerows like these for eleven years. They were doing that great unfurling thing that used to send me . . . I was still feeling nauseous, all choked up somehow. I had thought I knew the story of my evacuation, thought I'd packed it away carefully in a sealed container to be brought out exactly as I'd left it whenever I chose. But I hadn't bargained on being older. It didn't occur to me how much more of it there would be than when I left it, and how it would shed new light on itself, just in the telling of it.

I went to Tugwell's – the only shop left in the village, apart from the post office – and the door pinged as I opened it. I had completely forgotten how it did that. Mr Tugwell was not behind the counter, and I was glad. I felt awkward – like an impostor, almost – as I bought a banana from a sullen-faced girl at the till. I didn't want to reveal myself just yet. Even buying a banana from the store that never once saw a banana when I was there, seemed a treacherous thing to do. I felt I ought to be sharing it out amongst the inhabitants: cutting it up into a thousand slices.

The road through Sheepcote was tarmacked now and, although still quiet, it took me by surprise, with cars hurtling round the bends every now and then. I found the five bar gate I was looking for and climbed it. I made my way through the familiar field paths, choked by the beauty of the cowslip field, the fragrant yellow clusters nodding in the breeze and yellowing the whole pasture land. I climbed through sheep fields and across stiles until I could see it up ahead. The stile on the horizon beyond which lay our spot: the buttercup field, the oak tree and our valley.

I began to grow fearful, as I approached, that it would all be changed. I was panting with the climb, but unsure if it was fear or exhaustion or excitement that made my pulse race as I swung my leg over the last boundary.

A fresh flood of smells swept over me as a breeze hit me full in the face, and there it all was: the oak tree and the woods behind, littered with wood anemones – the sneaky smell fox – and wood sorrel. And over the ridge of the path was the valley, the lush, vast, rambling valley of my memories: leafy, green, unfurled to spring, waiting indifferently for me to feast my eyes upon it, as if not a second had passed since the last time I pounded its grass with my fists.

I must've stopped breathing, because the next thing I was gasping, and I had the galloping feeling I'd had as a child when I first saw this place, and I could see myself twirling and running, feel the cardboard racing over the grass. I remembered the studied gaze while being sketched, the plans that were made here, the dreams that were hatched, the promises . . .

A little lap of wind seemed to curl about my neck briefly, and I could feel his hand on my shoulder. I turned my head and I could see him, towering above me, eyes fixed on the horizon and his future projects, a furrow of determination between his brows. This very smell of warm metallic earth after rain hurtled through me as if it belonged to him. I could see his hair flopping about in the breeze and his stubby pencil tucked behind his ear. And I would've put my arm around his waist, and leant my head into him, had I not made him vanish eleven years before by opening my mouth at the wrong time.

He had told me a secret, and I had betrayed him. If only I had kept my mouth shut, he would've had no need to run from Fairly, and he might've been here now, on this beloved stretch of land, living peacefully and tending his sheep.

I had lived with these thoughts for years, but they had become such familiar companions that the sheer force of them in this place took me by surprise. I was punch drunk on guilt, gasping for air again.

I lay down on the grass and tried to breathe, and let the warm spring-excited earth nurse me back to a sort of calm.

As I climbed the lane to Weaver's Cottage I reached the exact spot where we had met Miss Lavish, and I remembered how Aunty Joyce had flipped over the label on my coat to read my name – and then only because someone else wanted to know it. I was all but shaking at the memory of that heartless welcome, as if the very ground under my feet was feeding it all back to me. But when I stepped out of the spot I saw her only as a happy woman, transformed by guilt and grief, and I continued up the lane.

A familiar figure came cycling towards me downhill. After she'd passed me, I turned, and she too had turned, propping her bike up with one foot on the road. She was greying but very sprightly, and with lively wise eyes I recognized straight away.

"Miss Lavish!"

I ran back towards her and she looked at me smiling. A few seconds passed.

"It's not Kitty, is it?"

"Yes! Don't tell me – I haven't changed a bit?"

"Kitty! Kitty!" She held out a hand whilst keeping the other on the bicycle, and clung on to my arm. "Yes, of course you've changed. My, you're a real lady! No, I only guessed because Miss Pegler said the new student teacher had been here as an evacuee, and that narrowed it down to a few dozen! Oh, Kitty! You've no idea how wonderful it is to see you!"

I seemed to have broken the ice, and I felt less nervous standing on Sheepcote soil than I thought I would.

"Miss Lavish! It's so good to –"

"I'm not Miss Lavish any more, actually," she giggled girlishly. "I'm Mrs Edwards!"

"Mrs . . . ?"

"I married Harry . . . the headmaster?"

"Boss Harry! You married Boss Harry! Miss Lavish! You dark horse!" We giggled a bit more, and I realized how pleased I was that she had found a companion. "I'm so happy for you."

She dismounted her bicycle in a decisive sort of way and started to walk it uphill alongside me. I pictured her taking some items from her front basket and asking jauntily, "Can I say 'knickers' to you?" But it slipped away. She genuinely wanted to talk to me, and I noticed that she was quite a few inches shorter than me too. It felt so odd being a grown-up here.

"Two wheels, I notice."

"Yes, the old tricycle fell apart! Now, what about you? We've all been wondering what happened to you."

"Really? I wasn't sure whether Aunty Joyce and Uncle Jack would be pleased to see me or not . . ."

"Heavens! Thrilled, I should think! You've no idea how hard they've tried to find you over the years."

"Over the *years*?"

"Yes. They tried writing to the address your mother gave them, but the letters were returned. They went up to London and hunted every Green in the telephone directory."

"Oh – well, if we *had* a phone, it would be under Trigg."

She came to an abrupt standstill, as if in shock. "You got married?"

"No – my mum remarried – that man, remember?"

"Oh!" It was a sigh of relief. "Well, that explains a lot. Lord, they were up in London knocking on doors – several trips they made, over a number of years."

"Uncle Jack and Aunty Joyce?"

We were outside Weaver's Terrace.

She looked startled. "Oh Lord! You haven't spoken to them yet, have you? You don't know!"

"What? What don't I know? Are they still . . . ? Have they had more children?"

"Oh yes, yes, they have. Three – Kitty, Tom and Patricia." She continued to look shaken. "You'd better come inside."

It was smaller than I remembered it, but the smell of piano and old books came hurtling through my memories as I sat in her front room sipping tea.

"What happened to that Mr Fairly?"

"You'll remember Lady Elmsleigh . . ."

"Yes, of course."

"She tried very hard to get Fairly convicted, but nothing came of it. None of the boys would say anything to the police. In the end his wife left him – and his housekeeper – and he just went away, scot-free. Lord only knows where he is now, or what he's up to."

"That must've been hard for Aunty Joyce and Uncle Jack. I remember, Tommy wouldn't even say anything about Rosemary."

"No, that's right."

She put down her cup of tea and looked directly at me. "You'll hear this anyway, now you're around, so it might as well be me who tells you. I just hope it doesn't upset you too much." There was a fearful, apologetic look, and one I recognized: the harbinger of bad news. I felt a rush of panic, but it was too late to stop her.

"Tommy did something much worse. Something I think you never knew about . . ."

"You know the school bell's ringing, do you?" said Boss Harry, coming in from the garden and smiling fresh air around the room. He held out a round warm hand to shake, and I wondered if he knew who I was. "Go on, Kitty Green. You don't want to be late on your first day!"

Wild garlic

The sickly hollow feeling of my afternoon was made worse only by the kindly attention of Miss Pegler, whose inclusive questions ("Don't you think so, Miss Green?" "Ask Miss Green – she knows more about that than I do." "Miss Green, have you anything to add?") simply drew everyone's attention to the fact that I had turned into a peaky-looking deaf mute.

Since I had further to travel than the other student teachers, it had been agreed with my college that Miss Pegler would provide me with tea for the first week of term, so that I could catch a later bus back to Cheltenham without missing a meal. This would enable her to give me essential 'debriefing' at the end of each day, and discuss lesson plans with me. Miss Pegler's aim was to debrief as briefly as possible the very moment the bell rang for home time, thus freeing her later to prepare tea and relax.

All I wanted to do was escape for a quiet walk, so I was grateful to Miss Pegler for her efficiency. Her assessment of my performance today was 'excellent', after waxing lyrical about my voice projection, my presence and my ability to hold the attention of a completely unknown group of children this morning. Not surprisingly her tip for happy teaching was "praise, praise and more praise". She snapped a completely unnecessary book shut on her lap and replaced the lid on her unused pen.

"But what if they're being naughty?"

"Oh, then you must admonish them, of course. But even the most difficult child should be praised at least twice as often as he's told off."

I thought of some of the children I had been taught with in this very class. "But what if they don't do *anything* worthy of praise?"

"Oh, there's always *something* you can find: sitting quietly for a change, nice straight back, nice big smile, shirt tucked in . . . and if you don't praise them when they're getting things right, how will they ever know when they're on the right track?"

I nodded vigorously, and wondered if this accounted for my own excellent assessment, despite my slacking off into a po-faced void this afternoon. Then she did venture to ask if I'd been feeling quite myself since the dinner hour. I could see the tempting possibilities of unburdening myself to her, but the story was too long and too harrowing to relive again so soon, even if I did long for her to practise her tip and absolve me from all guilt past or present in a glorious smiling affirmation that I had done the right thing, and quite possibly deserved a star.

As we stood in the school porch I asked if I had time for a short walk before I helped her with the tea. But Miss Pegler was a woman who liked her kitchen to herself, and she shooed me away with enthusiasm.

I made my way across the village through the same lanes I had followed home as a girl. I had it in mind to visit Joyce and Jack, but my courage weakened with each step. How was it that I had managed to write only one short letter in all these years and even that not in gratitude for taking me in? I wasn't ungrateful. I could see what a minefield it had been for them to take in a stranger, a child who reminded them in size and shape of the one they had lost. I had chosen to imagine, in my childish way, that there was a time limit on gratitude, and that if I let enough time slip past the need to express it would disperse into thin air. But now I could see that the very opposite was true, and the road up to Weaver's Cottage seemed suddenly unnavigable.

Then off to the right I saw the path. It was overgrown now with nettles and cow parsley, but it was no longer forbidden. There was no one to stop me visiting Heaven House, and with a delicious defiance I headed off towards the derelict building through the stingers.

I had seen it at a distance from the road many times, but never from the front porch. Even though it had been besmirched by Fairly, something of the old magic made me quiver. Here it was, right in front of me, the house I had ogled secretly every time I walked to and from school, whose windows I had so wanted to see into, whose strange routines I had longed to decode.

It stood there before me disgraced, scorn poured all over it, but dripping instead with new-leafed Virginia creeper and budding clematis. The front door, once a handsome bottle green, was flaking and revealing an older blue beneath. It was locked, and I wandered around to the back of the house to find another way in. My lungs were filled with a fierce pungent smell that ripped apart the seams of my memories like a wild animal. It was woodland garlic. I could see its snowball florets carpeting the roots of some beeches to the side of the overgrown garden. The back door was shut but the glass had been broken, and I found it unlocked.

Inside were signs of more recent life: this year's children's comics, chipped cups, a smell of chip wrappers, writing on the wallpaper ('Liz loves Don true NO SHE DONT'). I moved slowly up the hallway, looking in each room as I went. I gazed up at the high cornices; there were no clues as to what had happened here: the rooms were bare but for the odd bottle or chewing-gum wrapper.

Upstairs was no different except that the old beds, stripped of their mattresses, were still there in rows. The sadness of the two stark dormitories caught me by surprise. For the first time I could see how it was: two rows of beds, two rows of boys. All thrown in together. No love, no praise, nothing to aim for but escape. Above each bed was a hook and an unfaded rectangle of wallpaper. I found myself suddenly grateful for the lack of clues. Pictures of long-lost mothers would have been too sentimental to bear. I went over to a large cupboard by the window and looked inside. I was still searching and not sure if I wanted to find anything. It was empty: nothing but a musty smell and old cigarette packets.

I looked out of the broken window on to the garden. It had started to rain and the dampness made me shiver. I shouldn't have come. Searching for the truth is a dangerous thing to do, unless you're prepared to live with what you find. What was it he had done that was so dreadful? I felt trapped between my fear of knowing and my desperate need to find out.

I kept thinking back to the register I had taken, and the names on it. Chudd. There had been a Chudd. I kept seeing Betty in the lane with her big breasts and her tight buttons and her bare legs. I kept seeing the look in his eyes, torn between loyalty and lust. I had only partly understood it. Then it had spelt only disloyalty; now it spelt a child in a class I was teaching. I leant on the wall by the window and closed my eyes. And in this strange ambiguous state of things I hoped it was true. For if it was not, then I had to contemplate that other possibility, and that was too dreadful to consider.

If I was going to see Miss Lavish again, if I was going to face it, then I would have to prepare myself. I looked across at the rusty bedsprings. Could it be that the reason Tommy had not given evidence against Fairly was because he too . . . ? I screwed my eyes tight shut. It was so unthinkable I couldn't believe I had allowed the thought to pass by. It was this place, this building. I wondered how anyone could want to rehouse a *school* on such an evil site as this.

I had come back here to be close to him. There had been a choice. I could've accepted a placement in a nice quiet school in Cheltenham. I had volunteered for a rural location, hoping to be nearer. I hadn't expected to be right here. And now that I was, I could see how much my need had played a part in it. I had longed to see this place again, but without the guilt I felt every time I remembered it. I had imagined being an anonymous Miss Green, able to get close to my memories of Tommy without facing what anyone thought about me. Time had twisted my childish guilt into remorse. I had become Tommy's murderer: I had been responsible for the death of the only boy I had ever loved. For every boy I had met since had been compared to him. If there was a hint of Tommy in his voice or his look or his smell I would show a relentless, irrational interest in him. As soon as he betrayed himself by not being enough like Tommy, I lost interest. Tommy was my blueprint. I couldn't bear to hear Miss Lavish destroy him. I couldn't contemplate any damage to his memory. I shouldn't have come.

My heel stood on something and I bent down to pick it up. Right up by the skirting board a slim dark green object was wedged into the lino. It was only about three inches long. I turned it round in my fingers; a thin slice had been carved out of the green pencil for the owner's initials: 'G'. I was about to toss it aside when I saw that it had been sharpened right up to this letter, and that there had almost certainly been another letter which had been removed with the sharpening. I stared at it, then I kissed it and pressed it close to my cheek.

It was a timely reminder of everything good and tender about Tommy. I clutched it tightly in my hand and left the building as quickly as I could, before any more evil thoughts defiled my memory of him.

It had stopped raining, and the birds had begun to sing enthusiastically, restating their territory all over again. I stood for a while in the back garden of Heaven House. I spotted a fox in the bushes, but it only froze for a moment and then trotted off indifferently. A blue tit flew on to a windowsill and twittered about happily, seemingly unmoved by the demons all around. I put my hand up against the stone as if I might feel something similar. It was cool and damp. I loved this stone. It reminded me of the bruised grey film of hard-boiled eggs, its golden yellow just beneath the surface. It was Cotswold stone: good stone. The clematis saw no problem with it, nor the creeper, the ivy, the tits or the house martins, the song thrushes or the sparrows. The structure was sound and there was solid yellow stone under the surface. I walked away feeling glad that it had a second chance. Perhaps it could, after all, be transformed by children.

Tea for two

Miss Pegler's elaborate preparations produced scrambled eggs on toast and tinned fruit.

"Would you like salt and pepper on your eggs?"

"Both, please."

"I'm afraid I've run out of pepper."

"Oh, well. Just salt's fine."

"Good, good."

She ate slowly, watching me take each mouthful.

"Do you like pineapple?"

I hesitated. "Yes."

"I'm afraid I don't have any. I only have peaches."

"Peaches are lovely too."

She put them in front of me, and smiled. I knew I should make conversation but I could think of nothing cheerful to say.

"I'll buy pineapple tomorrow," she said.

Beyond her shoulder, perched on the piano, was a framed photograph of a young RAF officer, looking slightly embarrassed at having his picture taken. Normally I would ask about him, not just out of politeness, but out of curiosity. But this evening I couldn't face the unhappy, heart-rending story that I knew would follow. He would've begged to marry her, she would've said let's wait until after the war, he would've been shot down two days later, and she would've regretted it ever since. Better to let her chew on her peaches and chat on about how much she wanted a proper staff room. I didn't want to hear that other stuff. No thanks. Although I might as well have done, for the thinking about it affected my ability to swallow.

What was it with dead people? There he was, preserved forever in his frame, youthful as the day it was taken. Miss Pegler had had no chance to see whether, at their very next meeting, he might have pissed her off a bit, flirting with some other girl, getting a bit too drunk with his mates, making fun of her slightly beaky nose or her ever so slightly goofy teeth. She hadn't had a chance to see whether he patronized her opinions or beat her black and blue after a night's drinking or broke wind loudly after every meal. He was just there – like Tommy really – preserved forever in his perfection.

I could barely eat. The peaches had become sweet young flesh (young officer, perhaps?) preserved in some chemical fluid.

Miss Pegler began to pour the tea, and then looked anxiously at me. "Would you prefer coffee?"

It felt like a trick question.

"No, thank you."

"Good."

I took some forget-me-nots I had gathered into the classroom on my way to catch the bus. As I came out of the school I spotted Miss Lavish leaving the school house by the wicket gate and waving to Miss Pegler.

"Kitty!"

I looked away anxiously towards the bus stop.

"I was hoping I'd catch you. Harry had a phone call – oh . . ." The bus rounded the corner and sailed past before I could reach the road. "Oh, heavens! Was that your bus?" She must've taken my frown to indicate annoyance about the bus. Much as I longed for Miss Lavish's warmth and cocoa, I felt trapped by her bad news. "When's the next one?"

"Seven o'clock. It's the last one."

"Of course it is. Come on back with me for some cocoa. Harry's going out to his Sheepcote Players thing. They're doing *The Pirates of Penzance*."

I feigned interest, and went reluctantly up the hill to her house.

Those little white lies

Miss Lavish was smiling when she sat me down (good sign). She poured me cocoa and force-fed me biscuits, then she sandwiched one of my hands between hers and frowned at my lap (not good at all).

I could feel the nausea coming back. It was so sudden I had to put down the bourbon biscuit I had just munched into.

"It's Betty Chudd, isn't it? It's all right, I know. She's had a child, hasn't she?"

"Betty Chudd? Heavens, she's only been married two months. A dentist – lives in Gloucester. Tabby Chudd is pleased as punch – "

"But there's a Chudd in my class."

"Mrs Chudd's! She said it was an accident, but we're not so sure. What with Joyce and Jack starting all over again, I think she got a bit broody."

"I see."

The clock on the wall seemed to tick very loudly, and Miss Lavish renewed her squeeze on my hand. I was certain I didn't want to hear what was coming, but she was going to tell me, and I would have to bear it.

"Tommy was so afraid of what Fairly might do to him that

he ran away. Only he didn't go to sea at all. Apparently he found work on a farm in Wiltshire or some place, and he telephoned Lady Elmsleigh every week to hear whether Fairly had gone or not, and begging her not to say where he was."

"But . . . he wrote to me – from his ship."

"He sent it to Lady Elmsleigh – she gave you the letter. I've had long, long chats with her, I can tell you. She's never forgiven herself. Anyway, when he heard Fairly was looking for him he faked that telegram you had."

"Faked it? But he –"

"Thought it was better you heard, you see, because if it went to Fairly, he'd have known it was a fake straight away. Also he was afraid you were too small to keep a secret like that – especially if Fairly got hold of you. He thought that if Fairly heard about his death second-hand, and especially if he saw you genuinely grieving, then it would be more convincing."

"But he wouldn't have –"

"He was going to tell you a few days later."

Right, of course. I couldn't have kept my mouth shut for more than two minutes about anything. But this didn't make sense. I knew Tommy was dead. I knew Tommy was dead because I had grieved for him for eleven years. I had ached with guilt and longing throughout the dregs of my childhood and right through my teens. Every old song on the wireless, every lark in the morning, every moth, every spider, every reeking lane in spring, every whiff of wild garlic, every cow's breath, every owl's hoot, every boy's head from the back . . . It had been a long, slow, messy burial. But he was dead. The smells of this room with its old piano came rushing at me like a gale. These too had been buried, but here they were: that musty, dusty, dead smell, redeemed by the vibrant one of leather from the sofa and apples on the sideboard. I saw my free hand on my lap and it didn't seem to belong to me.

"Of course, when he told Lady Elmsleigh what he'd done

she was appalled. She came tearing round here – can you remember? – to tell you, only it was the day you were leaving –"

"– and I'd just had some other bad news . . ."

She reached out a cool hand and placed it on mine. "I'm so sorry, Kitty."

I stared at her elegantly veined hand. Strange words shot out from my lips. "Tommy's alive!"

She smiled. I looked at her intently. Everything seemed to hang on that smile.

"Is he here now?"

"I think so. But –"

Her clock started to chime the half-past loudly.

I stared at her sparkling grey eyes, trying to read what else there was to be said, parched for more information. But I was so excited by now that I wanted her to cut to the chase, I wanted to wind her up so she'd reach the conclusion. I was dying to hear as fast as possible, and the tension was so numbing that I couldn't open my mouth to ask what I really wanted to know.

"Come back after school tomorrow if you like."

I swallowed, disappointed, impatient. I felt unable to move, as though if I went out of her front-room door any number of unknown things could happen to me, and I wouldn't be ready for them.

"Go on," she said, smiling in exactly the same conspiratorial way she had twelve years ago when she bent down and whispered, 'Call me Lavinia.' "Don't be late for your bus!"

Dear hearts and gentle people

She took pity on me and walked with me to the bus stop.

"I suppose he's . . ."

"Mm?" That glint in her eyes again. "He was so desperate to get married that he proposed to the first girl he met. That was after looking for you in London with Jack, of course."

"So . . ."

"She turned out to be no good, with a man in Painswick, a man in Stroud, another in Cheltenham. Gracious, she was a terrible mistake! Then he made another big effort to find you again. He went to live in London to study – heavens! – he must've worn some shoe leather looking for you, Kitty. Anyway, he got engaged again last year – "

"So he's . . ."

"Married?" Her eyes sparkled gleefully at me again. "No. She broke it off."

"Poor Tommy!"

She stopped and gave me a rebuking sort of a look. "You don't mean that."

"I . . ."

"She said he was too clingy. But we all knew the real reason."

"What?"

She raised one mischievous eyebrow. "Well . . . it's no fun being second best, is it?"

There ahead of us was a woman whose walk looked familiar, and whose hairstyle had not changed in eleven years. She was wearing a splendid green-flowered dirndl and was flanked by children: a boy about eight, a girl about five or six, and another girl of about ten trailing behind — the Shepherd girl from my class. And beside them a man walking a bicycle — the same bicycle, lovingly maintained down the years.

Miss Lavish looked at me and smiled expectantly. But the sudden vision took me by surprise, and I felt a little over-whelmed. I took deep breaths and gazed at Aunty Joyce's hands holding the two smallest children, and at the five pairs of Shepherd feet clopping on the tarmac that used to be yellow stone.

I slowed my pace. I didn't want to catch up with the Shepherds, not yet anyway. I was seeing them as I'd always hoped they would be, all those years ago, and I wanted to keep my big mouth shut.

"They're going to the rehearsal in the hall. All the little Shepherds are in Harry's production. Oh — and someone else you'll remember: Heinrich Schmidt."

"What happened to him?"

"Heinrich? You know the Russells? Russells' farm up the other valley? Well, not long after you left he went up Russells' sheep farm to work. And old Mr Russell, he was pleased as punch with him. And then when he died he left him the farm. Didn't surprise anyone either — and no one minded! Oh — and you'll never believe who he married . . ."

"Miss Hubble?"

"My goodness!" She looked at me closely. "You have done your homework!"

"Just took the register, that's all."

She laughed and looked down at her handlebars.

"You see all the good things that have come out of all those wretched years?"

"Maybe not come out of, maybe just come *after* . . ."

Miss Lavish brought her bike to a sudden standstill, although we were still thirty yards from the bus stop.

"Perhaps we have no power for good at all, no way of helping to change the course of events whatsoever. You're the last person I would expect to hear that from . . ."

"Why?"

She raised her eyebrows as if expecting me to answer my own question. "The little girl from London who comes and changes everything?"

"I didn't do anything."

I started to move on but then stopped: the Shepherds had come to a halt further on, outside the village hall.

Miss Lavish said nothing, just smiled and looked ahead. Aunty Joyce was laughing, and almost toppling over as she knelt down to give her youngest girl a giant hug. Uncle Jack had said something to make the other two laugh and they were giggling. I looked back at Miss Lavish.

"Come on!" she said. "You don't want to be late."

She was full to bursting with something. Whether it was tears, laughter or some mischief I couldn't be sure.

"Harry had a phone call earlier."

"You said."

"Yes. It was from Tom."

"Tommy?" The nose of the bus appeared through the thickening hedgerows. "What? What did he say?"

Miss Lavish stepped up to the road and put out her arm, since I was clearly not going to.

"He's coming to tea tomorrow – can you join us? About five or so?"

The bus stopped. I stared at her radiant scheming face. I

saw suddenly how beguiling it could be, and thought of Tosser's Lavinia story of love under the beech trees. And then I could see why she wanted me to grab my chances, and I hoped she wasn't misconstruing things a bit just to try and nudge events along which were never going to happen.

"Not wishin' to hurry you or nothin'." The bus conductor was hanging out of the door. "Which one of you lovely ladies is wanting my carriage this evening?"

I stared at Miss Lavish in panic. "Does he know I'm coming?"

"No – go on! They'll go without you!"

I'll be with you to change your name to mine

I didn't want to meet him over tea with Miss Lavish and Boss Harry. What on earth would I say to Tommy over scrambled eggs and tinned peaches? I had spent a tortured night in the bed at my digs, frustrated at the time we had lost, angry with him for his deceit, furious with myself for not staying in touch, fearfully, painfully, outrageously excited to be seeing him again.

I was up so early I caught a bus at six thirty, and went for a walk before school. I swung over the five bar gate with my briefcase and stomped through the long damp grass up over the fields. I began to hope I would meet him here, away from everyone. I thought if I kept on walking he would appear on the horizon, possibly with a few violin players.

My feet were getting wet, but I hurled them down one after the other, raking them through the dew, in rebuke for not leading me back here years ago.

I stopped at the next stile and caught my anguished breath. What if I had come back sooner? What would I have been to him? A little friend, a chum, a pal. He had never shown the remotest interest in me romantically. That had all come from the daydreams of a little girl. At least now I had something new to show him; the grown-up Kitty I'd so wanted him to see. I looked down at my breasts. I would never be Betty Chudd, but I might just do.

Even so, I knew that the reason my pulse pounded was not only a nervousness about how he would find me, but a terror of finding he was not anything like the Tommy presented in my memories.

Miss Pegler was still full of apologies for my 'baptism of fire', begging me not to mention it to my college. I could just sit and observe this morning. I was relieved. Joy and terror were having a tug-of-war in my throat, and I didn't feel like speaking.

After the children had filed in, she held up a plan of the new school buildings. They all leaned sideways and elbowed each other to squint at a collection of thick black rectangles with gaps in them. As soon as they saw it they frowned and lost interest. She might as well have been holding up a copy of the Financial Times.

"This is what we call a plan. It's like a view from the air." She drew a rectangle on the board to represent the classroom, and put in a little diagonal line to represent the door. "Now, what you're going to do this afternoon is design your own plan of your ideal school." There was a muffled sigh from the back row, and a ripple of excitement from the rest of them. "Don't forget to include the sort of facilities you'd like to see in your ideal school. By that I mean cloakrooms, assembly halls . . . a gymnasium even – why not? Anything you would like to see in your dream school."

"A juke box!" shouted one of the boys.

"A smokin' room," grunted another.

The girls, on the other hand, could think of no greater luxury than indoor toilets. Miss Pegler tried to hush them, and she set the monitors to work, handing out sugar paper and pencils. I wandered between the desks from time to time, smiling and pretending to show an interest, but I saw nothing.

I kept imagining how he would be, and different versions of him kept popping up. There was an old sea-dog with a great scrubbing brush of a beard, trailing wafts of tobacco and farting without apology. He slapped me on the shoulder and said he'd waited eleven years for me, and I ran so fast I actually found myself accelerating up the aisle between the desks with my hand clapped to my mouth. Then I saw him with his hair slicked back, a teddy-boy suit, winkle-pickers and his own London flat. I walked up to his front door just as he was coming out, and he said, "Hey, doll!" and a swarm of pony-tailed girls came from nowhere and thwacked me with their roomy handbags. Then he just turned up in Sheepcote school one day with his gum boots on, sucking on straw and smelling of dung. He kept asking me to marry him and when I said I'd think about it he pushed me up against the corridor wall and said I had to: I couldn't let him down, he'd bought the buttercup field – no, he'd even built a cottage on it and now he needed some children to help work the land. It was all arranged. Aunty Joyce had made my wedding dress and Miss Lavish had already knitted the baby bootees. I tried to say no, but Mrs Chudd shouted, "Shame on you!" and threw her knitting down, then Mrs Glass and Mrs Tugwell and Mrs Marsh and the whole of Sheepcote were throwing stones at me and slabs of mud. So I said yes, and the next thing I knew I was knee deep in cow dung for the rest of my life.

Then I remembered him drawing my picture, and he was suddenly a depressed and damaged artist, forcing me back to his studio where every picture was a picture of me – in oils, watercolour, gouache; portrait, nude, abstract, classical, two-headed – but always me, staring wistfully or ghoulishly out of the canvases which he had manically amassed in crateloads, and he had done so many that he had had to rent a warehouse to store them all, and he had turned to drink, belching out a proposal which was more of a command as he handcuffed me to his easel and hissed, *"Together for ever!"*

Then something interrupted my ramblings, and it was something Miss Pegler was saying:

"That's right. An architect is someone who *designs* buildings. This is the architect's sketch of what it will look like when it's finished. And do you know, the architect who drew this was actually an *orphan* at Heaven House when it was a boys' home – "

"He's comin', miss!" A boy from the back was looking out of the window. "Just got off the bus! I can see him comin'."

Miss Pegler looked at me and raised her eyebrows. "Would you . . . ?"

But I was out of there.

I was running out of the door, my head turned sideways at the windows, catching glimpses of the umbrella bobbing up and down above the railings. It must have begun to rain. I sped down the narrow corridor and out of the front door, breathless, my eyes still fixed on the bobbing umbrella, watching it come closer.

Raining violets

As you turned into the gate I stood there, panting, blocking the way so that you couldn't help noticing me. You smiled and tipped your trilby hat, rushing onwards.

Did you hear my heartbeat, at thirty feet, like the owl?

You put down your umbrella and then you turned your head a little – just a fraction – as if to check something. You were just turning it back again to face the door when you saw that I too had turned, and you swung your head swiftly round to consider me with your conker eyes. The pulse in my head was soft urgent footsteps on gravel. Your face was much longer and your jaw much wider than I'd known it. There was nothing terrifying about you, and if I was at all frightened it was on account of the raging stew of emotions that I was trying to conceal.

I found myself slowly whispering, "Facky . . . Nell . . . !"

You removed your trilby and took a pace towards me.

"Kitty!"

I was willing that space between us to close up, but I didn't know how to do it. The couple of yards of playground seemed like miles and miles. And then there was a hoot from the school window: a boy was leaning out – no, three boys –

girls too – the whole class lolling out of the windows, crowding to see.

"G'won, miss!"

"Is it 'im, miss? Is it Tommy?"

"Kiss 'er!"

You smiled. I found that I was smiling too. You kept on smiling, and we seemed to just stand there, simmering, the sound of crude suggestions coming at us from the windows.

I stupidly held out my hand to shake yours, and you took it with your left hand, because your other one was full of umbrella and briefcase. And we stood there holding hands on one side like a couple in a gavotte, only we were shaking them up and down foolishly as if some Charlie Chaplin film had got stuck. All the time you were tracing my face with your eyes, as if you recognized it from drawing it all those years ago.

Up and down went our joined hands, and we waited in the fine drizzle for something to happen. Then you dropped your briefcase and umbrella, and I threw my arms around your neck, and you hugged me back. It was easier than looking at you.

"G'won! Kiss 'er!"

Then, to hide your reddening eyes and perhaps to hide mine too, you did as you were told.

The classroom behind us was in uproar, and children were pulling up plants from the flowerbeds outside the windows, throwing great wads of flower petals at us.

A sketch of heaven

It's been good to catch up with all the news. I can't believe how much has changed: most of the shops gone; and the school will soon be moved to Heaven House; Aunty Joyce and Uncle Jack have three children; the village hall has got central heating and a proper stage with velvet curtains; and you are all grown up with a trilby hat and umbrella and a face like Gregory Peck.

No, really. That's how you look.

If I'd only known . . . Lady Elmsleigh panting up the road that day . . . Ah Tommy! You'd've been welcome in our house, you know. And we weren't that far away. We moved to Bristol in the end and Maurice got a good job with Wills where he used to work before the war.

It's funny really, what evacuation did. I mean, most people have to wait till they grow up and leave home to take a long look at their parents, but there I was by the age of eight seeing my mother through new eyes. It was like I'd stood back from it all, and could see she wasn't all-powerful, all-wonderful after all. She was just my very blemished, bumbling mum, muddling through and making the most of it. I gave poor Maurice a run for his money, but looking back, I'm ashamed now, really. He was just doing the best he could to get through it all, doing the best he knew for his own child: finding her a mother. And my mum was just doing the best she could for us. They weren't made for each other – and they knew it. But they had that one thing in common: they knew the children mattered. And the funny thing is, they've become pretty inseparable now. They go for long walks on the Downs holding hands like lovers, sharing memories, talking things through. I take my hat off to old Maurice – to both of them – I do really.

And what a hotchpotch it all was for you – the war, I mean. You say it brought you me, and that I changed everything. Me and my big mouth, that would be. Well, I'm glad if I changed everything, but it wasn't intentional. Children do that, don't they? They change everything.

And now you're talking about us having children ourselves.

I don't know . . . reliving the past has made us both see things we didn't quite see before. Those poor hurt people, with childhoods sabotaged by poor hurt people, with childhoods . . . all unwittingly . . .

I know you told me things, but I was only small. I sensed things, like an animal makes out wafts in the air. It's only talking of it now that lets me really pick up the trail. Now I know what made you run.

I'm not saying let's not have children – I'm not even saying let's wait. It's just . . . Well, there's something that's got to happen first, isn't there? It's no problem for me or anything. I mean, birds do it, bees do it, even educated . . . okay, I'll shut up.

No – I mean, fall in love. Although *that* as well. The bunny thing. Not that it would have to be quite like the bunnies. Not that I object to that . . . I wouldn't know whether I would . . . I mean . . . please stop smiling and shut me up.

As you say, it's a huge and exciting thing to embark on. The hugeness and excitement of it all is almost too much.

But we know things now, you and I, so it can't have been all for nothing.

And Uncle Jack. Crumbs! All that stuff about trying to be someone, trying to leave his mark . . . When all he needed, to be a hero, was to lift a child on to his shoulders and make her laugh.

If we're lucky enough . . . if we do . . . if everything works out . . .

Yes.

You're right.

Let's not scribble some indelible script on their tender childhood, or allow a single blot on the blank page. Instead, let's take a soft pencil from behind our ear, and lightly sketch something beautiful.

An interview with Jane Bailey on how she came to write *Tommy Glover's Sketch of Heaven*

I wanted to write a mystery and a love story, but something gripping, not mawkish. I wanted to move people, but also make them laugh.

Unlike other novels I have written, the entire story of *Tommy Glover's Sketch of Heaven* came to me one day as I was gazing out of the window. I let it ferment for a year, played around with the tense and narrative voice a bit, but then it just seemed to write itself.

It was sparked by the idea that it might be interesting to look at a dysfunctional couple through the candid eyes of a child. I knew the child would have to be an outsider, because offspring are far too enmeshed in the politics of family relationships to view things with the candour I was looking for. The obvious answer was to make the protagonist an evacuee, a child from an impoverished but loving background, thrust into the bizarre private relationship of an inscrutable couple.

Although I hadn't chosen it deliberately, as soon as I started writing, I knew the Home Front of the Second World War was the ideal setting. Everything was stripped down to basics then: love and death. It was a good, clear canvas to work on.

When I was about three-quarters of the way through the novel, I woke in the middle of the night and scribbled down the last paragraph. It wasn't until I wrote those lines that I realized what the book was really about. It is about how much children matter. In the book we see a whole range of ways in which human beings hurt each other, the deepest and cruellest being those hurts inflicted as children. They range from physical child abuse involving the lonely Tommy Glover to the devastating emotional cruelty suffered by Aunty Joyce at the hands of her mother, and which she subsequently took from her husband. This damage and hurt is passed on from generation to generation, and it takes the unwitting astuteness of a child – the outspoken evacuee Kitty Green – to break the chain.

I found it very easy to slip back into that childhood persona who wants to know everything but is told nothing. I well remember finding out the most juicy information from sitting behind the sofa at home and humming softly so that chatting adults would think I was fully engaged in a game. Similarly, Kitty uncovers breathtaking secrets by keeping her head down at the women's village knitting group. She may not always interpret things correctly, but she is certainly proactive with the information. Everything that happens to us in childhood is magnified one hundredfold in our experience. And yet children are dismissed, talked over, pushed out of conversations and deemed not to feel things which they cannot articulate.

Tommy Glover's Sketch of Heaven is a book about the many ways people find to hurt each other, and the immense redemptive power of children, if only we look after them. It did turn out to be a mystery. It is also, by the way, a love story.